BLACK FOX
ONE

ELYSE
HOFFMAN

ISBN (ebook): 978-1-952742-27-9
ISBN (paperback): 978-1-952742-26-2
ISBN (hardcover): 978-1-952742-28-6

Project 613 Publishing
elysehoffman.com

PROJECT613

To my grandfather David,
my grandmother Shirley,
my mother Lydia,
my father Richard,
my sister Liana,
and to God, Who makes all stories.

THE VENGEANCE OF SAMUEL VAL

While *"Black Fox One"* can be enjoyed as a standalone story, it is also a continuation of Elyse Hoffman's previous book, *The Vengeance of Samuel Val*. Characters and plot details from *The Vengeance of Samuel Val* might be referenced in this book.

You might enjoy this story more if you read *The Vengeance of Samuel Val* first.

Thank you, and enjoy!

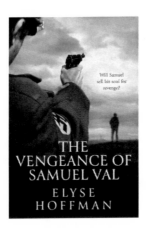

ONE

Germany, 1927

"Ava!"

Ten-year-old Jonas Amsel was entirely certain that his best friend was going to kill him. He had followed Avalina Keller into the woods as he often did, but the girl had been too excited and had run ahead, leaving the boy to stumble through the thrush and desperately try to track her down.

"Ava!" he cried again, and this time he heard a musical giggle somewhere close by. Jonas perked up his ears and tottered forward, trying to figure out where she...

"*Boo!*"

Jonas let out an unbecoming shriek and nearly fell into a thornbush. Ava's laugh filled his ears, and by the time he recovered from the surprise and turned to face his oldest friend, he wasn't even angry at her anymore.

Ava was a pretty girl. She had onyx black hair that was slightly curly and would have fallen just past her shoulder if she didn't tie it up in a ponytail, black eyes that to Jonas seemed like a portion of a star-filled night sky that had been taken from the heavens and put in her irises, and a smile that could have melted ice.

The radiant dark-haired, dark-eyed girl contrasted mightily with her closest friend. Jonas Amsel was a tall, lanky boy with sand-blond hair and lapis-colored eyes. Ava's mother, Gisela Keller, always fondly said that while Ava was a roaring fireplace, Jonas was a candle: quiet, thoughtful, a boy that hated any sport where he had to be part of a team, a boy that preferred to either climb the monkey bars by himself or sit in a far corner and bury his face in a spy novel or a crossword puzzle.

Unless he was with Ava. When he was with Ava, Jonas was happy to do whatever crazy thing she wanted.

The fact that Ava was his best friend had also rendered her his only friend. The other boys would see Jonas walk home from school with her and would relentlessly jeer at him. "Jonas has a girlfriend! Jonas is in looove!"

But Jonas cared about Ava more than he could ever care about the opinions of a gaggle of boys, and besides, they weren't entirely wrong. She wasn't his girlfriend, but he *wished* she was.

Jonas couldn't remember a time he hadn't had a crush on her. His father, Dieter, was fond of telling the story of when they had met: little Ava had been sitting in the hallway of their apartment floor playing with paper bricks that she had carefully stacked into an impressive structure. Dieter had come out of his home, gripping his son by the hand. Jonas had seen Ava, wriggled out of his father's grasp, and tottered over to her with all the speed of a three-year-old with a mission. He had knocked down her tower by accident and timidly said, "I'm Jonas, you're pretty!"

Then Ava had yelled at him for being a town destroyer and slapped his face. They had been friends ever since.

Jonas didn't remember that incident. In fact, he couldn't remember a time that he hadn't known Ava. He also couldn't recall a time when Ava hadn't tried to give him a heart attack whenever she saw the opportunity.

"Ava!" Jonas yelped. "You scared me!"

Ava giggled and punched his arm. "Sorry, Dummi!" she said, which was what she had always called him, a teasing insult that didn't befit Jonas at all, him being the best student in their school.

"Ya scream funny, you sound more like a girl than me!" Ava cackled.

Jonas grumbled and felt a blush creep across his cheeks. He rubbed his arm, which was still sore from her playful punch. Her night-sky eyes shifted to his sore spot and glistened with mischief as she folded her arms over her chest and said, "Sorry, you wanna kiss to make it better?"

Jonas was entirely certain that his cheeks were on fire. "No!" he lied, knowing that she would make him suffer if he was honest. Her musical laugh made his ears ring.

"Good! Now c'mon, quit gettin' lost! Let's go!" She adjusted the bag she had slung over her shoulder and grabbed her friend's wrist. Jonas struggled to keep from crying out. Ava was abnormally tough for a little girl: her father Otto Keller had been one of the best soldiers on the front of the Great War. He had only recently been blessed with sons: a pair of twin boys, Fritz and Oskar. For a long time, he had assumed he would never be able to pass down his skills. Since the day Ava had beaten the shit out of one of her schoolmates for saying she looked like a Jew, however, her father had decided she was worthy of learning to fight despite her sex. "Better you know how to fight either way," he'd said. "Girls get into trouble as much as boys, and you can't always rely on Jonas to save you."

Jonas probably could have saved her if she'd let him, but whether it was bullies or make-believe villains they confronted during their escapades, Ava preferred to be the one to fight for herself, and she could fight for herself better than Jonas could ever hope to fight on her behalf. Jonas was able to hold his own when he joined Otto's lessons, but he lacked the viciousness that had earned Ava the playground moniker of Bärchen— Little Bear.

"Uhm...we're pretty far from town, Bärchen..."

"So?" the girl giggled. "The further the better! No chance I'll have to hear Fritz and Oskar cry!"

Jonas nodded. In truth, he was just as eager to get away from his home. He loved his father, but Dieter Amsel was a man in a perpetual state of mourning. The Amsel household had the atmosphere of a memorial: any space that wasn't taken up by pictures of Jonas' milestones was occupied by photos of Magda Amsel, who had died bringing Jonas into the world.

Typically, when Dieter was away or when the miasma of mourning grew too thick for Jonas to bear, the boy would retreat to the Kellers' house. Unfortunately, Ava's mother was at her wits end dealing with two yowling newborns, and thus he and Ava had been spending more and more time exploring outside. Last week, Jonas had been laid up with a cold, and so Ava had gone deep into the woods to scout out a new place for them to play. She had returned with a victorious grin, declaring in a secretive whisper that she had found something incredible.

Now Jonas' cold was nothing more than a minor cough, and so Ava dragged him deeper and deeper into the forest. Over thornbushes, past craggy stones, and over mossy hills until at last, she announced that they had arrived.

"This is it?" Jonas muttered. "I don't see anything."

Indeed, it seemed there wasn't anything special about this spot. Two twisted trees among a throng of small saplings. One tree was alive, sprouting leaves and covered in weeds. The other was grey and dead.

"Here, it's right..." Ava scurried to the space between the twisted trees and knelt down, feeling at the forest floor until she found what she was looking for. "Aha!"

Jonas watched with wonder as Ava grabbed a hatch handle hidden by false grass and moss. She threw open the disguised door, revealing a brick staircase leading into utter darkness.

"Here," Ava said, reaching into her bag and pulling out an electric lantern that she must have swiped from her father. She handed it to her accomplice. Jonas fumbled with the device and finally turned it on.

"Go on!" Ava cried, pushing him towards the stairs.

"Is...is it safe?" the boy muttered, obeying nonetheless and trudging down first.

"Well, there wasn't anyone here before, but I didn't have a lantern when I found it, so maybe there are dead bodies!"

"Ava!" Jonas squealed, turning and briefly flashing the light in her glistening night-sky eyes. She laughed wickedly and pushed him again, nearly sending him toppling down the stairs before she turned and shut the hatch, making it so that Jonas had no choice but to continue his descent.

They reached the bottom of the steps and found themselves in an empty bunker with brick and concrete walls covered in mold and dying moss. A few fluorescent lights dangled from the ceiling, connected by frayed wires.

"What is this place?" Jonas mumbled as they searched the underground hideaway, peeking in the myriad of rooms. No dead bodies, much to Jonas' relief and Ava's disappointment. In fact, there wasn't much of anything. Almost every room was barren save for a few that offered twin bedframes and one which had a musty mattress. No crates, no ammo, nothing. It was almost like the architect had constructed the structure only to either die or decide that it wouldn't do for whatever purpose it had been built for.

"Maybe it's from the war?" Ava suggested, kicking at the walls to test its structural integrity and finding that the Bunker was solid: the walls and roof didn't collapse right on top of the two children, anyway.

"Looks like it wasn't ever used," Jonas noted, flashing his beam on the mattress and wincing when a huge spider skittered out. "And it's strange to have something like this in the woods."

"Maybe they built it before everyone ended up in the trenches," muttered Ava. "Nobody's been here in forever, though...so now it's ours!"

"Er...what?" Jonas muttered as she ran to him, grabbing his arm and dragging him back towards the entrance hall. He nearly dropped the lantern, but before it could fall from his fingers, she grabbed it and set it on the staircase, pointing it at the wall.

"Here!" Ava reached into her bag and pulled out two black containers and two paintbrushes. Jonas immediately recognized the labels on the containers and felt his face heat up.

"Ava, those are Papa's paints!" he squeaked. "They're for his models!"

"So?" Ava cackled. "He wasn't usin' 'em."

Fair enough. Dieter Amsel hadn't had work as an architect for almost two years, and so his little model buildings had been rendered playsets for Jonas. Dieter hadn't seemed to mind, declaring with a smile that it was better they make his boy happy than sit around and collect dust. He'd probably have a similar mindset about the paint.

"Okay," sighed Jonas. "But we're gonna have to pickpocket someone tomorrow, someone with a fat wallet so we can pay Papa back."

"Done! I'll hit that Jew Goldhagen! C'mon, let's make it ours!"

The two children set about painting the walls of their newly claimed clubhouse. First, they scrawled out a simple message: PROPERTY OF JONAS AND AVA, KEEP OUT!

Ava added a warning: OR ELSE YOU'LL DIE! Then she drew a painting of a bear mauling a potential intruder, an intruder with a hooked nose and Semitic features. Jonas giggled. With paint and plenty of playtime to spare, the children made the wall their canvas.

"Is your papa going to the *Reichsparteitag* festival in Nuremberg?" Jonas asked, scrawling a swastika.

"It's backwards, Dummi!" Ava giggled, painting over Jonas' crooked cross and drawing the correct version beneath it. It was only reasonable that Jonas wouldn't be as familiar with the symbol of the Nazi Party as she: Ava's father had supported Hitler since the Nazi leader's failed Beer Hall Putsch while Dieter Amsel had only just become an admirer.

"Papa wants to go, but he can't get off of work. Even if he could, he'd wanna stay with the babies and help Mama," Ava said. "What about your papa?"

"He said he's gonna try." Jonas dipped the brush again, somberly watching the paint drip onto the floor before the bristles touched the wall and he drew another swastika, this one facing the right way. "He doesn't have to worry about work, after all."

"Papa says Hitler'll fix everything and give everyone jobs," Ava declared.

"I hope so..."

"Don't worry! I won't ever let ya starve to death! Even if you run outta money, you can come live with us!"

"Really?" Jonas felt like a weight had been lifted off his heart.

"Yeah! But you'd have to sleep on the floor. You can't have my bed!"

"That's fine. I think it'd be fun to live together."

"You think?" Ava looked at him, her smile shining brighter than the flashlight. A speckle of paint was staining her cheek.

"Yeah, I'd definitely like to live with you," Jonas confirmed, suddenly wishing his own cheeks were paint-stained to hide his burning blush.

"When we're older, we can live together!" Ava suggested. "Hitler's gonna make everything better, so you won't have to move in because you go broke, but if you wanna live together anyway, then we'll have to wait until we're adults."

"Ah, like...married people?" Jonas squeaked, his heart hammering.

"Sure!" Ava declared. "You're the only boy I'd wanna marry. All the others are idiots."

"But you always call me Dummi..."

"You're not an *idiot*, you're my Dummi! It's different!"

"Av..."

"You wanna kiss?" Ava asked suddenly, her eyes sparkling. Jonas almost choked on his tongue.

"I! I!"

"If you wanna get married when we're older, you should get a kiss! Here, close your eyes and do this!" She puckered her lips. Jonas clutched the paintbrush so hard he almost broke it in two as his mind buzzed. A kiss? A real kiss! His instinct told him not to trust it, that it was far too good to be true, but his heart decreed that it was well worth the risk. He shut his eyes and puckered his lips.

He felt something brush against his mouth: not Ava's lips, but moist bristles. Jonas sputtered and spat, rubbing his mouth on his sleeve in an attempt to wipe off the paint Ava had smeared across his lips.

"A-va!" he gagged, and the girl cackled wickedly, leaping to her feet and grabbing the lantern.

"You're so gross!" she declared, bolting into the great chamber. Jonas grabbed a brush and chased her, dripping paint all along the Bunker's concrete floor.

"I'm gonna get you back for that!" he vowed, laughing even as he tried for a vengeful snarl.

"Can't catch me!" Ava cried, and her merciless giggles echoed about their new Bunker.

Germany, 1931

"Ava?"

Fourteen-year-old Jonas Amsel cried out for his friend as he descended into the Bunker, pausing only to shut the hatch lest someone else discover their secret spot. The lanterns were lit, which meant Ava was down there. She had fled from the schoolyard after decking Bruno Ackerman in the face. He'd taunted her for her dark hair and dark eyes, and Ava had responded with more viciousness than even she was typically wont to show. She'd swept his legs, knocking him to the pavement, and then punched him in the face until his handsome features resembled minced meat.

She had fled before the teachers or Bruno's parents could arrive on the scene. Jonas had known right away that she wouldn't be rushing home.

He found Ava sitting on one of the sleeping bags they had dragged into their hidden lair, scowling as she wrapped a bandage around her bruised knuckles. There was a trail of dried tears streaming down her cheeks. Vicious as Ava was, her fury had been borne from pain. It wasn't the first time she'd been called a Jew.

"Hey, Dummi," Ava muttered as Jonas sat beside her, drawing his knees to his chest and glancing down at her bruises. Protectiveness and affection made him want to ask if she was all right, but he knew better. She hated it when he treated her like a girl instead of a bear.

"I think he'll never smell again," Jonas said. "You definitely broke his nose."

"Easy to do," Ava huffed, tearing the bandage with her teeth and gazing down at her sloppy first-aid handiwork. "He's got some nerve calling me a Jew when he's got that big Jew nose."

She wriggled her fingers and then curled her hand into a fist, punching the air as though she wanted to strike Ackerman once more.

"So I'm expelled?" she grumbled. "Or just suspended?"

"Neither. You're not in any trouble," Jonas said, resting his cheek on his knee. "I told Herr Ackerman and Herr Weiss that I beat up Bruno."

Ava turned to him, night-sky eyes glistening. Puberty had made a childhood crush become a deathly distracting infatuation. Jonas had always known that Ava was pretty, but now every soft look she offered drove him mad.

"You did?" Ava said, and she sounded surprised. Jonas nodded.

"And they bought it?"

"Bruno ran with it. He didn't want his pa to know that he got beat up by a girl."

"Are...are you in trouble? You wanted to go to that chess contest..."

"Can't," Jonas sighed. "Maybe next year."

"Jonas!" Her freckle-flecked cheeks turned scarlet. "You shouldn't have done that!"

"It's all right, Ava," Jonas assured her.

"No, you're a good student!"

"Exactly: they went easy on me. *You* might have actually been expelled, and right before your gymnastics contest. I'll be okay."

"I..." Ava's shoulders sagged, and she gave him a smile, that beautiful smile that made his heart turn into a ball of flames. "Thanks. You're the best."

"I know." Jonas leaned against their painted wall, putting his hands behind his head and drinking in her praise. She punched his side, knocking the wind out of him.

"Ooooowww!"

"You're gonna have to train more with me and Papa now!" Ava declared. "Bruno might have to try and beat you up now."

"But I didn't actually..."

"Yeah, but he *said* you did, so he'll have to challenge ya once his face gets better. *If* it gets better. For his honor, you know."

"Oh, I can handle him," Jonas said. He couldn't match Ava

in terms of viciousness, but he had done well during Otto Keller's shooting and knife-wielding lessons. If Bruno Ackerman ever felt obliged to seek revenge, he'd have his work cut out for him.

"I guess. Is your papa upset?" Ava asked.

"He's not home. Left for Munich yesterday. He'll be back by the weekend."

"Oh! That's lucky, I guess! He's working for the Party, right?"

"For the *Schutzstaffel*," Jonas proclaimed with not a small amount of pride.

"Are those like...Stormtroopers?"

"Smaller, more elite. They're supposed to defend the Führer. Papa's working for the intelligence division, getting info on Jews and communists. It's real small right now: they're keeping filing cards in cigarette boxes, and Papa's boss has to keep borrowing a typewriter from another department. Has to carry it back and forth whenever he needs it."

"You mentioned your papa had a new boss! What was his name?"

"Heydrich, I think," Jonas said. "He and Papa both do horseback riding. Papa says he's a real talent, and a great fighter. The commies call him the Blond Beast. Hey, if Papa hears about my 'fight,' maybe he'll be happy: I can just say I was being like Herr Heydrich!"

"Well, beating up communists and beating up someone for calling me a Jew...it's a little different," muttered Ava, pinching a lock of her dark hair between her fingers and winding it around her hand. "Jonas, you don't think I look like a Jew, do you?"

Jonas sat upright. "No!" he cried so loud that his denial echoed about their hiding spot. "No, definitely not!"

"I have dark hair..."

18

"Don't let him get to you!" Jonas commanded, all but slamming his fist on the paint-splattered concrete floor. "You're not a Jew! You're prettier than any blonde in the school!"

The light that their lanterns offered wasn't great, but it was enough for him to see that Ava was blushing.

"Ass!" she said, punching his arm like she always did when he gave her a compliment. This time, however, her strike was soft, barely a brush. "But there are pretty Jews, y'know. Papa said that's why inbreeding is such a problem."

"Yeah, but pretty Jews are still evil. Then again, you're mean as Hell, so…"

She hit him again. He snickered. "I'm kidding!"

"You don't think I'm mean?"

"No, you're mean, but you're good even when you're mean, and you only hit people who deserve it."

"Like you?" She struck him again. He cackled.

"Yup!"

"You *do* deserve it. But you also deserve this."

She leaned forward too suddenly for him to think of defending himself, but this time she didn't tease or spit or lick his cheek or do anything else to ruin the moment. She planted a chaste little kiss right on his lips.

If Jonas Amsel's brain were a car, it would have combusted right then. He was entirely certain he had died and gone to Heaven. The only thought that went through his mind was *what what what Ava kiss what what.*

Another punch on his arm brought him back to life. "Hey, jerk!" Ava cried. "You've been trying all your life to get me to kiss ya and now you look like you're gonna throw up! I'm never kissing you again!"

She didn't keep that vow.

Germany, 1933

"Ava!"

Avalina Keller was every bit as vicious between the sheets as she was in every other capacity, which meant that stealing an intimate moment with Jonas at home was nearly impossible. The two of them were entirely too noisy to get away with screwing in their apartment complex.

Fortunately, they had the Bunker. And while it had been a hassle to drag a clean mattress all the way into the woods to replace the ancient moldy one that was filled with spiders, it was well worth it. They could be as vicious and noisy as they liked in the Bunker and their parents would be none-the-wiser.

They weren't being particularly noisy this time since Ava was in an affectionate mood, kissing her boyfriend deeply, breaking away barely long enough for Jonas to catch his breath and let out a delighted cry before her lips crashed against his again.

He wasn't about to complain, though. He grasped her tousled onyx hair with one hand while the other stroked her just so, earning a muffled moan from Ava as she deepened the kiss. A few more well-practiced caresses and she tumbled over the edge, at last breaking the kiss long enough to give him a chance to be noisy.

"Ava, Ava! Ah, God, Ava!"

"Jonas! *Jonas!*"

She collapsed on top of him, offering him another deep kiss before resting her cheek on his shoulder and fighting to catch her breath. Jonas sighed happily and kissed her temple.

"You're crushing me," he said after a moment, and she chuckled. The twin mattress didn't offer much space for snuggling, and so Ava was only barely able to shift herself off of her boyfriend, clinging to him tightly.

"We need an apartment," Jonas declared, chuckling as he wrapped an arm around her, saving her from falling off the bed. "Wanna get married?"

"Stop asking me that!" Ava giggled. It had been established long ago that her answer was *yes*, but the timing and circumstances would have to be more in their favor for them to actually tie the knot.

"You want me to marry you, you need a house and a job," Ava said, raking her hand through Jonas' sweaty sand-colored hair.

"You know, Bärchen, most girlfriends give pillow talk, not pillow nagging."

"It's not *nagging*, it's reality! We'll be out of school soon and I wanna move in with you! Screw in a queen bed in our house instead of the Bunker."

"Oooh, you don't like the Bunker?" chuckled Jonas. "You've staked your claim all over it."

He gestured to the wall above their heads, which was covered in graffiti, almost all of it naughty except for a few heartfelt, chase proclamations of love that Ava had scrawled on their anniversary or Jonas' birthday.

"I like the Bunker, but I wanna have a house, damn it. A *nice* house. We're not going to be neighbors once your papa buys a new house."

"Your family is moving too! Your papa got a raise!"

"About time, too! Fritz and Oskar need the space, they're driving me insane. But I want a place for just *us*. Besides a scary bunker with jimmy-rigged electricity."

She gestured to a flickering light above their head. Ava had managed to install a small generator to give their little hideout power again, but it was still a crude setup, barely better than what they had enjoyed as children.

"Once I finish school. We're still going to be close, Ava! We're practically still going to be neighbors! You're in the same cul-de-sac!"

"I know. Hm...you should join the SS." She ran her hand across his chest. "You'd look so handsome in the uniform."

"I'm not handsome right now?" Jonas teased, and Ava giggled impishly.

"Oh, you're handsomest when you're naked, but I can't show you off around town naked."

"You could *try*..." His quip earned him a light smack upside the head that made him chuckle.

"I think you'd be great in the SS," Ava said. "Besides the fact that you would look drop-dead gorgeous in the uniform, you've always loved puzzles and those detective books. Why not join your papa in the intelligence division? You could solve problems all day and get paid for it, plus you'd be serving the Führer!"

Jonas offered a thoughtful hum. In truth, he had considered it. There were certainly many upsides to the SS: prestige, respect, and yes, it would be very nice to have Ava brag about how handsome he looked in the uniform. Serving a great Cause, Hitler's Cause, the Cause that had made Germany strong, that had given hope and purpose to his father, that would be lovely.

Nevertheless, Jonas remembered how often his father had been away from home when he was a teenager and Dieter was throwing everything into the Nazi Cause. Hitler was Chancellor now, which might have made things a bit different.

Perhaps Jonas could get a cushy position that would let him be a good husband to Ava and a good father to their inevitable brood of Aryan babies while he served the new Reich.

If not, however, he would rather become a postman and be able to come home early to Ava every day. He couldn't count the number of times he'd heard Dieter mutter that he wished he'd spent more time with Magda. Jonas wouldn't let his country get between him and Ava.

"Maybe," he said. "If I can get a flexible job. Someone will have to watch the children when you're winning gold medals at the Olympics."

"Ah, good point," Ava sighed, nestling against him and tracing his bicep with her finger. "We'll have to wait until *after* the Olympics to get married."

"You've got to be the center of the world on your wedding day, eh?"

"Damn right! Then a honeymoon...Paris?"

"Rome."

"Done. Then babies."

"We could start on the babies now if you'd just stop..."

"No, no, no! I've got six gymnastics competitions! I may not be going to the Olympics, but I'm gonna get close!"

"You'll be in the Olympics one day," Jonas said.

"I'm sure, and by then we'll have a litter of babies! Not now, though. Jesus, Dummi, you're suicidal. If you got me pregnant, Papa would kill you. He loves you, but he'd still kill you."

"Oh, I don't doubt it...hey!"

Ava suddenly threw her leg over him, straddling him once more.

"Don't rush," she said, pressing her lips to his cheek. "Marriage certificate or not, we're together."

"Right..." Jonas muttered, smiling as he reached up and cupped her face in his hands. "God, I love you."

She kissed him deeply in response and he felt whole. Little bits of uncertainty dotted his path—the SS? A simple civilian life? Tiny potholes to be filled in later. He had Ava. As long as he had her, he was happy.

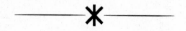

Germany, 1936

"Ava?!"

Nineteen-year-old Jonas Amsel clutched a small ring box in one black-gloved hand and brushed the leaves and thorns that clung to his SS uniform away as he descended the staircase. He hadn't been in the Bunker for a very long time. No need: he and Ava had been living together for the past year, since Jonas had finally joined the SS and they'd bought an old fixer-upper house barely a block from the cul-de-sac where the Kellers and Dieter resided.

Life was good. He was already up for a promotion, the Olympics had been dazzling, and now it was time. A few weeks ago, Jonas had bought a golden ring with a swastika in place of a diamond and told his father that he was finally going to propose.

"About damn time!" Dieter had laughed, clapping his son's shoulder and sparing a glance at the portrait of Magda that hung on his wall. "You'll give her a wedding for the ages?"

"You think Heydrich would attend?"

"If I can drag him away from his desk for a few minutes! Between running security for the Olympics and everything else, he's a busy man! Maybe I could convince him to be your firstborn's godfather—that would be a real honor!"

Jonas had nodded in agreement, grinning at the thought of finally having a child. He had been spending his few free moments looking down at the little ring and eagerly envisioning showing off his beautiful *wife* and perfect firstborn child to the rest of the SS men. He had been waiting practically his entire life to marry Ava and now that the day was close, so close that he could already hear the wedding bells, he felt like he was going to explode from excitement.

"Ava's my Magda, Papa," Jonas had declared, glancing at his mother's eternally smiling visage. "I want to give her everything she deserves."

"I know, my boy..." Dieter had said, squeezing his son's shoulder proudly. "Don't you worry: I'll handle all the boring paperwork and submit all the family trees to *Reichsführer* Himmler. Maybe *he'll* be able to attend the wedding! Ah, then again, her father will want it to be a Christian ceremony and I *know* Himmler won't like that, you know how he is about his Nordic paganism."

Everything had been planned out after that. Dieter would submit the paperwork, Jonas would set the mood. A nice dinner, a walk about town, and then he would propose to her at night, when the star-filled sky matched her eyes, beneath the fluttering swastika banners in the middle of town square.

Jonas had been ready. He had waited at the restaurant, brimming with happiness. Everything was going so well. He was an up-and-coming SS man, Reinhard Heydrich had called him a promising recruit, the Reich was rising, and he would soon be married to the woman he loved, the woman he had *always* loved. Visions of Rome and holding his firstborn and cheering with his children as Ava claimed a gold medal for

Germany at the next Olympics had danced in his head even as the minutes ticked by.

At first, he hadn't worried. Ava was always late. Late to class, late to parties, late to church. Always late. Never *too* late, but always late.

But when minutes had turned to hours, his excitement had morphed into worry. Jonas had waited some more, but dread had gnawed at his heart until he had set off to find her.

The Kellers' house was the first place Jonas had checked. He feared that something had happened: one of her brothers had finally fallen out of a tree and gotten hurt, or her mother had an accident, something terrible that had required her immediate attention.

Jonas had arrived at the Keller abode and found their door open. He had taken out his gun, prepared to fend off an invader, but he'd walked in and discovered that the house was empty. Not completely empty: a few of the Kellers' most prized possessions were gone, along with some of their coats and clothes, but everything else was still in place. Fritz had even left behind his favorite toy sword.

Jonas had run to his father's house, knowing that if something had happened, Ava would have left word with his father.

"The Kellers are gone?" Dieter had mused. "Strange. I know nothing about this."

"You...you don't think they were arrested, do you?"

It was an odd thought: Otto Keller was a loyal National Socialist. He would sooner cut off his own tongue than speak ill of Hitler or his Cause.

"I'm sure I would have known about that," Dieter had declared, his tone gentle, the sort he had used when Jonas had been little and he'd assured the boy that there were no monsters under his bed. "Let's wait and see. Perhaps they had a family emergency."

"No, no, she would have told me, I have to..."

Jonas had run out then, still clutching the ring, and torn the town apart searching for his beloved. The hospital yielded nothing. The men at Gestapo headquarters announced that they hadn't touched the Kellers. Nothing at Fritz and Oskar's school. Nothing. They were gone, all of them...

"Ava!"

He ran down the stairs of the Bunker, his last hope for finding her. He threw on the lights and dashed down the old paint-stained halls, the chill of the Bunker eating into his very marrow when he found nothing.

Gone. She was gone.

His knees gave out, and he collapsed to the ground, clutching the ring close to his chest as ice slunk into his heart and terror tore at his soul.

"Ava..."

TWO

Nazi-Occupied Prague, 1942

"Special Agent Amsel, the *Reichsprotektor* will see you now."

Jonas Amsel barely resisted the urge to let out a small sigh of disappointment as Reinhard Heydrich's secretary woke him from a brief but pleasant waiting-room nap. He had been dreaming of Ava again, and even though being reminded of her always made his chest ache, he liked to dream about her, to remember her eyes and her smile.

He stood up and thanked the secretary, straightening out his grey SD uniform and making sure that his many medals were glistening. Jonas didn't often wear all of his awards since, proud as he was of his accomplishments, the many swastika-emblazoned trinkets weighed him down, but Reinhard Heydrich would be upset if his favorite agent arrived bare-chested. Jonas Amsel's accomplishments were also Heydrich's, and Heydrich did love to be reminded of his own victories.

"Jonas!"

29

Jonas had barely taken a step towards Heydrich's office when a familiar voice struck his ears. He paused, turned, and offered his father a small Hitler salute and a smile. SS Major Dieter Amsel returned the salute, his blue eyes, typically so sorrowful even two decades after the death of his wife, crinkling fondly. Dieter whipped off his SS cap and brushed back his greying hair.

"You're here to see Reinhard?" the Major said. "I'll go with you. I needed to talk to him anyway."

"Papa, I don't need an escort to see my own boss," Jonas said, his voice harsher than he intended. His father's smile dipped and the misery in his eyes intensified. Though Jonas wanted to apologize, regret was an emotion not befitting an SS man, much less one of Reinhard Heydrich's agents.

"Ah, sorry, son..." Dieter said. "I guess you don't. Not now, especially. He's in a good mood for once. I think he's going to chat with you about our newest project."

"Project?" Jonas repeated, but his father grabbed his shoulder and pushed him towards Heydrich's office.

"Mustn't spoil the surprise! Go on, don't keep him waiting!" Dieter commanded, and Jonas nodded, quietly vowing to talk more with his father once he was through with his meeting. He marched into the office of the Head of the Gestapo.

Reinhard Heydrich had certainly moved up since his days of sharing a typewriter with Richard Hildebrandt and begging Ernst Röhm for extra funding. His new office was sprawling and grand, with a glittering chandelier casting a dazzling pattern of light onto a huge German eagle banner that hung above Heydrich's grand oakwood desk. Jonas maneuvered past a set of floral-print furniture and stood between two chairs that sat opposite to Heydrich's own leather seat.

Heydrich had more than earned his exquisite accommodations. He had gone from a shadow in the Nazi Party to its North Star. The SD Chief had collected honors and titles at a rate that would make even Hermann Goering blush, and though he had been sent to Czechoslovakia at the insistence of Martin Bormann in order to stifle his career before he got too big for his britches, Heydrich had taken the rebellious nation and transformed it into a model of Nazi occupation.

Heydrich didn't look up at Jonas as he entered. He was scrawling an untidy signature onto some sort of official paper, his long face screwed up in a look of aggravated concentration. Whatever he was signing off on, it must have been something he was barely willing to agree to. A silver ring on one of Heydrich's long fingers, emblazoned with a grinning death's-head skull and several Nordic runes, glittered as he flourished his pen. An *ehrenring*, the highest SS honor, a personal gift from *Reichsführer* Heinrich Himmler for his best knights. Jonas wanted nothing more than to find Ava, but his second dearest wish was to earn an *ehrenring* for himself.

Heydrich's ring in particular seemed vibrant, as though it reflected his character as a perfect National Socialist. Reinhard Heydrich had quipped more than once that his ring was lucky, and while Jonas was a skeptical man by nature and didn't typically believe in fortune good or ill, he believed it in the case of Heydrich's *ehrenring*. The SD Chief had dodged death far too many times for his good luck to be coincidental. He had been shot down over Norway and the Soviet Union during a somewhat ill-advised stint in the Luftwaffe, and yet he had walked away with little more than a scratch. It seemed like the man was invincible; perhaps that invincibility could be attributed to the little smirking skull that decorated his finger.

The *ehrenring* was supposed to be worn on the left hand, but Heydrich always wore it on the right, much to Himmler's apparent annoyance. Jonas wasn't sure why Heydrich insisted on wearing it improperly: perhaps out of a devilish desire to prod at his boss, perhaps because he liked knowing that he was so irreplaceable that he *could* prod his boss and get away with it.

Reinhard Heydrich was an enigma. Jonas remembered that when Ava had teasingly asked him if his father's boss was hand-some, he had genuinely not been sure how to respond. He *wasn't*, but he wasn't quite *ugly* either. On the surface, Heydrich seemed to be the perfect Aryan, in fact the only perfect Aryan in the upper ranks of the Reich. While Himmler was dark-haired, Heydrich was blond. While Goebbels was short, Heydrich was six-foot-two. While Goering was fat and slovenly, Heydrich was slim and a dedicated athlete who played more sports than Jonas could commit to memory—fencing being first he recalled, horse-riding the other since that was how Heydrich and Dieter had become acquaintances.

Upon closer inspection, however, flaws started to stand out: Heydrich's fingers were long and thin like a duo of spiders. His hips were a bit too broad, almost feminine. His features were a touch too soft in the right light, his nose was big and slightly crooked (ostensibly because of a horse-riding accident, but it was hard to know what was true and what was rumor when it concerned Heydrich.) Most particularly, when Heydrich spoke, his voice was strangely high-pitched. His enemies, perhaps suicidally, often called him Billy-Goat Heydrich because of his bleating voice.

Jonas had heard whispers about Heydrich becoming the Führer after Adolf Hitler passed since the Nazi dictator had no biological heir and was apparently quite fond of Heydrich. Jonas wasn't sure what would happen if Heydrich was ever offered the position. On one hand, Heydrich thirsted for power. On the other hand, the Gestapo Chief hated the spotlight. He hated giving speeches, he hated being watched, and he was used to being unliked, perhaps even comfortable being despised. Heydrich would only be able to govern through fear, and the position of the Führer required both fear and love.

It was a mark of Jonas Amsel's talent that he had gleaned the respect and admiration of a man like Heydrich, who didn't seem to like anybody. Heydrich had many nicknames: the Hangman, the Blond Beast, the Butcher of Prague, but in SS circles he was most often called *der Oberverdachtschopfer,* the Chief Suspicious-Mind, a man who trusted nobody.

Nobody except Jonas Amsel, whom Heydrich seemed to trust more than any other soldier in his employ.

Heydrich plopped his pen back in the inkwell and finally lifted his gaze. Jonas was well-versed in reading eyes, but Heydrich's were a language all their own. Bright, icy-blue, and strangely hollow. Jonas had stared into the eyes of criminals and sociopaths and had seen an emptiness that was similar, but not quite the same. Those eyes had the vacancy of an unfilled grave, of a space that had never been occupied by anything good. Heydrich's eyes reminded him of a once well-loved home that had been abandoned and left to rot.

"Dieter kept you?" Heydrich said, his tone even and crisp. Heydrich never used two words where one would do.

"You know I wouldn't be a second late otherwise, Chief," Jonas said. The corner of Heydrich's mouth quirked upwards, and he folded his long fingers on the desk. He always preferred to be called "Chief," no matter how high he climbed. Dieter often joked that deep down, Heydrich was still a fresh SS recruit giddily devouring British spy books and desperately trying to bring those novels to life.

"Did he tell you anything?" Heydrich asked, and Jonas shook his head.

"Good," Heydrich said. He cast a cold yet strangely contemplative glance at the fern that sat above his mantelpiece. A few of its leaves were turning brown.

"Your capture of Black Fox Ten has made rounds," Heydrich said, his squeaky voice barely allowing a trickle of pride to seep in. "The Führer was very impressed."

"I have to earn my title, Chief," Jonas said, barely repressing a proud smirk.

"Ah...*der Fuchsjäger*," Heydrich said, a true smile coming to his face, the smile of a dog-trainer whose hound had caught a nice, fat rabbit.

Ava's disappearance had given Jonas little to live for except the Nazi Cause. He had thrown himself into the deep end of the SS and had gained a widespread reputation for his ability to hunt down and capture resistance fighters, particularly the slippery Black Foxes.

The Black Foxes were a strange, expansive resistance movement. Led by a man known only as Papa Fox, they were a diverse bunch of Jews and gentiles who had one goal: to help the "undesirables" that the Nazis were determined to slaughter reach safe haven. The Black Foxes acted as a sort of underground railroad, shepherding the enemies of the Reich out of her borders. They weren't as violent as other anti-Nazi groups: they didn't conduct assassinations, many didn't even carry arms, but they were a very public enemy. A foe that brought bad press, and worse, a foe that was determined to free as many Jews as possible.

Jonas was well known for his ability to find and capture Black Foxes, so much so that he had gained a moniker of his own. *Der Fuchsjäger*. The Fox Hunter. Joseph Goebbels, the chief propagandist of the Third Reich, liked nothing more than to put out an article or a newsreel bragging about the Fox

Hunter's triumphs over the foolish Black Foxes. Papa Fox, during his daily broadcasts over Black Fox Radio, often warned his underlings about the ruthless Jonas Amsel. Heydrich had been bragging about his talented protégé during his meetings with Führer.

"You know, the last time I spoke with the Führer, he mentioned that he would like to meet you someday," Heydrich declared, leaning back in his seat and stealing a glance at the dying fern once again. "If you can do the job I have for you, I'm sure you'll get an audience with him."

"That would be an honor, sir," Jonas said, his eyes almost instinctually flitting down to the *ehrenring* shimmering on Heydrich's finger. The Hangman saw the Fox Hunter's envious gaze and his smirk broadened.

"If you're successful, I can personally guarantee that you'll receive an *ehrenring* of your own," the Butcher of Prague promised, running a finger over the smirking skull on his SS award. Jonas was unable to repress an eager smile.

"You see," Heydrich continued. "The resistance movement in Bohemia and Moravia is all but dead. I've successfully crushed any rebellious inclination in the Czechs. The Black Foxes, however, continue to evade me. They rarely sabotage our weapons or pop our tires...but they do worse than that by sending Jews to the Allies. Spreading enemy propaganda. They are a virus, and we have to crush their spirits completely. I've come up with an idea to do just that. Your father and I have been working on it for months. It's called the Fox Farm."

The Blond Beast plucked a folder from the tidy stack on his desk and slid it towards Jonas. "Sit and have a look," he commanded, and Jonas obeyed, plopping down in front of his boss and opening the folder.

It contained a few typed-up documents labeled with his

father's signature and some diagrams of what looked to be a small concentration camp. There were several pictures of the nearly finished product: a small concentration camp dotted with sturdy barracks. Jonas' photographic memory quickly captured a mental snapshot of every little detail.

"Is this a camp or a compound?" Jonas queried.

"Both," Heydrich clarified, stretching out his spidery hands and snatching the folder out of his underling's grasp. "This is my personal project, one I'm very proud of. While most of the time, we don't like to publicize the camps, the Fox Farm will be different. Everyone will know about it, and the Black Foxes will fear it. Every Black Fox that we have in custody, as well as their immediate family, will be sent to the Fox Farm once it opens next month. The Fox Farm will be in the minds of every citizen of the Reich, every soul in Europe. Nobody will be able to hear Papa Fox's voice without thinking about what will happen to them and the people they love if they assist him."

"So you'll be sending all of the Foxes I've caught to the Fox Farm?"

"Yes."

"I imagine you already have approval from the *Reichsführer*."

"He was very enthusiastic about the idea, but not as much as Goebbels. *He's* chomping at the bit to be the first one to make a film about it. And the Führer liked the idea as well, gave it his stamp of approval. The camp is almost finished, the captured Black Foxes are ready to be shipped in, but before the grand opening, there's something I want."

"Something to make the grand opening really grand," Jonas guessed, and Heydrich let out a small bleat of a chuckle.

"Correct. I want this to be a true strike against the heart of the Black Foxes. Ideally, we would hang their leader. Finally silence that Papa Fox..."

Jonas's lips thinned. If Heydrich was going to ask him to capture the leader of the Black Foxes, well, he would certainly try, but it was a tall order. Papa Fox never actually conducted any missions, and they had absolutely no leads about who he was, where he was from, or even what he looked like. He seemingly spoke every language in Europe fluently. With only a voice to go on, Jonas had little hope of tracking down Papa Fox in a month.

Fortunately, the Blond Beast saw the Fox Hunter's hesitancy and gave him the closest thing to a disarming smile that a man like Reinhard Heydrich could manage. "Don't worry. He'll get his due in time, but for the Fox Farm's grand opening, I want you to capture Black Fox One."

That made Jonas raise an eyebrow. Papa Fox may have been the leader of the Black Foxes, but his first lieutenant and best man, Black Fox One, was almost as infamous. All Black Foxes were mysterious to a certain extent: they never referred to one another by name, but by their rank, their number. Black Fox One, the most talented fighter in the resistance group, was a mystery even amongst the Black Foxes. None of the Black Foxes that they had captured so far knew anything about Black Fox One. Not his age, nationality, race, nothing. No SS man that had seen Black Fox One up close lived to tell the tale.

Heydrich wanted him to catch the uncatchable. Black Fox One would be a crown jewel, a prize for the Fox Farm.

Jonas smirked, pressed a black-gloved hand to his medal-clad chest, and vowed, "I'll get him, Chief. If I have to work day and night."

"Excellent," Heydrich said. "Then I'll be sure to provide whatever you..."

SLAM!

"HEYDRICH!"

Jonas' hand flew to his sidearm. He leapt out of his seat, nearly knocking the chair to the ground in his haste to defend his boss. Heydrich didn't even flinch, as though he knew somehow that he would not be harmed. As though he thought that he *couldn't* be harmed.

Jonas' hammering heart calmed slightly when he saw the intruder's garb: it was an SS man who had burst in. A few years younger than Heydrich with dark brown hair, blistering blue eyes, and a crescent-shaped fencing scar that cut from the bridge of his nose down to his left cheek. He was a recognizable figure to anyone in the SD: Viktor Naden, commander of one of the Reich's many *Einsatzgruppen* units. A man who conducted mass-shooting operations on the Eastern Front, mowing down entire villages of Jews and Slavs.

Viktor Naden, the so-called Beast of Belorussia.

Viktor Naden, husband of Black Fox 10.

Jonas had investigated the matter thoroughly and concluded that the Beast of Belorussia had not been involved in his wife's subversive activities. Nevertheless, it was an embarrassment for him, for the SS, and for Heydrich as Naden's direct superior. Fortunately for Heydrich, his all-star Fox Hunter had alleviated the humiliation by capturing Black Fox 10, Naden's wife, and her close associate Black Fox 27, Naden's twelve-year-old daughter.

Jonas had personally arrested both Black Foxes, even nabbing Naden's youngest, five-year-old Heidi, just in case. Arresting the little girls had been tough, the screams and howls still echoed in Jonas' nightmares, but it had to be done. By saving Jews, Katja and Nadine Naden had betrayed the Reich and negated so much of Heydrich's hard work. Black Fox 10 alone was probably responsible for the safe escape of hundreds of Jews and other undesirables.

Of course, Viktor Naden was none-too-pleased about his entire family being arrested. Jonas had been expecting the *Einsatzgruppen* Captain to come knocking on his office door any day. He wouldn't have thought, however, that the Captain would be brave and stupid enough to go right to Heydrich.

"*Reichsprotektor*, I'm so sorry, he just shoved past me—" Heydrich's secretary poked her head into the room. Dieter Amsel came running in a second later. Quickly, the Major shut the door in the secretary's face before marching towards Viktor Naden. Jonas' father grabbed the Beast of Belorussia's arm and muttered something forceful yet comforting under his breath, but the Nazi Captain evidently decided not to follow Dieter's counsel. He shoved him off and marched past the floral-print furniture, right up to Heydrich's desk.

Jonas braced himself for a fight, but the Captain's attention only flitted to the Fox Hunter for a mere second, hatred burning in his blue eyes briefly before he redirected his attention to the Hangman of Prague.

"Ah, Captain Naden," Heydrich said in a tone of slightly aggravated amusement. "I was wondering when you'd come by. You made it to Prague rather quick. You could have just called, you know."

It almost sounded like Heydrich was attempting to tell a joke, but in a strangely self-aware manner where he knew fully well that he was the only person who found any of this funny.

"Your little *pet*," Naden said, briefly turning his head to indicate *der Fuchsjäger*, "arrested my wife and my daughters!"

"He did," Heydrich said, and a heavy silence hung in the air for a moment, the discomforting sort of silence that

Heydrich seemed to relish. It was Jonas' father that finally broke it.

"Naden, let's…"

Naden let out a feral snarl and his fingers twitched as though he would have liked nothing more than to personally wring Heydrich's neck. However, something about Dieter's tone, cool but advisory, must have reminded the Beast of Belorussia that he was powerless in this situation and angering the Hangman would do nothing to help his family. Inhaling deeply as though to cool his inner fire, Naden leaned slightly over the desk.

"Look," the Beast of Belorussia whispered, his tone forcefully neutral, "I know we've never exactly seen eye to eye…"

Heydrich's frosty gaze traced the line of Naden's moon-shaped scar, and his smile widened almost imperceptibly.

"But this is my family, my wife, my *children*. My youngest is five and your agent still arrested her…"

"The youngest was placed into protective custody," Jonas said, finally daring to speak up. His reward for his contribution to the conversation was a snarl from Naden and an icy scowl from Heydrich that communicated more than any words: *shut up and let me handle this.*

"Protective custody?! We *all* know what that means! Let's not play pretend! Nobody here is a civilian!" snapped Naden, slamming an open palm on the desk.

"The older child is a confirmed Black Fox, and there is reason to believe the youngest may have known or participated in Black Fox activities," Heydrich said.

"She's *five*!" Naden cried, holding up five fingers as though to emphasize his child's young age before slamming his hands on the desk again. "Her sister is *twelve*!"

"Regardless, the youngest will need to be deprogrammed."

"Depro—?! What are you going to do to her?!"

"Not your department," Heydrich said, lacing his spider-leg fingers together and leaning back in his leather chair.

"Heydrich..." Naden's voice was trembling with fury and fear. "I know you have a daughter."

Heydrich's eyes flashed with fire, a rare guest in normally frosty irises. The message was clear: Silke Heydrich, his beloved daughter, was strictly off-limits.

Naden must have read the Hangman's look and realized that trying to get Heydrich to empathize with his plight would be like trying to wring kindness from a rabid dog. Nevertheless, he bowed his head and abandoned his SS pride, stepping back and clasping his hands in front of him.

"Please, please, release my children, and show my wife mercy," Naden begged, and Jonas felt his guts writhe when he heard a sob almost escape the Beast of Belorussia's throat.

The fire borne from Naden's ill-advised attempt to bring Silke into the conversation faded from Heydrich's eyes, but the Blond Beast's self-assured smirk did not return. The Hangman did not regard Naden's pathetic pleading with sociopathic glee or gloating. No, his eyes glazed over with utter contempt.

"Why?" Heydrich spat the question with more vitriol than Jonas had ever heard. Nervously, almost instinctually, the Fox Hunter glanced at his father. Dieter was quaking.

"Reinh—" Dieter dared to utter a word, but Heydrich didn't even seem to hear him. The Hangman sat up, leaning over his desk, prodding at the oaken surface with one long finger, emphasizing every word he spoke with a *tap*.

"You are a member of the *Einsatzgruppen*," Heydrich declared, and Jonas had never seen him so riled up. "Your job for the past few months has been to subdue Enemies of the State. Men, women, and yes—children, where necessary, where *appropriate.* You have performed this task without hesitation, and never once did you show them any mercy. And yet..."

Heydrich slammed a flat palm onto the table. It seemed like all of Prague trembled. Naden leapt back, shaking in his jackboots.

"Now that it's *your* woman and *your* children!" Heydrich pointed one long finger at the *Einsatzgruppen* Captain. He was almost shouting now, and it was strange to hear. Heydrich's high-pitched voice didn't befit a Hitlerian rant, and it wasn't quite the same as Goebbels' howling tirades. It was almost grating on the ears, like the shriek of an air-raid siren. It seemed almost inhuman, like the voice coming from the Hangman was that of a demon possessing his body.

"*Now* you want to show our enemies mercy. Tell me, Naden, do people like your wife *deserve* mercy?"

"I...I..."

"***Answer.***"

"My wife deserves..."

"And *why*? What makes *you* so special? Why do *you* deserve to have an exception?"

"I...I have served the Reich, I have done my duty, I've been loyal..."

"Until now." Heydrich stood up. He was barely taller than Naden, but right then he seemed like an absolute giant. "Get out of my sight. I have no tolerance for hypocrites."

It seemed as though a spell of silence had fallen upon Prague Castle. No SS man in the room even seemed to breathe for a moment until Naden, trembling, took a step away from Heydrich's desk.

"Fine..." Naden said, barely a whisper, more of a hiss. "*Fine.* I suppose I should have known better than to ask *you*. The Man with the Iron Heart, that's you. I'll go right to

Himmler, he at least has a soul. I'll go all the way to the Führer if I have to."

Heydrich's face was unreadable, but his tone when he spoke one single word was frightening. "Don't," he said, and Jonas couldn't tell if it was an order or a warning.

It didn't matter either way. Naden was already stalking out of the office. Dieter muttered something about following him, smiled at his son, saluted the Blond Beast, and then scurried out, nearly knocking over a swastika banner in his haste.

Jonas stood in silence for a moment, waiting for the awkward atmosphere to dissipate. When it didn't, he braced himself and turned to his boss.

"That was...something," the Fox Hunter said, trying to keep his voice neutral, to let Heydrich decide whether or not this was a joke or a serious remark.

Heydrich decided on the latter, of course. "He'll regret going to Himmler. He'll be lucky to survive if he goes to Hitler."

The notion that Heydrich had somehow been comparatively merciful to Viktor Naden was a strange one, though Jonas knew better than to say anything on the matter.

"It's funny," Heydrich said. "I was going to mention...do you remember Anniska Engel, the wife of *Leibstandarte* SS Major Engel?"

"Black Fox Twenty-Five," Jonas said with a nod. He remembered well: that had been one of his more famous catches even though most of the credit couldn't go to the Fox Hunter. The wife of one of Hitler's own personal bodyguards had been unmasked as a high-ranked Black Fox that smuggled Jewish families to safety almost literally under the Führer's nose.

"Do you remember who turned her in?" Heydrich's smile widened cruelly.

"Her son, Norman," Jonas answered. Major Leon Engel was lucky: his son's act of loyalty to the Reich had meant that his honor was preserved. He wasn't the husband of a traitor, he was a father who had raised his son to adore Hitler more than his own mother.

"It's an absolute travesty," Heydrich declared, gesturing to the door, "that one of my men can't demonstrate the ideological strength of a thirteen-year-old boy. This will kill Naden's career. Meanwhile, Major Engel rightfully shot that traitor in the skull and he's going places. Matter of fact, he's going right to the Fox Farm. He'll be the Kommandant. The Führer's personal recommendation."

"I'll be seeing Major Engel soon, then," Jonas said, fighting to maintain a casual tone. While the entire Reich had celebrated Leon Engel for following in his son's selfless footsteps and personally executing his beloved wife for her treachery, the entire affair had made Jonas queasy. He should have admired Engel like everyone else did, but instead he pitied him. The Fox Hunter didn't even like to imagine what the man had gone through in his soul when he'd pulled the trigger.

Sometimes, when he thought of his small role in their misery, when he remembered little Norman calling his hotline and begging the brave Fox Hunter to come and arrest his mother, Jonas almost wished that he had dismissed the boy as delusional and hung up.

Of course, that was a terrible thing to think: every Jew was an existential threat to Germany, and if the price of wiping them off the face of the Earth was ripping a few families apart, so be it. *Deutschland Über Alles*, Germany above everything.

That was what Jonas had been taught even before he had gone through SS training.

"When you capture Black Fox One," Heydrich said. "Goebbels is making a movie about him and his son, you know. You'd better hurry and capture Black Fox One or the Engels will have a film before you."

"They deserve the honor."

"I hope you won't let this incident bother you, Jonas," Heydrich said, and the Fox Hunter was startled to hear his first name come out of the Hangman's mouth. Heydrich had *never* called him by his first name.

Jonas was quiet for a moment. Heydrich didn't trust anyone, but he had given Jonas his favor, and outright lying would lose him that. And *that* would be dangerous.

"I'll do my best, sir," the Fox Hunter sighed. The edge of Heydrich's lip quirked up. He was satisfied.

"Good," the Blond Beast. "Then get to work."

THREE

"Jonas?! When was the last time you slept?!"

Jonas let out a noncommittal grunt in answer. The Fox Hunter had retreated to the small apartment that he shared with Dieter whenever he was in Prague: Jonas hated to be completely alone, and he knew that Dieter was glad for his company, so it was an arrangement that worked well for both of them.

Jonas barely looked up from the papers spread across his desk as his father entered their apartment and greeted him with an exclamation of concern. He was too busy squinting down at a document that listed the names of every Jew on one particular transport that Black Fox One had struck. The Fox Hunter had been burning the midnight oil trying to fulfill Heydrich's wish. He could probably count the hours of sleep he'd gotten in the last few days on one hand.

"There has to be a pattern, there *has* to..." Jonas mumbled, rubbing his exhausted eyes and hunching deeper as he let his pupils flit from document to map, map to photo, photo to roster. He was beginning to fear that there would be no common denominator to link all of Black Fox One's attacks, no way to draw him out. It seemed that the top Black Fox struck everywhere and anywhere: from France to Poland, from Bohemia to Denmark. He would flit from nation to nation, place to place, with seemingly no pattern to where and when he struck except that he struck quickly and left no survivors. That lack of survivors made Jonas' task particularly difficult: confirmed Black Fox One attacks bled in with conjecture.

The Fox Hunter felt a hand on his shoulder and looked up. Dieter was giving him *that* smile. That smile he had given Jonas when he was a ten-year-old trembling with anxiety the day before a big test.

"Hey, son," Dieter said gently. "I'm very proud of you, but you won't catch anything if you kill yourself working. Even the Führer sleeps."

The Major gestured to a painting of Adolf Hitler that hung on one of their walls. The Führer stood with one hand on his hip, blazing blue eyes obscured by a sheen of dust that covered the portrait's glass pane.

"Take a break, and I'll make you something to eat," Dieter said, at once an offer and an order. "I have a feeling if you haven't been sleeping, you also haven't been eating."

Practically on cue, Jonas' stomach snarled. Dieter cackled and slapped his son's shoulder.

"There we go!"

"Let me finish going through this *one* roster and then I'll take a break," Jonas vowed, smiling teasingly at his father. "And *I'll* cook."

"Oh, you rotten little shit!" Dieter laughed, giving his son a small shove. "Can you go back to being ten? At least back then you *pretended* to enjoy my cooking."

"I didn't pretend to *enjoy* it, I genuinely *appreciated* it,"

Jonas countered, connecting a line between two surnames he had seen on six different rosters of transports. *"Appreciate* and *enjoy* are two very different things."

"You know, your mother..."

Oh dear, here we go. Jonas braced himself, glancing over his shoulder as his father stepped beneath a grand portrait of Magda Amsel that hung above a small shrine of candles and bouquets. Dieter plucked a dying petal off one of the roses he'd left for her and let it flutter to the ground.

"She wouldn't even *pretend* to like my cooking," he said. "Not that she was a particularly good cook herself, mind! I remember once she somehow burned carrots! My initial plan when I was going to propose to her, you know, I was terribly broke at the time, so I couldn't afford to take her to a good restaurant..."

Jonas did his best to ignore old, familiar story about how Dieter had botched a romantic dinner and ended up proposing in a smoke-filled kitchen. The words his father spoke brought back awful memories. Proposal, ring, one knee, an enthusiastic yes. All things he had dreamed of but never achieved, as elusive as an *ehrenring*.

Work, Jonas commanded himself as the familiar weight of sorrow settled on his soul. Work was the only cure for such sadness. If he could work, he could do *something*. He could fight back. He could find her.

Jonas hissed as his pen ran out of ink. He tossed it onto the pile of empty utensils he'd accumulated. "Papa, do you have a pen?" the Fox Hunter asked, digging through his desk drawers and finding nothing.

"Ahhhh...damn, hang on, there must be one somewhere."

Jonas finally left his desk to join his father in searching their cluttered abode for a pen. He dug through one drawer, and beneath the glut of abandoned office supplies, he found a small box. Arching an eyebrow, he opened it and was surprised to discover a silver pocket watch engraved with a familiar custom rune: the rune Heydrich had on his plane, the Hangman's personal rune.

"Papa, what's this?" the Fox Hunter queried, holding up the box, and Dieter let out a flustered laugh.

"Oh, *there* it is! Ha! *Of course* we find it *now!*" the SS Major cried, strutting over and snatching the case from Jonas' hands. "This was supposed to be Heydrich's birthday gift. Went through all the trouble to get it specially engraved and then I went and lost it. It's a miracle either of us get anything done, you know: you inherited my sloppiness." Dieter jabbed his thumb back towards Jonas' messy desk, and the Fox Hunter snorted.

"Is that why you were panicking and ended up spending half your salary on those fancy fencing sabres?" Jonas queried.

"I know about horseback riding, nothing about fencing! And I couldn't get him *another* saddle. Ended up just buying whatever the shopkeeper told me to. Fortunately, Reinhard seemed happy with it. Even invited me to fence with him sometime."

"You didn't agree, I hope."

"I'll stick with horseback riding with him: I don't want to end up like Naden in more ways than one," chortled Dieter, tracing his fingers across his face before tossing the pocket watch on top of the table. "Ah, well, maybe I'll give it to him once the Fox Farm opens as a gift for the big occasion. Otherwise, there's always a use for it down the line. Can never have too many gifts for Heydrich, anything to cool his head when he gets moody."

"True," Jonas said with a nod before returning to the

drawer and yanking out some more clutter: crumpled paper, notes, bizarrely enough a single clean sock, and then...

He found another box, smaller than the one which had held the lost birthday gift. Jonas drew it from the depths and his heartbeat stalled.

A ring box. He dared to open it enough to peek at the trinket inside: a ring with a swastika instead of a center stone. Shimmering, still unworn.

Ava consumed his thoughts again. Tears battered at Jonas' eyes, and only his training kept them at bay. Six long, miserable years had gone by since the Kellers had vanished without a trace, and the pain, when he was willing to pay it mind, was raw as ever. Jonas wished he could know what had happened to them. The uncertainty of it all was almost worse than the agony of not having his Ava, his other half. It felt like a part of his soul was missing, like someone had ripped it out of his body.

And who was that *someone*? Jonas knew there could only be one answer: an Enemy of the State, an undesirable. Perhaps they had targeted Ava because of her National Socialist father, or because of her ties to the Amsels, or perhaps it was simply an unhappy coincidence. Jews, ever rapacious, were known to kidnap lovely girls for their disgusting ends, though Jonas had never heard of an entire family being taken. Maybe Ava's father had fought them? He gritted his teeth and shut the ring box, squeezing it in his palm.

Jonas had become the Fox Hunter for many reasons. Patriotism, obviously. He wanted to defend his nation against the plague of Jewry and crush their weak allies. It suited him too: like Ava had said, he had always loved puzzles, problems, detective books. He would have never made it as a camp guard or an interrogator, but he could connect dots, sniff out tracks, find clues and hunt down a villain.

That being said, one of the main reasons that Jonas had become the Fox Hunter was Ava. Her absence and the lack of a brood of Aryan children to tie him down made it easier to accept the job, and when he worked, he was driven by the hope that he would find her one day. A Jew would be captured, Papa Fox would be snared, and he would finally have a lead that would let him find his stolen love. Find her, save her...

"Jonas!"

His father's voice brought him back to reality. Hastily, Jonas shoved the box back into the drawer and slammed it shut. The Fox Hunter plastered a smile onto his face as he turned to Dieter, who victoriously held a pen aloft.

"Found one!" Dieter announced.

"You're the best, Papa!" Jonas chuckled, plucking the pen from his father's fingers and returning to the puzzle with a new fire of determination burning away his exhaustion. He would find Black Fox One, and hopefully doing so would bring him one step closer to Ava.

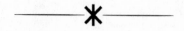

"Papa, get up!"

Dieter did not get up. He offered a groan to tell his son that he was awake and annoyed at the interruption, but he didn't get up.

The Major craned his neck a bit and opened one exhausted eye halfway to steal a glance at his boy, and despite how tired he was, he felt affection and pride bloom in his chest.

This was a familiar little ritual: Jonas bursting into his

room at an ungodly hour, brimming with pride brought about by an accomplishment that for one reason or another he could only achieve at 2 AM. It reminded Dieter of when his boy was little and had run to him with a perfect test score or a difficult crossword he'd managed to complete. Of course, ten-year-old Jonas Amsel's puzzles hadn't been as complex and important as those that the Fox Hunter was duty bound to solve.

Then again, ten-year-old Jonas Amsel had been bound to a reasonable bedtime and had never woken up his father anytime past midnight.

"Gah wha son?" grumbled Dieter, and Jonas held up a paper. Even in the darkness of his father's room, his lapis-colored eyes sparkled brightly.

"I've got it! The connection! Every single transport that Black Fox One has attacked, every *single* one had at least one Jew from the French city of Annuville."

"V'ry goo' son..." muttered Dieter, meaning it even though he could barely speak. His brilliant son *would* be able to find such a tiny connection, to parse out something nobody else had noticed. Dieter was as proud as he was desperate to go back to sleep.

"This is it! I'm going to call Heydrich and set a trap! We'll have Black Fox One in custody by the end of the week."

"Call him in the morning, son," Dieter said, lifting his face off the pillow enough to give his boy a paternal warning. Heydrich may have admired Jonas' dedication, but even the Hangman was likely to be asleep by 2 AM. That, or the Blond Beast was prowling about the local nightclubs. Either way, the Gestapo Chief wouldn't want to take any work calls at this hour.

"Ah, right, right," Jonas sighed, sounding rather disap-pointed. "I'll be patient."

"Get some sleep! You've done enough work!" Dieter commanded, sitting up on his elbow and pointing towards Jonas' room. He had adopted the papa-tone he had used on the rare occasions when his obedient boy had tarried before bedtime as a child. Jonas let out a groan that was almost identical to the sort he would let out as a little boy when confronted with *that* tone.

"Yes, sir," the Fox Hunter said, and he finally retreated into his room, practically skipping with glee.

The puzzle was almost complete. Soon, he would have victory, an *ehrenring* shimmering on his finger, another newsreel bragging about his exploits, and another lead to find his precious Ava.

FOUR

Operation Hubert was, by necessity, small. Although Heydrich had promised that Jonas could have whatever resources he would need to bring down Black Fox One, the Fox Hunter knew that he couldn't afford to bring the whole cavalry. If Black Fox One found himself confronted by an entire battalion of SS men, he would probably just flee, and if he got away, he would probably be able to put two and two together and realize that the Fox Hunter had discovered his *modus operandi*.

And if *that* happened, well, then Jonas would certainly never catch the Black Fox. Not before Heydrich's deadline, at least.

So he asked for a small troop of talented men and a transport of Jews, half of whom were from Annuville. A truck with a purposefully popped tire resting at a gas station in the middle of a sleepy city in the Sudetenland would prove to be a perfect lure.

Jonas' men, all decked out in plainclothes, were milling about the gas station shop as supposed civilians, fixing up cars as mechanics, and waiting in cars pretending to be irate customers eager to fill up their tanks.

"You think...uhm...do you think he'll toss a grenade?" muttered one undercover SS man who was sitting beside Jonas in a beat-up old car. Jonas, who was pretending to read an old newspaper, cast a scowl at the cadet for breaking character.

"No," he answered quietly. "He won't be foolish enough to open fire here. He won't want to harm the Jews."

"And that's why *we* can't open fire."

"Not unless you'd like to accidentally blow us all to smithereens. Not unless it's necessary *and* you've got a really clean shot."

The locale had been chosen for just this reason, of course. Heydrich wanted Black Fox One alive, and Jonas didn't want his men to get too trigger-happy. The gas station created an environment where the only possible way to get the Jews out safely would be for Black Fox One to wait until the Nazis fixed the popped wheel and then stealthily steal the truck. Black Fox One would likely try to wait on top of the van, using the darkness as a shield and hoping that the apparently distracted and agitated SS men wouldn't notice.

"Remember: aim, but don't fire unless I say so," the Fox Hunter commanded. "We want him alive."

"Yes, sir."

Jonas lifted his gaze above the torn pages of his newspaper, tired of reading the same diatribe against world Jewry for the nine-hundredth time. He had already picked out every typo. (The fact that the author had misspelled "*Reichspro-tektor* Reinhard Heydrich" as "*Reichsprotektor* Reinhart Heidrik*" being the most amusing one; Jonas would have loved to have been in the editor's office when the Hangman inevitably phoned him to complain about *that* one.) Now, anxiety and excitement had given way to boredom. Jonas could deal with discomfort, but boredom was truly torturous.

He glanced at the windows of the station shop, wondering if he could exit his car. Maybe he could pretend to be a frustrated customer voicing a complaint about the hold-up. Jonas had always been a very effective liar: hunting Black Foxes required such a skill. To tell when someone was lying, one needed to be acutely aware of the little tells, aware enough to know how to subdue such microscopic hints when he himself fibbed.

Jonas looked into the shop and debated whether or not to go inside. He glanced down at the error-ridden newspaper and decided that it would be worth it just to get something else to read.

"Stay here," Jonas commanded the cadet. "I'm going to check on the men inside the shop."

"Yes, sir," the cadet said, twitching nervously as he stared into the darkness.

The cloudy night offered enough cover that Jonas likely would have been just fine with minimal acting, but nonetheless, he was keenly aware of his every miniscule motion: his frown pulled down just so, how he paused to stretch his muscles before marching into the store, his every step carefully performed to show his anger without over-exaggerating and making the ruse too obvious.

The Fox Hunter reached the front door and realized right away that something was wrong: he couldn't see his men milling about the aisles or the soldier he had assigned to the register.

Jonas broke character and let his hand flit towards his hidden sidearm as he carefully entered, ducking behind a rack of cigarettes as the little bell rang to announce his presence. He prepared for an ambush but received nothing.

"Hello?" the Fox Hunter called out, shuffling towards the counter and catching a whiff of a familiar coppery scent. He already knew what had happened, but he looked behind the counter to confirm, grimacing when he saw three dead plain-clothes-clad SS men piled behind the cash register.

Shit! Black Fox One knew this was a set up! He must have snuck in and taken them out one by one! Then where...?

As though in answer, he heard a scream outside.

Jonas wrapped the mantle of the Fox Hunter about himself and grabbed his firearm, rushing outside. He was greeted by a chaotic scene. A few SS men were laying hither and thither, their throats slashed. The rest had abandoned their posts and were flashing lights into the dark, blinding each other as they tried to glimpse a moving shadow.

One of them, perhaps hoping to use the Jews trapped in the van as hostages, started to undo the lock on the back of the trunk. Hardly had he done so when a figure in black leapt down, slashing his throat in one swift movement before chucking a knife at another SS man. The blade hit the Nazi's heart with expert accuracy, toppling him.

One SS man flashed a beam of light onto the attacker, and finally Jonas saw his quarry. Black Fox One was much shorter than he would have suspected. The mysterious figure was dressed entirely in black: black boots, some sort of black armor, a black hood pulled over his head and a black gas mask that hid his face.

The armor must have been light, however, as Black Fox One leapt on top of the truck with the agility of a cat and then hopped to another car, pulling out a gun and killing the SS man stationed in the driver's seat. Another SS man, deciding that the risk of firing a gun at a gas station was well worth it, shot at Black Fox One. He hit a gas tank, but to Jonas' surprise the truck didn't blow them all to Kingdom Come. Maybe the bullet hadn't been hot enough to ignite the gas.

Another dagger flew from Black Fox One's hand, striking the SS man that had shot at them. Jonas ducked behind a car, gripping his gun and gritting his teeth. Plan! He needed a plan. The damn Black Fox was too quick and the darkness too thick: he would never get a shot off.

Black Fox One finished off what he must have thought was the last of the SS men. He yanked a throwing knife from an SS officer's throat and glanced about. Jonas peeked over the hood of the car, his heartbeat quickening when the empty eyes of the gas mask fell on his hiding spot.

But Black Fox One merely rolled his shoulders and turned, strolling towards the van filled with Jews.

Back turned, Jonas thought, shoving his gun into its holster. He had never been the best shot and didn't trust his ability to hit the darkly dressed target when he could barely make him out, but he could slip close and stab the Black Fox, capture him alive.

Careful not to tread on the broken bits of windshield glass scattered across the ground, Jonas crept towards Black Fox One. He was much taller than the Black Fox: for as quick as he was, Jonas would surely get the upper hand if it came down to a hand-to-hand battle. The Fox Hunter lifted up his dagger, plotting where to strike: chest or arm? He needed to make sure Black Fox One wouldn't bleed out before he could deliver him to Heydrich.

He didn't get to decide: Black Fox One must have heard his breathing or his pounding heartbeat.

In a split-second, the Black Fox spun around, grabbing

Jonas by the wrist and twisting it, wrenching the knife from his hand. The Black Fox was small, but he was able to use Jonas' own weight against him, ducking and then striking, bringing the Fox Hunter down.

Jonas' back slammed against the pavement. He felt chunks of glass stab into his spine and gasoline splash his cheek. The beam from a flashlight one of his comrades had dropped shone in his eyes, stunning him for a moment as the Black Fox lifted up the SS blade he had stolen, preparing to end the Fox Hunter.

Jonas barely had a second to think, but he was braced to die. He had tried, at least. He would die for a great Cause. His only regret was that he would never...

"Jonas!"

At first, he thought he was hearing things, hearing her voice one last time before he met oblivion, but then he realized that the quiet exclamation had come from beneath Black Fox One's mask.

Shock struck him worse than a dagger in his heart.

"Ava!?"

The scent of gasoline was overwhelming, and for a moment Jonas was certain that he was merely hallucinating. But then Black Fox One lowered the knife and spoke again, a sharp command in a voice he could still recognize after all these years: Ava's voice.

"Quit your job."

Then she slammed the back of his head on the concrete, and the world went dark.

FIVE

"Jonas...Jonas!"

He knew when he awoke and found himself in a hospital rather than a heavenly courtroom that his ears hadn't been fooling him. Black Fox One would not have spared him for any other reason.

"Ava...Av..." Jonas sat upright too quickly, and blinding pain sent him falling back onto the pillow. Dieter's voice came from somewhere above him, panicked, begging him to lie still for a moment while he got the doctor.

Vaguely, Jonas heard the doctor say that the Fox Hunter had a concussion. He heard the doctor mutter that as of today, Black Fox One had finally left an SS survivor. Someone had finally seen "him" up close.

"H-home..." Jonas mumbled, trying to sit up again. "Wanna go home..."

"Oh, dear..." Dieter mumbled, pressing his palm to his son's forehead the way he had when Jonas was a child with a nasty cold. "Doctor, would it be possible to transfer him? Can he recover at home?"

"Err...I suppose it's possible, though I'm not sure *Reich-sprotektor* Heydrich will approve. He'll want to speak to him."

"Just..." Dieter exhaled sharply, glanced about the ward, and leaned confidentially close to the doctor's ear. "Just let *me* handle Heydrich. Let me take my son home."

"All right, Major," the doctor relented, his voice laced with nervous empathy.

Jonas sighed happily. Home. No ears, no bugs, no spies listening. Once he was home, he could say what he needed to. *Ava is alive. Ava is Black Fox One.*

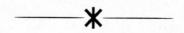

"W-WHAT?!"

"I know it sounds insane, Papa, but it was her," Jonas said, fidgeting with a peeling part of the bandage wrapped about his arm. He sat on the edge of his bed: his head had cleared enough that he could speak and think somewhat coherently, though the revelation that his greatest foe was his dearest love still made his skull ache worse than any injury he'd sustained. Dieter, who had been presenting his son with a mug of tea, nearly dropped the cup in his shock.

"S-son," the Major stuttered. "That's...you must be...your head is still..."

"Father, I'm not crazy!" Jonas snapped, bringing a fist down on the end of his bedframe, making his furniture tremble. "It was Ava! She told me to quit my job and she let me live! I don't..."

The Fox Hunter's anger tapered into confusion, and he fell silent. He bit his lip and glanced past Dieter, at the living room, at the drawer where he still kept the swastika ring.

Ava, *his* Ava. He gritted his teeth. His lovely, sweet Ava had been a loyal National Socialist, more ardent than even he. It didn't make any sense. She had been happy with him, happy and eager to serve the Reich at his side. She would never join the Black Foxes of her own free will.

Maybe she was kidnapped...kidnapped by Jews? Brainwashed? Turned into some sort of weapon? She's obviously in there somewhere. She wouldn't have spared me if she was completely gone, if she hated me...

The Fox Hunter planted his feet on the carpet and shakily stood up. "I'm going to find her."

"J-Jonas...?"

"Don't you see, Papa?" Jonas said, stalking out of his room, into the living room. "I don't know what happened to Ava, but it must be something awful. Brainwashing, or perhaps they're holding her family hostage until she brings them one particular Jew from Annuville."

"Son..."

"I *know* she's not doing this willingly, I *know* it, but nobody else will understand. She's killed so many SS men."

"She's dangerous, son!" Dieter exclaimed, shuffling after his son and glancing almost beseechingly at Magda's portrait as he did so, as though he hoped to somehow summon her ghost for support. "I know this...this is hard for you, but if you tell Heydrich, perhaps he'll give you a different mission."

Jonas stopped and turned to his father with a scowl, shaking his head. Dieter nodded once, conceding his own stupidity. As Naden had said, the Man with the Iron Heart couldn't be trusted to offer mercy.

"No, out of the question. Heydrich can't know anything about her. He'll..." Jonas inhaled sharply, imagining Ava captured, Ava in a camp, Ava beaten and...

He shook his head and knelt down, pulling the dusty ring box out from the depths of the drawer.

"You remember what he said to Naden," Jonas whispered, gripping the box tightly. "He'd kill her. I can't...I *can't* let anything happen to her."

"I...I..." Dieter clutched at his chest, breathing sharply, trying to calm his hammering heart. "Jonas, he's *Heydrich.*"

Jonas almost laughed. *He's Heydrich.* That alone meant so much. Keeping anything from that man would be a feat of Olympic fibbing. *He's Heydrich.* That meant he was dangerous. If he found out that Ava was Black Fox One, he would rip the Reich apart to get at her. If he found out that Jonas knew Black Fox One's identity and hadn't told him...

Jonas was more than willing to risk Heydrich's wrath to keep Ava safe. Of course, now Dieter knew too. And if the look of terror on his father's face was anything to go by...

"Papa, please," Jonas begged, clutching the ring box to his heart, and casting a glance at the picture of his mother hanging on the wall. "She's my Magda. I have to save her. I *have* to."

"Jonas..." Dieter sounded like he wanted nothing more than to melt into the shadows and simply stop existing.

"I can trust you, right, Papa?" Jonas said, standing up and reaching out almost desperately. "I can trust you?"

Dieter glanced down at his uniform, then at the portrait of Hitler. He tightened his jaw, his gaze gliding to Magda's shrine, at the wilting flowers he still set beneath her portrait all these years later. The Nazi Major let out a squeak as though he was repressing a hiccup.

"Y-Yes, son...of course..." he said, and his voice was pained, like the words he spoke were needles. "I won't tell Heydrich. Just...please stay safe. I can't lose you too..."

Dieter stepped forward and wrapped his arms around his

son, squeezing him tightly and quietly muttering, "I'm sorry," as though he feared embarrassing his son even in their own home.

"I'll be okay, Papa," Jonas promised, patting his father's shoulder and squeezing the little box. "I'll be okay."

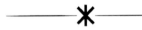

"Ah! The sole survivor!"

When Jonas arrived at Prague Castle just as the sun was beginning to dip beneath the medieval city and Heydrich greeted him with a grin and a slap on the shoulder, he knew he was going to have trouble. The smile that Heydrich gave was a viper's smile. Jonas should have been greeted as a failure. That Heydrich was seemingly regarding him as an injured hero was a tell: the Hangman already suspected something.

"Come," Heydrich said, pushing the Fox Hunter away from Prague Castle's grand office.

"Err...sir? Don't you want my report?"

"I already read your report, Amsel, I don't need it again," Heydrich said, waving a dismissive hand. "No, we're going to celebrate."

"Celebrate?"

"You're alive. Is that not something to celebrate?" The Hangman's voice became slightly too high-pitched. It almost grated on Jonas' ears. The Fox Hunter glanced at the Butcher of Prague's *ehrenring*, the shimmer of the silver almost blinding. The skull grinned menacingly from Heydrich's long fingers.

"I...suppose," he muttered.

"Don't be so dour," Heydrich commanded. "Besides, I

want to introduce you to Major Engel. He just arrived in Prague. You two will be working together frequently after the Fox Farm opens up."

"Oh, that's great, Chief," Jonas said, his mouth feeling dry. Major Engel, the man who had been married to Black Fox 25, the man who had shot his own wife. A week ago, Jonas had pitied Engel, unable to even imagine what it would be like to be in his shoes. Before, remembering what he had done to the Engels had made him somewhat queasy, and he had despised himself for such weak feelings of hesitation. *Now...*now that slight queasiness had become gut-churning guilt.

He followed Heydrich down the hall, past stiff guards and portraits of Hitler. Outside, they strolled into the small paved area behind the well-guarded ornate front gate and were quickly approached by an SS officer bedecked in a uniform that bore the telltale markings of the *Leibstandarte* SS—Hitler's personal bodyguard.

Major Leon Engel was a handsome enough gentleman, and Jonas could see why Hitler had chosen him for his guard: he was a model Aryan. Neat blond hair, bright blue-green eyes, only an inch or two shorter than Heydrich.

When Engel drew close and greeted the Hangman and the Fox Hunter with an enthusiastic "Heil Hitler!", however, Jonas was able to get a closer look and see cracks in the perfect Aryan facade: bags beneath his eyes too heavy to merely be the result of long work nights, a listless emptiness to his perfectly German irises, a smile that was twisted and warped at the edges like a hunk of metal struck by a bomb. Tiny details, imperceptible to anyone except someone like Jonas, someone trained to see what others wanted to keep hidden.

Engel offered Jonas the hand he had used to shoot his own wife and Jonas shook it, vowing to himself that he wouldn't make the same terrible choices as the Major. He would rather die than become this hollow shell of a man.

"You're going to have to tell me everything!" laughed Engel as Heydrich led both of his underlings to an open-topped Mercedes. A driver opened the door for Jonas, letting him in first. Leon sat beside him, and Heydrich hopped into the passenger seat without even opening the door, wearing a mischievous, almost boyish smirk.

"You'll have plenty of time to chat, though I doubt you'll want to for long!" the Hangman declared giddily, like a child that was being driven to the candy shop. "We're going to have fun tonight, boys. All on me."

"You're too generous, sir!" cackled Engel.

"You really are, sir," Jonas concurred, trying to lean out of the car so he would be as far from Engel as possible. "Uhm, where are we going?"

"Single fellow like you, Jonas," Heydrich chuckled, turning his body so he could face the Fox Hunter. "You really should know all the prime spots in Prague. We're going to the First Circle. Boring place during the day, but at night, it really comes to life!"

The Blond Beast glanced at his driver as though to make sure he wasn't listening before he leaned a bit closer to his comrades and said, "The girls are very talented."

Engel let out an excited bray of a laugh, and Jonas copied him even as his heart started hammering. *Shit!* He remembered how Walter Schellenberg, a fellow high-ranked SD officer, would bitch and moan constantly about Heydrich's unfortunate tendency to corral some of his underlings and drag them along on his romps through the nightclubs and whorehouses of Europe. Jonas had always been spared such indignities, perhaps because Heydrich was acutely aware that such outings were embarrassing punishments rather than exciting rewards and had chosen to show mercy to his favorite agent.

Heydrich's mercy, however, was as limited as his self-control when it came to his libido. The Hangman didn't have a mistress, preferring one-night stands, seemingly never visiting the same lady-of-the-night twice. That was either because he meant it when he said he only loved his wife and the other women were but a means to an end, or because...

Jonas really didn't want to think about the other potential explanations for Heydrich's behavior.

Regardless, it didn't matter. Jonas knew this wasn't just an incidental little field trip. Heydrich was doing this on purpose: he knew that such a venture would make the Fox Hunter, who was well-known for being a conservative that was married to his work, nervous. A nervous man was more likely to let a mask slip.

Jonas studiously hid his nervousness and pretended to laugh along with Engel even as his heart battered his ribcage. They stopped at a townhouse that must have been one of Heydrich's little hideaways to change into civilian garb before switching cars. Heydrich always looked a bit odd in plain-clothes: a suit didn't suit him as well as the rune-emblazoned SS uniform. He stuck out too much.

They arrived at the First Circle just as dusk turned to dark and the "boring" daytime bar became a thriving nightclub. As Jonas followed Heydrich and Engel (the latter of whom was practically skipping) into the building and towards a circle of cozy chairs in one corner, he felt his head grow light.

The First Circle was packed. Scantily clad girls flitted from customer to customer, trying to determine who would pay the most for the least. The pungent scent of alcohol, cigars, and salt attacked his sinuses, and Jonas was glad when he was finally able to sit down. He could see why Heydrich liked this place: good cover. Nobody would be able to pick one John out among the sea of casually dressed Germans getting serviced. Even Heydrich, who usually stood out in a crowd, could blend in and enjoy himself without having to worry about his nocturnal activities coming back to bite him in the morning.

"To the Führer and the Cause," Heydrich declared when, with a snap of his fingers, he summoned a waitress with a tall, expensive glass of brandy. She poured the three SS men drinks, smiling and winking at Jonas as she handed him his glass. The Fox Hunter gave a polite nod and joined Engel in toasting Hitler and his thousand-year Reich, downing the shot. Heydrich only took a small sip.

Ah, that's how it's going to be, Jonas thought. Drinks and women, both fantastic ways to loosen lips. Jonas wouldn't be utilizing any of the girls tonight, and he had always been a tight-lipped drunk anyhow. He would be fine if he could just keep a cool head until the *Reichsprotektor* grew sick of testing the Fox Hunter and left to enjoy himself with one of the girls. And if the Hangman's eyes, which hungrily leapt from lady to lady, were anything to go by, that wouldn't take too long.

"I hope there aren't any Czechs here, Chief!" cackled Engel, eyeing one dark-haired beauty a few feet away.

"Don't be picky, Engel. You're not finding a new wife here," Heydrich replied, and though his tone was cheerful, there was a biting edge to it. Engel winced as though the Hangman had struck him.

"Ah...right...well...Amsel!" Eager to get off the subject of wives, Engel slapped Jonas' shoulder. "When the nation finds out you defeated Black Fox One, the women will be paying *you* for *your* attention."

"Ah, well," chuckled Jonas, "I haven't defeated h...him yet."

ELYSE HOFFMAN

He took a swig of brandy, and despite the way it burned his throat as it went down, Heydrich's eyes, pinned unblinking to the Fox Hunter, made him feel like he'd swallowed ice.

"I was hoping to discuss the issue with you, Chief," Jonas said. "I had another plan to get him."

"Another brilliant idea?" Heydrich muttered, one hand curling into a fist. The *ehrenring* glistened. "I don't suppose you got a good look at him."

"How tall is he?" Engel interrupted, finishing off his shot and immediately calling a waitress over for a refill. "I heard he was taller than the Chief."

Heydrich's eyes flashed.

"Oh, he was much shorter than the Chief," Jonas assured his comrades. Heydrich's lip curled and he took another sip of brandy. Engel thanked the waitress for her service by slapping her bum. She let out a playful shriek. Jonas winced.

"Don't get too carried away, Engel," Heydrich advised, and the future Kommandant cackled.

"Just having fun, Chief! The Fox Farm won't be this exciting! Ah, how is your father, Amsel? You know, I've met him, but I've never met you."

Miraculously, Engel finished another cup of brandy. He called for the waitress again. Heydrich's brow was starting to crinkle.

"You've met my father?" Jonas said. "I don't think he mentioned–ah!"

A woman appeared behind the Fox Hunter. She set her hands on his shoulders and smiled, her eyes misty. Out of the corner of his eye, Jonas saw Heydrich smirk and wondered if the Hangman had every prostitute in this place under his employ. It wouldn't be the first time the Blond Beast had utilized such tactics. Jonas

70

knew all about the Salon Kitty brothel that Heydrich ran in Berlin, a building meant to service German higher-ups and foreign dignitaries. A whorehouse with microphones under every pillow and one-way mirrors in every room, where every prostitute was trained to pluck politically sensitive material from her mark.

"Fräulein," Jonas said politely, shrugging the woman off and downing most of his drink before holding up his glass. "Another?"

Heydrich's smirk twitched, and the girl sighed, but obeyed, running to the bar.

"Your father and I were both in the same boat!" Engel chuckled, and somehow in the short time Jonas had been busy with the woman, he'd finished off another glass. If Engel's liver lasted the night, that would be a true miracle. "We've been working together on the Fox Farm for a while, but even before —oh, thank you, Fräulein!"

The lady that had tried to offer her services to Jonas returned with another bottle of brandy. She topped off Heydrich's glass, gave Jonas and Engel a refill, and then cast a scowl at the Fox Hunter when Major Engel copped a feel as she scurried off to find another mark. Jonas flashed her an apologetic smile. Heydrich by now was looking at Engel like the SS Major was an unruly toddler making a scene in a nice restaurant.

"Anyway," Engel said, and now his speech was slightly slurred. "Dieter and I, we're both artists, you know. Artists couldn't get by in Weimar, not with Jews infesting the place. I was an art student, but the Jew professors, you know, they only appreciate their own ilk. Subverting our culture with their degeneracy. They don't appreciate true beauty. Same issue for your father as an architect: Jew leaders didn't want truly beautiful buildings. Ah, well, that's all changed. The Fox Farm will be a real beauty!"

"Right, right..." Jonas said, pretending to listen to Engel's drunken diatribe while his gaze was trained on Heydrich. The Hangman had stopped smiling.

"Engel," Heydrich said when it seemed that he could bear no more prattling. "That blonde in the red number has been eying you this whole time. If you don't take her, I will. Fair warning."

Jonas wasn't sure if he was grateful to Heydrich or aggravated that his perfect distraction was being banished. Engel's misty eyes followed Heydrich's long finger, and he cackled when he saw the fair Fräulein.

"You're too generous, sir!" the Major cried, clumsily rising to his feet, swaying as he finished off his final drink. "If you'll excuse me, gentlemen. Give my best to Dieter, Special Agent."

"Right," Jonas said, smiling at the Major and pitying his poor target.

"You don't seem very excited, Amsel," Heydrich observed once Engel had disappeared into the throng of drunkards and prostitutes. "You can be both a good husband and a nightclub prowler. You can be one or the other. Neither, though? People will call you a faggot."

"I, ah, just don't want to catch anything, sir."

"Oh, you don't have to worry about that here. This is *my* stomping ground. I'm very careful. Always very careful about *everything*."

"*Reichsführer* Himmler would disagree, sir," chuckled Jonas, hoping that his jocular tone would be acceptable in this casual setting. "He did tell you to stop flying for the Luftwaffe and driving around in that open-topped car."

Heydrich took a thoughtful sip of his drink and hummed

in agreement. The Hangman of Prague despised nothing more than being viewed as a desk jockey who exclusively served the Reich from a cozy little office while his underlings took on all the risk. Heydrich not only liked to drive around occupied Prague without an armored car or a battalion of guards, a risky move that had sent Himmler into hysterics last time he had visited his subordinate, but he had actually joined the German air force. Heydrich had fought in the skies of Norway and the Soviet Union. The Führer himself had been forced to permanently ground Heydrich after the Gestapo Chief had been shot down behind Soviet lines, noting that the Reich couldn't afford to lose him. It had bruised Heydrich's ego something awful, but he had obeyed even though he clearly wanted nothing more than to go back and see some real action.

"All right, fair enough," Heydrich said. "I would just think that after surviving an encounter with Black Fox One, you would wish to...live a little."

"Far from it, sir," Jonas declared. "I'd like to get back to work. It's difficult to get excited when I'm this anxious."

"Ah, you're riled up about that deadline. So what's this about a new plan to capture Black Fox One, Special Agent?" Heydrich queried, shifting his weight slightly as though he was beginning to get anxious with all this waiting.

"Deep cover, sir," Jonas explained. "False papers. I'm hoping to feign being a fugitive Jew and then catch him off guard. Now that I have a better feel for Black Fox One's patterns, for his *modus operandi*, I think a stealth mission would be best."

"You don't think he would recognize you?" Heydrich mused, head tilted slightly to the side, a smirk playing at the edge of his lips as he took a tepid sip of his drink. He wasn't even finished with one-fourth of the cup.

"No, sir," Jonas declared, taking a brazen, confident swig from his glass. "He didn't get a good look at me. I truly believe this will work, sir. And we won't have to worry about any more assets being harmed."

"Assets, hm..." The Hangman looked down at his glass, thoughtfully tilting it back and forth and watching the golden liquid slosh about. The grin on the skull of the Blond Beast's *ehrenring* seemed to stretch.

"I offered you whatever resources you require to bring Black Fox One down," Heydrich finally said. "That offer still stands. If you need an army, fine. If you need false papers, very well. I care that the job is done, I don't care *how* it's done."

Relief flooded Jonas' heart, and it took every bit of his self-control not to let out a sigh. He merely smiled and nodded at the Hangman, feigning casual contentment. "Thank you, sir, I promise I wo—*unk!*"

Jonas' well-practiced little speech was interrupted as another woman, this time a blonde with smoke-grey eyes, plopped down on his lap with a drunken giggle, looping her arms around his neck.

"Hey, handsome," she crooned. "You look lonely. Poor thing, I think I know just what you need..."

Jonas felt his face and body burn, and he was more than grateful when Heydrich evidently decided that he was through dealing with the Fox Hunter.

"Fräulein." Heydrich's timbre was anything but smooth, but it made the girl look up. The edge of the Hangman's lip curled as he took a small wad of Reichsmarks out of his breast pocket, offering them to the girl and nodding his head towards the staircase.

"Room five," he said. "Do well and you'll be rewarded."

Jonas could feel the girl stiffen, but she either recognized the Butcher of Prague or sensed that she would regret it if she rejected him. She stood, flashed Heydrich the smile of a girl who was conceding that she had been paid less for worse, and plucked the money from his fingers, sauntering to the desired room.

"Sorry, Amsel: find yourself a different girl and unwind for the night," Heydrich said, waiting for one more moment before finishing his glass of brandy, standing up, and raking a hand through his golden hair. "Deep cover won't be this pleasant."

"Yes, sir. Enjoy yourself as well," muttered Jonas, leaning back and pretending to let his eyes peruse the other girls. Heydrich chuckled and started towards the staircase.

"I will. And Amsel."

"Chief?"

Heydrich turned, his smile gone, giving Jonas a look that could have frozen lava.

"Don't fail me again," the Hangman said before stalking up to room five.

"ARE YOU CERTAIN...?"

"Papa, you know there's no talking me out of this."

"I know...you're stubborn like your mother, my boy..." Dieter chuckled, glancing at his wife's portrait before letting his gaze return to his son. The Fox Hunter's "deep cover" was little more than a suit topped with a trilby. His SS trappings would be left behind, and his Luger would be hidden under his jacket. There would be nothing to indicate his status as a Nazi except for the swastika ring he would be taking with him.

"How long do you think you'll be gone?" Dieter asked, and Jonas shrugged.

"As long as it takes to find her."

"Jonas, how will I know if you need help?"

"Ha! I'm sure if the Black Foxes catch me, Papa, you'll hear about it on their radio station. Papa Fox won't be able to shut up about it."

"So...what? I'm just supposed to dance around Heydrich and listen to Black Fox Radio, wait for them to announce that they've got you and..."

"Papa." Jonas finished buttoning up his coat and grabbed his father's shoulders, pulling him into a tight embrace. He felt Dieter stiffen: Jonas hadn't initiated a hug since he had been small.

Gingerly, as though he was frightened of this sudden affectionate display, Dieter returned his son's embrace.

"I'll be fine, and I'll be back with Ava. I promise." Jonas pulled away and held up three fingers, mirroring the gesture he had made when he'd taken his SS vows. "Swear on the Führer."

Dieter let out a bitter bray and nodded, his eyes flitting to the portrait of Hitler. "On the Führer. Just promise that if something goes...wrong...you'll return. Swear on the Führer, all right? Swear that to me."

"I promise I'll come back. Swear on the Führer."

"And no matter what, you must remember your vows, remember who you are," Dieter said, grabbing his son's shoulders and giving him a small shake. "You're a loyal SS man, an Aryan. Don't forget your nation, no matter what happens. At the end of the day, Germany must come first! *Deutschland Über Alles!*"

"Papa!" Jonas laughed, brushing off the possibility of treason verbally even as fear struck his heart. In the past, he might have completely dismissed the idea that he would even consider betraying his nation, but somehow the Jews had gotten to Ava. Ava, stubborn and inflexible, had been broken. If they could break her, control her, they could break anyone, even the Fox Hunter.

After all, they already had his Ava. If they tried to use her against him, what would he do?

Jonas barely suppressed a shiver at the thought. He would sooner die than betray his nation, but he would sooner betray his nation than see anything awful happen to Ava.

Praying that he would return to his father alive and as he was, a good SS man, he embraced Dieter one final time and then turned to leave.

"Where will you go to look for her?" Dieter asked as Jonas reached for the doorknob. "She won't be easy to find."

Bitterly, Jonas smiled and turned, zipping his lips and shaking his head. Dieter let out a huff.

"Jonas, I need to know just in case! You said you would trust me!"

"I trust you, Papa," Jonas said, opening the door and stepping out into the chilly hall. "But a promise is a promise."

SIX

The journey back to the *Altreich* was grueling. Normally, Jonas' status as the *Fuchsjäger* let him breeze through the checkpoints, but being incognito and coming from Prague meant that the SS guards were extra suspicious of him. They thoroughly searched his car, his person, his fake papers. When they found nothing but seemingly legitimate identity cards and a swastika ring that he cheerfully proclaimed was for his fiancée, they let him go with a grumble and a Heil Hitler.

At last, after a drive that was far too long for a man as important as Jonas Amsel, he made it to a familiar little town. He parked his car in a lot that had once been the apartment complex where he and Ava had grown up. The complex had been leveled years ago. He had been grateful for that at the time, for the building had held nothing but bitterly sweet memories, but now he looked at the cars parked around a statue of a German soldier standing triumphantly on the neck of a hideous Jew and felt a strange hollowness.

Jonas trudged towards the forest. He had been worried

before, when he had first realized where Black Fox One would surely be hiding. He had feared that time would have fogged his memory and made it impossible to find their old hideout. Jonas hadn't made a map, after all, and he hadn't gone back since Ava had disappeared so long ago.

But as Jonas stepped over barbs and weaved around familiar rocks, he found that journeying to the Bunker was like riding a bicycle: an instinctual motion that gripped him as naturally as the impulse to draw in breath. In no time at all, he was standing between two familiar twisted trees, one still brimming with life while the other remained as much a husk as it had been so long ago. It was strange: their homes had been razed and everything was different, but this, their oasis, was still the same even decades later. The nation, the world had changed so much, but their spot was still whole.

Jonas dropped to his knees and felt about the grass and stones until he found the hatch handle. He threw it open and knew from the smell that Ava had been inside recently: a sweet scent came up from the Bunker. Soap, cinnamon, unmistakably Ava.

He descended the staircase. It was dark in the Bunker, but one click from a flashlight he had packed illuminated their old hiding spot.

"Ah..." he muttered as he looked about. Differences leapt out at him right away: gone were the sleeping mats they had kept in the bunker, replaced by piles of pillows and blankets no doubt reserved for the escaping undesirables that Ava brought to hide in her old stomping grounds. Crates of food and bottles of water lined the walls they had drawn on as children.

Jonas shone the flashlight's beam on the segments of wall that peeked out from behind the supply crates. A few familiar markings stood out, bringing a smile to his face: the drawings of the two knights defeating wicked demons. The warning he and Ava had written when they'd claimed the Bunker as their own: PROPERTY OF JONAS AND AVA, KEEP OUT! OR ELSE YOU'LL DIE!

But it also appeared that some of Ava's rescuees had added their own contributions to the wall. They had crossed out the swastikas and SS runes Jonas and Ava had drawn when they were little and scrawled Stars of David and crude remarks about Hitler on top of them. Villainous Jews Jonas had painted were erased and replaced by drawings of monstrous SS men being stomped on by the heroic Black Fox One. Rebellious screeds had supplanted Nazi proclamations. *Heil Hitler* was gone and replaced with *Fuck Hitler*. *Germany Arise* had been erased and instead there was *Am Yisrael Chai!*

Jonas grimaced at this defacing of his private childhood drawings, but one set of scrawls that took up a huge section of the wall caught his eye.

"The Hell?" Jonas muttered. A few stark images were painted on one corner of the wall: an upside-down yellow triangle. He arched an eyebrow. Yellow triangles were typically camp badges for Jews. Why would Ava or one of her charges paint such a symbol?

Right above the yellow triangle was another drawing: a silver eye with a flame for a pupil. Jonas had learned about Judaic symbols during his SS training. He recalled that one Jewish symbol, the *Hamsa*, was an eye in the palm of a hand. This wasn't quite the same, but something about it looked oddly familiar.

Above the eye was a serrated script. A warning.

You're Being Watched

Jonas was rarely a man who took graffiti seriously. He'd seen bold, rebellious proclamations written on walls plenty of times in the past. But something about the desperate, frightened way this message was scrawled made him take a step back.

Before he could ponder the meaning further, however, something hard struck the back of his skull and he fell to the concrete ground, unconscious.

SEVEN

"Ah, you're awake."

Barely. Jonas opened his eyes and groaned when he discovered that a fluorescent bulb was dangling above his head. Evidently, Ava's jimmy-rigging held fast and some rooms in the Bunker still had power.

Jonas sat up and immediately realized there was a chain locked tight around his ankle, restraining him to the metal bunk he'd been laid upon, the very one he and Ava had utilized when they were teens. He rubbed the back of his head, stars spinning before his vision still.

"Brain still in working order, Dummi? I don't think you can afford any damage."

She *had* hit him pretty hard, but nonetheless Jonas smiled. He looked up at his fiancée. Ava was sitting in a small chair on the other side of the room, having shorn her gas mask and pulled back her hood. She looked a bit different. Her night-black eyes were a bit dimmer. Her hair, which had once been long, was cut just above her shoulders. Her rosy cheeks were placid, perhaps from the lack of sun. Still, she was lovely as ever.

Jonas' heart ached at seeing her and he wanted nothing more than to run to her, cup her face in his hands, and kiss every inch of her. Instead, he tore his eyes away from his love and glanced about the familiar chamber. It was furnished now, much more so than it had been when they were young. There was a faded carpet, a bucket in the corner, a small table, a radio by the door tuned in to Papa Fox's subversive Black Fox Radio program, and a bookcase piled high with forbidden tomes about Judaism.

"You like?" Ava said, waving her black-gloved hands to gesture about the room. "Not exactly a honeymoon suite in Rome, but it's still cozy."

"You've been living down here?" Jonas muttered, glancing at his would-be wife, and forcing his heart to endure seeing her morose face. Ava strolled over to the radio and lowered the volume so that Papa Fox's diatribe against the Third Reich didn't interrupt their conversation.

"On and off. When I'm not being an Enemy of the State. Well...I suppose I'm always an Enemy of the State, but you know what I mean." Ava's confident smirk became twisted and bitter. "Now, Dummi, I know you're usually good at *following orders,* but I sort of figured you wouldn't listen when I told you to quit your job."

"Of course," Jonas muttered.

"Frankly, I'm just surprised you were fool enough to come by yourself."

"You were expecting me."

"I was expecting you to come with an army."

"And if I had?" Jonas said, his voice almost trembling. "You're by yourself down here?"

"For now. Made sure to empty the place after I found you at the gas station."

"Then you were expecting to take on an army alone?"

"I was expecting to go out in a blaze of glory if you'd betrayed me." Ava's shoulders sagged. Jonas felt his heart sink.

"Ava..."

"You've told Heydrich about me..." Not a question. A statement. An *accusation*.

"No! I told him nothing!" Jonas insisted, the chain rattling as he scooted to the end of the bed and grasped the bottom frame. "I didn't come here to arrest you, Ava, I came here to *save* you!"

Ava winced as though this revelation was a sudden slap in the face. For a moment, there was silence between the former lovers save for Ava's heavy breathing. Then, Black Fox One let out a mirthless chuckle.

"Remember how I used to ruin our games?" she said. "Whenever we'd play knight?"

"I remember," Jonas confirmed, letting a smile tug at the edges of his lips. "I wanted you to be my damsel. We'd set everything up, pretend like you'd been kidnapped by an evil Duke, and I was the noble knight rushing in to save you..."

"But," Ava interrupted, fondness brightening her tone, "I wouldn't let you just save me. I'd always change it up before you could finish the story yourself. I'd pretend I'd freed myself and killed all of the Duke's guards..."

"And then we'd kill him together. Both of us. Heroes together."

"Unfortunately, one of us needs saving now," Ava said, her smile withering into an expression not dissimilar to the one she had sported whenever Bruno Ackerman had accused her of looking like a Jew. "And it isn't me."

"What do you mean by that?"

"You're..." She inhaled deeply, as though whatever she was about to say burned her throat. Ava pressed a hand to her heart and softly mumbled, "You...don't seem mad. I figured you'd be furious..."

"Mad?! I was never mad, Ava, I was terrified!" Jonas leapt off the bed too quickly and stumbled, collapsing to the concrete floor. Ava stood up as though she would have liked to help him up, but she held back.

Jonas rose to his feet by himself and tried to approach her, but the chain didn't allow him to get close enough to pull her into his arms. They stood a few feet apart, Jonas leaning as close as he could despite the chain, Ava holding her hands against her chest as though she was afraid she was about to have a heart attack.

"I figured you would be angry at me for abandoning you without a word," Ava mumbled, bitterly smirking as she added, "Figured you'd come down here screaming that I'd left you, run off with someone else..."

"You would never do that. I *know* you would never do that."

"Maybe you don't know me as well as you thought." There was a biting iciness to Ava's tone that almost reminded him of Heydrich. Jonas flinched and stumbled back, but then he saw the deep sorrow in those night-sky eyes of hers and reached out, desperate to stroke her cheek and assure her that everything was all right.

"Ava, Bärchen," he mumbled, and the edge of her lip quirked upwards as the old pet name fell off his tongue.

"Never thought I'd hear you call me that again," she said, and it was clear that she was barely strong enough to stop her voice from cracking.

"Bärchen, please tell me what happened," Jonas pleaded, putting emphasis on the affectionate epithet. "I know you wouldn't have willingly left me. I knew all along that you were taken from me. I thought it might be Jews or Black Foxes…"

"Oh no…" A strangled sound came out of Ava's throat, half a laugh and half a cry. "Don't tell me you became the Fox Hunter just to find me…"

"Not *just* to find you. I always *hoped* to find you. Ava, you knew I was in the SS, you knew I was working for Heydrich. *You* pushed me to join."

"I didn't know," Ava's breath came in sharp. Tears fell from her dark eyes. "Jonas, I'm so sorry, I didn't know, I'm *so* sorry…"

She backed against the wall and collapsed, muffling sharp sobs with her gloved hand. Jonas could think of nothing more torturous than seeing his Ava cry and not being able to wipe the tears away. Helpless, he dropped down to his knees.

"Ava, darling, please don't cry," he begged. "Ava, whatever happened, it's all right. No matter what happened, I love you."

"That coward…" Ava hiccupped. "That fucking coward, he didn't tell you a thing, did he?"

"Who didn't tell me what?" Jonas asked, fighting not to sound exasperated. "Bärchen, please, tell me what happened. I promise I can fix it."

"Nothing can fix what's happened." Ava's tear-filled eyes became fiery. "Jonas, your father covered everything up. I'm sure he's been leading you in circles for years trying to protect you, trying to protect *himself*."

"Protect…from what?"

"From *me*, Dummi," Ava said, a bitter smile stretching across her lovely face. "Jonas, I wasn't kidnapped by Jews. I *am* a Jew."

Ava could have announced that she was a werewolf and Jonas would have believed it more than that proclamation. At first, he almost laughed, thinking this was some sort of extremely poorly timed joke from his ever-vicious Bärchen.

But when he saw the gleam of determination in Ava's black eyes, he realized she wasn't lying. "You're..." Jonas choked. "That's...that's not possible..."

"My family tree would disagree, but I'm sure Papa Dieter burned that. Probably slunk his little fingers into Heydrich's own files and burned everything about me, made it so I never even existed."

"But you're *not* a Jew!" Jonas cried. "You're Christian, you're German! You were a National Socialist before I was! Your father adored Hitler! Your brothers wanted to be in the SS!"

"And then the SS murdered them!" She slammed her fist against the wall and the old plaster cracked, sending dust and debris flying and making the fluorescent light above his head swing to and fro.

"W...what?" Jonas mumbled, recalling the puckish giggle of Oskar, the shrill shriek of Fritz whenever Ava had pulled his hair, the way they used to skitter around the apartment complex halls playing Jews vs Germans and arguing about who had to be the Jew. Dead? No. Jewish? Absolutely not.

Jonas' head felt fuzzy, as though she'd struck him again to knock him out. For a moment, he thought all of this might be a strange dream brought about by brain damage, but though he blinked and jabbed his thumb against a sharp part of his chain, he didn't awaken.

Ava sighed heavily and sat up. "I didn't know I was a Jew. You're right: we weren't Jews by any stretch. I was loyal to Hitler. I was German...I *thought* I was. Papa thought he was too. He and I, my brothers...we all really believed all that bull-shit about Jews. But...well, they say apostates always despise the faith they leave. Turns out my father's parents were Jews, and their parents before them. When my father was just a baby, his parents abandoned their faith and had him baptized. They raised him to hate their own people. I guess they figured they'd be safe if they did that, they'd be accepted as Germans."

She laughed bitterly. "So much for that! And my mother? Turns out she's from a home of Orthodox Jews. They were stifling, horrible people. She ran away from home when she was a teenager because they tried to make her marry a man twice her age. Hated everything to do with Judaism because of that, and what do you know? My father hated Jews too. They made a good match even though Mama never told Papa about her own Jewish blood. He found out, though. Same day I found out, ha ha..."

Ava grabbed her own wrist and squeezed tight, as though she wanted nothing more than to rip off her own hand. "Get it, Jonas?" she hissed. "I'm not just a mongrel, I'm a full-blooded Jewess. And I didn't know. I never would have known..."

"But when I proposed," Jonas whispered, his face turning pale. "Papa...he...he promised to do the paperwork. He found your family tree."

"Suffice to say, he wasn't happy to know his little boy had been screwing a Jewess for years." Ava chuckled bitterly before her slight smirk died and her jaw tightened.

"He came stomping into my family's house. He threatened me...threatened to kill me if I didn't get the hell out of Germany. Threatened to kill my mother and my little brothers if I ever spoke to you again."

Jonas almost couldn't imagine it: Dieter, red-faced, kicking down the Kellers' door and screaming at them. Threatening the family he had been eager to join. Threatening Gisela, who had offered a shoulder to cry on when Magda had passed. Threatening Otto, who had practically been his brother.

But then again, they were Jews, and he was an SS man. More than that, however, he was a father. If he had felt that Ava's true nature would be a threat to his son...

"You don't believe me," Ava said, her tone half pained, half biting. Jonas shook his head.

"I don't think I want to, but...I know you're not a liar, Bärchen. He just...lied right to my face."

"To protect you. To protect your future..."

"I wanted *you* to be my future!" Jonas exclaimed.

"Even though I'm a Jewess?" Ava sat up slightly, and her eyes glistened in a beautifully hopeful manner.

"Ava, you know there's nothing in the world that could make me hate you," Jonas said, and as she excitedly began to speak up, he held up a hand, his smile morphing into an expression of severity.

"That doesn't mean I condone your activities, however," he said. "I think you've been dealt a bad hand. I think you're an anomaly."

"An anomaly, hm?" Ava leaned back, the hope in her dark eyes turning into a bitter sort of scorn.

"National Socialism is scientific, Ava, and science accounts for natural anomalies," Jonas explained. "Wolves, generally, are vicious animals. But some are born docile. These anomalies don't render the whole notion of wolves being vicious moot, they're simply exceptions. Similarly, Germans are generally good. But every once in a while, even a prime example of Aryan stock is defective: weak, stupid, perverted, what have you. Jews, in the same vein, are generally rapacious, wicked, soulless creatures, but it's also true that exceptions to that rule would exist.

Jews by blood who do not exhibit the natural racial behavior of Jews and, being raised apart from the innately subversive Jewish culture, are entirely good, as good as any Aryan. A Jew with an Aryan soul."

Jonas straightened up a bit and leaned forward as though to tell a secret, dropping his voice as he confessed, "Heydrich informed me once that Hitler went through quite a bit of trouble to save his mother's old doctor. A Jewish doctor. Bloch, I think his name was. The Führer said, 'If every Jew was like Bloch, there would be no Jewish Question.' He called him an *Edeljude*."

"An honorable Jew," muttered Ava.

"That's you, Bärchen," Jonas proclaimed. "I know you're confused, and my father had no right to treat you so terribly..."

"Confused...no, Jonas, I think *you're* confused," Ava sighed. "Believe me, I was too. You can imagine: I was raised all my life to think Jews were the Devil, and then I was told *I* was the Devil. We didn't have much time to think about it, though: give your father some credit, he at least made arrangements for us. Got us tickets for a ship to America. Jonas...I *so* wanted to risk it and tell you, but my mother begged me not to and it was so insane and..."

"Ava, I'm not angry, I promise you."

Her lip twitched upwards. "Regardless, we got on the ship, and believe me, I did some compartmentalizing. It was a long two-week trip across the Atlantic, and I had a lot of time to run my little brain in circles. At first, I thought along the same lines as you: 'I'm the exception,' I thought. 'I'm not like these other Jews.' My father, mother, brothers, and I, we stayed away from the other Jews on the ship. We weren't like them. We were *real* Germans. This was a mistake, a misunderstanding. We were *different*. We kept telling ourselves that over and over..."

"If Papa got you tickets to America, how did you end up back here? What about your family?"

Ava's slight smile wilted. "The Americans didn't want us. Captain was a good man. He tried to get us dropped off in Canada, Cuba...but *nobody* wanted us. They all turned us away. I remember one man slit his wrists and jumped off the boat. God, the look in his eyes...he would rather die than go back to the Nazis. I didn't understand it. The Nazis were honorable. The Nazis were *right*, but...when it came down to it, even though me and my family kept telling ourselves we were *different*, we were treated the same as the rest of the dirty Jews. In the eyes of America, Canada, Cuba, Germany, we were all the same. I realized that we would be treated like Jews from now on wherever we went, and that man who slit his wrists...I started to think he had the right idea."

She gripped her wrist even tighter, as though trying to stem the flow of filthy Jewish blood.

"Ava..." Jonas whispered, helplessly reaching towards her.

"But," Black Fox One said, and now a wide smile came to her face: morose, but fond. "There was a Rabbi on the ship. After that man slit his wrists, the Rabbi didn't want there to be any copycats. He found me on the deck of the ship and stopped me from doing something foolish. Rabbi Gedaliah. Fascinating fellow, Rabbi Gedaliah. Well-traveled, well-spoken...very convincing. Convinced me to hear him out instead of jumping into the water. I was so rude to him. Insisted that I was *different*, that he was a dirty Jew, that I wasn't like him. He had every right to throw up his hands and let me chuck myself off deck, but he listened, and he was kind."

"That's..." Jonas found himself at a loss for words. On one hand, a Rabbi was the symbol of everything he had been trained to hate. But if this Rabbi had saved Ava's life...

92

What are the chances of there being two Edeljuden on a ship? Jonas thought, shaking his head. *Of course he tried to save her, he thought she was one of them. A parasite will try to maintain itself, and so Jewry as a whole will defend individual Jews.*

"Ava, I certainly would never want you to get hurt, and I'm...glad that Rabbi helped you..."

"He did more than that, Jonas!" Ava sighed, exasperation entering her voice. "He was on the ship with his congregants. He had me meet with them. The whole trip back to Europe, he sat with me every day and talked. He introduced me to his people! They were *people*, Jonas. They were kind too. Kind and...scared. Just like me, they were all just like me, don't you get it?! I was wrong! I'm *not* different! Rabbi Gedaliah taught me about Judaism, about his people, he showed me the truth! We've been lied to, Jonas! The Jews are not evil; Judaism is not evil! I'm not *different*, I'm just like the rest of them, and they're just like me!"

"Ava, please, you're a smart woman, but *you're* the one that's been lied to," Jonas said. "That Jew took advantage of your emotional state to manipulate you into joining his flock!"

"That is not true!" Ava's fist met the wall again, and this time the whole Bunker trembled. "You don't get it! Besides me, you've never spoken to a Jew!"

"The Jews were no doubt kind to you, but that's because they thought you were one of them!"

"I AM one of them!"

"*No, you're not!*" Now Jonas was shouting, shouting so loud that he was sure Heydrich would be able to hear him all the way in Prague. Almost immediately, he felt a stab of regret. He had never shouted at Ava before. Even when they had argued over stupid little things like Ava using an entire toilet paper roll in a single day or Jonas' propensity to steal all the blankets in the middle of the night, they had never actually screamed at one another.

Ava started to stand, reaching for the gas mask lying by the door, clearly ready to march out.

"I'm sorry!" Jonas' hasty apology stopped her. "Ava, I'm sorry, just...please tell me exactly what happened. How did you become...?"

His eyes flitted to the gas mask. Ava curled her hand into a fist and retracted her hand, walking back to the chair and sitting down, now above him like a teacher who was about to tell an unruly student a life lesson.

"When the ship returned to Europe, we didn't have many options. Rabbi Gedaliah and his congregation ended up going to France. My father, he hated Gedaliah, he thought that he was corrupting me, but what else could we do? We joined them and ended up settling..."

"In the village of Annuville."

"Correct. My father still didn't want me to have any contact with the Rabbi, but...well, you know me."

"Never were one to be bossed around," Jonas said with a smirk.

"I kept sneaking out. We'd study in secret. He taught me so much about *me*, about being Jewish. He taught me that it was nothing to be ashamed of. But of course..."

"The war."

"France was invaded, and all of a sudden we had to figure out a way to escape again. Rabbi Gedaliah was good friends with Papa Fox, knew him for a long time. Like I said, he's well-traveled."

"Gedaliah helped form the Black Foxes, then?"

"Sort of. Papa Fox had been helping Jews escape Europe since the *Anschluss,* and he'd been anonymously spreading anti-Nazi messages even before then. The Black Foxes as we know them now formed after the war broke out, but Gedaliah got the train rolling in the West. He was Black Fox One before I was. He managed to smuggle most of his congregants out, but my father didn't want his help. Damn him, I love him, but he was so stubborn..."

"Was?" Jonas repeated, his voice becoming soft. Ava inhaled sharply and looked at a crack in the wall above Jonas' bed, her eyes glazing over.

"We argued so much..."

"Ava, you don't have to tell me."

"No, I do," she declared, her sorrowful eyes flashing with determination. "I do because you're just like him. When the Nazis invaded...it's like he didn't even have a plan, like he thought we'd be all right as long as we didn't provoke your father. He still thought we weren't Jews, thought we were *different.* He didn't trust the Rabbi to save us, but somehow he still trusted the Nazis to be decent."

"But..."

"We argued, like I said. One day, I marched out of the house and went to Rabbi Gedaliah, like I usually did. But while I was gone...God, I don't know what happened exactly, but the SS showed up. Maybe Papa refused to go, maybe he talked back too much, maybe they wanted to kill him from the beginning. But either way, the SS...they killed them, Jonas. My father, my brothers..."

"Ava, I'm so sorry," he muttered. "I...I didn't know...I..."

Otto Keller had been a man with an Aryan spirit. He had taught Jonas to shoot. He had carried Jonas back home when the boy had broken his leg while they were out chopping wood. He had looked after the teenage Jonas Amsel whenever

95

Dieter was forced to travel to Munich for work. He had been a second father to him. He had been *good*.

But he had been a Jew. And the SS men who had raided Ava's home had no way of knowing that Otto Keller was an *Edeljude*.

Does that matter? Jonas thought. *If they'd killed Ava, would it have mattered to you that they didn't know she was different?*

No. He would have hunted her killers down to the ends of the earth.

"They took my mother, deported her, I still don't know where she is," Ava whispered. "I came home to find they'd left one SS man behind to collect me when I returned."

"You killed him," Jonas assumed, glancing at the dagger strapped to her side. Ava nodded.

"He was standing over my father, my little brothers...I should have kept him alive long enough to question him, but I just..."

Lightly, she smacked her fist against her knee. Jonas nodded.

"That's why you joined the Black Foxes," he muttered.

"Went right to Rabbi Gedaliah. Threw myself into the thresher. Stole his rank, eventually."

"And what happened to him?"

"He's alive, thank God. Helps Papa Fox operate the radio station. Interesting man, like I said, and he has more technological prowess than you'd expect for a Rabbi. Gedaliah couldn't blend in, couldn't...do what I do, so he took a backseat, and I became the new Black Fox One."

"'Do what you do.' Your acrobatics, your knife-throwing, your shooting abilities..."

"Thank goodness Papa wanted his little girl to be able to

hold her own, though I doubt he thought I'd ever have to hold my own against SS men. Sometimes I wonder...I think if he'd tried to fight, he would have beaten them. I think he didn't really try. He *trusted* them."

Jonas' head felt like it was filled with furious bees. The SS *was* trustworthy. The men of the SS were good. But they had hurt Ava. They might have killed her, or at least deported her...

"Your mother," Jonas said. "You said she was missing. Is that why you've been targeting Jews from Annuville? You've been looking for her."

"Whenever I can, I try to free Annuville Jews," Ava confessed, glancing at her gas mask. "To find my mother, or to rescue Rabbi Gedaliah's congregants who were caught. I... doubt I'll ever find my mother, though."

"You didn't have to become a Black Fox to help her, Ava," Jonas declared, scowling at the radio which was not quite silenced. "If you had contacted me..."

"By the time I was Black Fox One, you were already *der Fuchsjäger*," Ava sighed. "I...I missed you, Jonas, but I didn't want to see you. I thought if you knew what I was, you would..."

Ava bit her lip.

"Would what, Bärchen?"

"I don't know...I was afraid to find out. I didn't want to find you and have you spit in my face and tell me you didn't love me. I preferred to just leave you be and...preserve the good memories."

"And you call *me* Dummi?" Jonas quipped with a bitter sigh. He reached into his back pocket, searching for the swastika ring. He wasn't surprised to find it was gone.

"I...uh...appreciate the thought of this..." Jonas looked back up. Ava was holding the box. She dropped it on the floor and kicked it towards him. "But I...well, you understand. You *do* understand, don't you?"

Slowly, Jonas reached down and grabbed the ring box. A part of him wanted to open it, glance at the beautiful golden swastika, but he knew that Ava would be upset if he did. The symbol that had once meant strength, goodness, a wonderful future, for her it now represented the destruction of everything she loved. He slipped the box into his pocket.

"I...this is a lot, Ava," Jonas said. "I do love you, but I still think you've been misled. Misled and abused. The SS men who did that to your family, I don't condone that..."

"Because they're my family. And you think my family was *different.*"

"Ava, I don't fault you for coming to the conclusions you've come to given what you've been through. I don't fault you for despising the SS. I don't even fault you for being Black Fox One. If National Socialism leaves a bad taste in your mouth after what you've been through, that's reasonable. But that *doesn't* mean it's wrong. And that *doesn't* mean the Jews are good."

"I didn't expect to break a lifetime of brainwashing in a day," muttered Ava. "Honestly...you're...well, you've exceeded my expectations. I'm grateful for that. But...I also can't risk the lives of my comrades. You're still an SS man, you're still *der Fuchsjäger.*"

Jonas glanced down at the chain on his leg and sighed. "So I'm a prisoner."

"I'll try to make it comfortable."

"Ava, we can figure something out, but you need to cease these subversive activities."

She giggled and marched back to the radio, turning the dial again, making Papa Fox's seditious station audible once more.

"Sorry, Dummi. I actually have to get back to those subversive activities since I know the Bunker's safe again. There's water, food, entertainment and a bucket. I should be back before the bucket needs to be emptied."

"W-what?!" Jonas cried, glancing at the pristine bucket and then looking back at Ava as she put her gas mask back on.

"We'll talk more later," she said, her cheerful voice muffled by the mask. "I might be able to save your ass after all."

"Save my...?!" Jonas cried, but Ava turned and left, shutting the door behind her.

"Hey, Ava! Bärchen, this isn't funny! Where are you going?!" cried Jonas, helplessly tugging on his chain. "Ava?! AVA!"

EIGHT

Jonas Amsel wouldn't exactly call himself spoiled. He had lived in a one-bedroom apartment for most of his childhood, fixed an old run-down roach-den of a house when he'd lived with Ava, and whenever he was out on missions as the Fox Hunter, he would sometimes be forced to accept less-than-ideal accommodations. He'd slept in cars, in bushes, on stony hills overlooking potential Black Fox dens.

But at least he'd had his dignity out there. In the Bunker he had once called a second home, chained to the wall, stripped of his SS furnishings, forced to listen to Black Fox Radio even when he tossed a shoe at the bleating device in a futile attempt to make Papa Fox shut up, he felt a crushing sense of dehumanization.

Idly, he wondered if Ava had purposefully left him in this dreary hole as a way of teaching him a lesson. A harebrained attempt to get him to empathize with the Black Foxes he'd arrested over the years, Black Foxes whose conditions likely mirrored his own.

If they were lucky.

Jonas didn't suddenly find himself sympathizing with his old marks. However, Ava did leave him all by himself for five days, which gave him plenty of time to think. At first, he tried to come up with a way to escape, but there was absolutely nothing to be done about that. He tugged on his ankle chain until the links imprinted on his palms, but it held fast. The door was unlocked, but he was still trapped.

With no way to escape, he began to mull over a different obstacle: how was he going to fix this mess with Ava?

The first hurdle would be the most impossible to overcome: he had to convince her that she was wrong. Getting Ava to change her mind would be like convincing a cat to stop hunting mice, particularly after what she had been through.

The thought of her torments made Jonas' heart quiver and sprouted a small seed of doubt in his mind, a seed he promptly doused in acid. No. It would be ridiculous if she were right. Everyone despised Jews for a reason. The evidence presented by eugenic scientists and German historians was simply overwhelming: the Jews were a plague upon the planet. Ava and her family were exceptions—*Edeljuden* that had unfortunately been caught in the crossfire of a just war on International Jewry.

Nevertheless, he couldn't expect Ava to approach this situation as a rational National Socialist. She had lost her family to the Reich. However justified the war against Jewry was, she had still suffered, and Jonas had no desire to break her heart by undermining her agony.

Maybe I'll never fully change her mind, he thought. *I don't have to. If she wants to love Jews, fine. If she wants to believe in their stupid fairytales, fine. I just need to convince her to leave the Black Foxes. That shouldn't be impossible. She's grown fond of the Jews, but I can get through to her...and if I do...*

Then, hurdle number two: Heydrich. When Jonas had set off to find Ava, he had hoped he would also discover that she hadn't been acting of her own free will. Sufficient evidence of *that* might have convinced even the Man with the Iron Heart to show her mercy, to let her be deprogrammed and then held up as an example of the horrific cruelty of Jewry and the Black Foxes.

So much for that. Heydrich likely would have barely been willing to give clemency to an Ava Keller who was blackmailed into becoming Black Fox One. Jonas knew that she was an *Edeljudin* who had been manipulated by the Jews and the Black Foxes, but obviously Heydrich wouldn't see it that way. The incident with Viktor Naden had proved that asking for an exception would be a waste of time at best.

Which meant that Jonas wouldn't be reporting back. Which meant that his days as *der Fuchsjäger* were over. He would have to give up the SS, give up his rank, give up Germany. His father's words rang in his ears. *You're a loyal SS man, an Aryan. Don't forget your nation, no matter what happens. At the end of the day, Germany must come first. Deutschland Über Alles!*

Is that why you lied to me, Papa? Jonas thought bitterly. *You wanted me to put Germany over Ava? Sorry, Papa, that wasn't your choice to make: Ava will always come first for me.*

Dieter would probably be upset at his son's desertion. Despite the Major's sins, it hurt Jonas to know that he would likely never see his father again, but there was nothing else to be done. He wouldn't lose Ava again. Once he convinced her to leave the Black Foxes, they would run off together, get false papers, make their way to Sweden or some other neutral nation, and leave Germany to her fate.

The thought of throwing away everything he had built up

over the years did leave a pang in his chest. He looked down at the little box with the swastika ring and remembered his old dreams. Marrying Ava, raising a brood of Aryan children, serving the SS, growing old together in the new, better Germany that Hitler would create.

Jonas was a proud German and a proud SS man, but Ava had always been more important than any of that. He would rather grow old with Ava in a faraway land than be alone in the Reich.

With a sigh, Jonas laid down, covering his ears to drown out the American jazz belting from Black Fox Radio and running through the arguments he would present to Ava in his mind. He gingerly set the swastika ring box under his pillow, hoping that a miracle would occur, and he would still find a use for it.

JONAS HAD ALWAYS BEEN A HEAVY SLEEPER. AVA HAD once said he slept like a dead man. It was fortunate that his work as the Fox Hunter didn't require him to slumber near his foes or he likely would have been dead years ago. He could have easily slept through a bombardment.

So he wasn't entirely surprised when he woke up and discovered multiple massive changes in his little prison. His food and water had been replenished, his bucket had been swapped for a clean one, and the classic music Black Fox Radio was offering was being drowned out by singing coming from the Bunker's grand chamber.

"Yiddish..." Jonas grumbled, perking up his ears. An effective hunter knew the language of his quarry, and so he knew Yiddish well enough to understand the lyrics.

"Girl, girl, I want to ask of you
What can grow, grow without rain?
What can burn and never end?
What can yearn, cry without tears?
Tumbala, Tumbala, Tumbalalaika
Tumbala, Tumbala, Tumbalalaika
Tumbalalaika, strum balalaika
Tumbalalaika, may we be happy!"

The tune wasn't precisely cheery, but it also wasn't precisely sad. More amusedly exasperated than anything. If Jonas were a more open-minded man that was in a better mood, he might have conceded that it was rather catchy. Instead, he fell back onto his bed and let out a loud groan.

"Damn it, Ava..." he muttered. The Bunker was supposed to be their sacred spot, and she had ruined it with her subversive activities. Contaminated it by letting Jews that weren't *her*, that weren't *Edeljuden*, into their sanctuary. It almost felt like a betrayal, a worse betrayal than her being Black Fox One. He sat by himself for some time, stewing, readying his tongue to rebuke her when she finally returned.

At last, the door slid open.

"Ava, you really had to...!" Jonas started to say, but when he sat up and looked at the door, he realized it wasn't Ava that had entered his prison, but a ruddy-faced little boy. He was dressed in a torn-up sweater vest with a bloody bandage barely covering a wound on his cheek. No more than ten years old with sandy blond hair and dark blue eyes. Jonas had often fantasized about what his future son would look like. This child was a spitting image of the boy he had lovingly embraced in his dreams.

Der Fuchsjäger gritted his teeth and averted his gaze, staring at a crack in the wall beside his bed.

Jonas had always been proud of his work in the SS, but he would have been lying if he declared that the occasions where he had been forced to encounter children had been pleasant. He felt sorry for the men guarding concentration camps who actually had to put down the screaming little Jews. All *he* had to do once he found Black Foxes hiding the Jewish whelps was take the Black Fox and look the other way while his comrades collected the little ones. Jonas had known what would happen to the Jewish children, but he had blocked out their shrieks and refused to think about the gristly details. It was an ugly necessity. If they were allowed to grow up, after all, then all of Hitler's hard work would be for nothing. The Jewish plague would continue, and Germany would never truly be safe.

The Fox Hunter had always refrained from looking the children in the eye. He tried to do the same thing now, but it was terribly difficult. This wasn't a chaotic scene of SS men collecting children and Black Foxes desperately defending their charges. It was quiet, and he was alone with the boy.

"Black Fox One said you'd be here," the child mumbled. Jonas forced his pupils to remain on the fractured wall.

A noise, however, made him look over: the child had grabbed the little wooden chair by the back. At first, Jonas was afraid the boy was going to try and pick it up and bludgeon the helpless Nazi, but instead the child merely started fidgeting as little boys were wont to do. The Jewish boy rocked back and forth, twirling the chair this way and that in a desperate attempt to burn his excess energy.

It would have been adorable if the little dirt-covered child was fully human.

"She said there was a Dummi-Nazi here," the boy said. He had a slight lisp. Jonas' heart faltered. Instinctually, he found his latent paternal instincts flaring up. Suppressing them with rational racial doctrine was difficult. He glanced away again.

"She sent you down here," the Fox Hunter grumbled, this time forcing his gaze to fall upon the bookshelf. He scowled at the Judaic tomes Ava had filled his small living space with, all of which he had refused to read despite his boredom.

"Ah ah," the boy said. "She actually said not to come. A couple'a the others wanted to kill you, but she said everyone should leave you alone 'cause you're not evil, you're just confused."

"Confused..." Jonas scoffed.

"You don't look like SS," the boy said, his tone brightening a bit. "Where's your scary hat?"

Despite his training, Jonas snorted. "Scary hat?" he repeated, and his inner SS man told him to stay silent. *Don't say another word, you know that talking to them will just break you down...*

"The hat with the skull-face, it's scary!" the boy said. "Where's yours?"

"It's *supposed* to be scary, it frightens enemies of the Reich," Jonas said, his tone low and vicious. He hoped he might frighten the child into leaving him be, but the boy just climbed onto the chair and stood on top of it, swaying back and forth. Jonas grunted. Paternal instincts flared once more against his will. The boy would tumble off the chair and break his neck if he kept doing that. *Good*, his SS training decreed.

The boy seemed to mull over the Fox Hunter's words for a moment before he spoke again in an oddly cheerful tone:

"Black Fox One said you hated us because you're confused. Is that really true?"

"I'm *not* confused," Jonas insisted.

"So why do you hate me, then?"

Me not *us*. That made the Fox Hunter lift an eyebrow and glance warily at the child. Hate was perhaps too strong of a word for what he felt for the boy. It was easy to hate an entity, a concept, a faceless mass, but gazing at a small child and trying to summon a fire of hate in his soul was difficult. Jonas didn't hate *him*. He hated what he was and what he would turn into as he grew, but he didn't look at the boy and feel the overwhelming urge to put a bullet between his wide, curious eyes.

He scowled at the boy and tried to let the silence between them speak for itself. The boy merely grinned. He was missing two teeth.

"*Now* you look confused," he said, and Jonas rolled his eyes.

"Return to your mother," the Fox Hunter commanded, and the boy's smile dampened.

"Can't. Mama's dead."

Discomfort consumed Jonas' heart. The boy's tone was morose, and Jonas' polite instincts told him to offer his condolences, but he bit his tongue.

The boy picked a little at the bandage on his face. "Did you ever kill anyone?" the child asked, and that question caught Jonas off guard. Jonas was a hunter, but he rarely killed his prey. The occasional firefight or operation gone south aside, he preferred to capture his quarry alive and let the men in the camps handle them.

"Only when they deserved it," he answered, and the boy tilted his head sideways like a curious puppy.

"Oh. So you never killed any mamas, then?" It was a question, delivered almost hopefully. Jonas had certainly arrested his fair share of women. Thoughts of Katja Naden and Anniska Engel invaded his mind. Their screams and pleas for mercy...

I didn't kill them, I only arrested them.

"No," he said, relatively certain that he wasn't lying. The boy's eyes brightened, and he gave the German a small nod, as though to silently offer his approval. Jonas felt an odd weight settle in the pit of his stomach. He was grateful when the door opened and Ava stepped in, mask on. She looked imposing in her full Black Fox One getup, but when she spoke she used a gentle, maternal voice.

"Jakob, the others are looking for you," she said, kneeling down before the child and patting his uninjured cheek. "Silly! I told you to leave the Dummi-Nazi alone."

"Sorry, Fräulein One."

Fräulein One? Jonas thought, barely able to suppress a smirk.

"Go back with the others," Ava said, picking little Jakob up off the chair and gently setting him on the ground. "I'll catch up."

"Okay!" The boy turned to Jonas, a slight twinkle in his eye. He opened his mouth and lifted his hand as though he wanted to wave and say farewell, but he must have remembered who Jonas was, *what* he was. Instead, Jakob merely nodded at the captive *Fuchsjäger* and skittered out.

"Kids," sighed Ava, walking forward and shutting the door behind the boy.

"Jews," Jonas countered. Ava whirled around and ripped off her mask, revealing exhausted eyes that nonetheless gleamed with a familiar vibrancy: it was the sort of glow her eyes had been wont to take on whenever she'd hit a target during her father's knife-throwing lessons or completed a complex feat of acrobatics. She was proud of herself.

"A whole orphanage worth," she said, jabbing her thumb towards the door. "Good haul. Sorry if they're keeping you up. Don't worry: they'll be safe in Sweden and out of your hair soon."

"Lovely. And in a few years, they'll be back with a vengeance," Jonas grumbled, casting a glare at the books stacked high on the nearby shelf.

Ava chuckled sadly and plopped down in the chair, crossing her arms and shaking her head. "You really think that kid's evil, Dummi?"

"Do *you* really think *everyone* in the world is wrong about Jews?" snapped Jonas. "It isn't just the National Socialists that hate them, Ava. Scientists, philosophers, educated people have found that they are genetically predisposed to wickedness. They've been banished from a hundred countries and barred from hundreds more. Before the Final Solution, Heydrich and the others attempted to solve the Jew problem via emigration, but nobody wanted them. There's a *reason* for that, Ava. They're hated for a *reason*."

"I didn't think you were such a lemming," Ava said. "So the majority is always right, hm? Then when Hitler lost the election in 1932, that *proved* he was a raving madman and Germany despised him?"

"Er..." Jonas felt his confidence begin to abandon him.

"Most countries believe it, so it must be true," Ava continued, gesturing to the radio, which was offering a static-filled rendition of Bach's concertos. "Most countries believe the National Socialists are bloodhounds, is *that* true?"

"That's..."

"People hate them for a 'reason.' Mobs are so reasonable,

yes? The average person has historically always been reasonable. That's why they burned witches for hundreds of years and thought the Plague was spread through smells. 'Educated people' and 'scientists' say it's true. Thank Heaven science never changes, that's why the earth is certainly the center of the universe, and the sun revolves around *us*."

"Ava, don't be childish."

"I don't think *I'm* the one being childish, Jonas," Ava retorted, giving him a look of disapproval that perfectly mirrored the sort that Gisela had given her daughter whenever she brought home a bad report card. "Really, I expect better from you. The world was wrong about witches, about the sun revolving around the earth, and yes, they're wrong about Jews. I know that seems ridiculous. I would have said the same thing until I was forced to dig deeper. You're right that people hate Jews for a reason: it's an old poison, old superstitions from the Middle Ages made up by preachers who were angry that they wouldn't accept Jesus. Old superstitions that have been modernized and turned *'scientific.'* People hate Jews because they've been *taught* to hate Jews, and when they're asked why, they'll just say, 'Everyone else hates them, obviously there has to be a reason.' You're a Dummi, Jonas, but you're not *that* small-minded."

"Then explain the communists," Jonas demanded, fighting to sound calm even as frustration ate away at his patience. "The Soviets are overwhelmingly Jewish..."

"Overwhelmingly?! Ha! Lenin wasn't a Jew, Stalin isn't a Jew, the only communist Jews I can think of are Trotsky and Marx. And Marx hated Jewish Jews. He was just like my papa: baptized as a boy and raised Christian, though he was actually an atheist. I think he even wrote about how the 'Jew's God is money.' Maybe he and Hitler would have gotten along. Trotsky? Same story: atheist, a Jew in name only, and obviously he didn't fare well in the end." Ava made a motion like she was stabbing someone, alluding to Stalin's assassination of his old comrade.

"As for why so many Jews joined the communists initially," she continued. "Can you blame them? The Czar was a beast, his Cossacks destroyed their villages simply because of their faith, and then they're sold a story about a worker's paradise where every race and creed will be treated equally. What did they have to lose? A lot, actually. Stalin might not view Jews as a race, but he has no tolerance for Judaism. The Soviet Union isn't Jewish, it's *Soviet*. The fact that Jews would gravitate to a utopian ideology doesn't make them *evil*. If anything, it indicates that they have good hearts and bad foresight. Not unlike the Germans, really. Also, does it make any sense to say that Jews are selfish bankers, but they're also responsible for spreading communism?"

"That's...it's part of a larger scheme!" cried Jonas, feeling his cheeks burn as his brain struggled to come up with a proper argument. "If Jews aren't a self-serving race, then why do so many of them end up in positions of authority and power despite their small numbers? Oddly coincidental that they had their grubby hands in so many higher institutions during the degenerate Weimar era."

"Culture, Jonas, culture," sighed Ava. "Even in the absence of Jewish religious values, Jews maintain their own culture, and that culture is a culture of education. Jews are rarely athletes, but they excel in other areas because Jewish culture emphasizes reading, writing, and education above physical prowess. In Germany, you're a man once you learn to fight. In Jewish culture, you're a man once you've learned to read the Torah. For thousands of years, while the rest of Europe was illiterate, every Jew could read and write because they *had to*. They *had to* read their holy books, that's part of their faith. Even women and poor people *needed* to learn how to read the Torah. That culture of education is continuous. Even when they were stripped of their wealth and lost everything, they could scrape it back because their culture values education and determination. They strive, and they attain."

"Jewish *culture*..." Jonas sneered. "The *culture* that teaches them to torture animals for their kosher slaughter, that teaches them to cheat gentiles..."

"I suppose you *think* you're talking about *kashrut*. And you *think* you're quoting the Talmud or the Torah. But you don't know what you're talking about. Doctored quotes and out-of-context lines don't prove anything about the character of a race. Most Jews don't even read the Torah or the Talmud anymore, and the ones that do are more like Rabbi Gedaliah: willing to give me a chance even when I spit in his face. Maybe if you actually read the books Jews read, you'd see that you've been lied to. *We've* been lied to."

"I'm not interested in Judaism, Ava, it doesn't even matter..."

"If it doesn't matter, then why did you bring it up? Or did you run out of Goebbels' talking points?" Her smirk became nearly insufferable, and Jonas' shoulders slumped in resignation as affectionate anger wormed its way into his gut.

"I really don't want to argue, Ava," he said. "I don't want to fight. I don't care if we disagree on the Jewish Question."

"Well, *I* do," Black Fox One declared, and her smirk melted into an expression of almost maternal severity that mirrored the sort of look Gisela Keller would give Jonas and Ava when they stayed out too late as teens. "And if you love me, you'll care enough about who I am to question who you are."

Jonas' eyes widened. Ava had never been one to pull the 'if you love me' card in the past, and he knew she wouldn't start if she weren't deathly serious. He opened his mouth to question her, but Ava put on her mask and left before he could utter a single syllable.

Jonas stared at the door for a moment after she had gone, her words echoing about his skull. His eyes flitted from the empty chair to the pile of books. The Hebrew lettering shimmered in the dull fluorescent light of the Bunker. The loyal SS man residing in Jonas Amsel's heart let out a bleat of protest that he was even considering it. *You already know what's in those books. Why waste time reading Jewish nonsense?*

Nevertheless, he had little else to do. Black Fox Radio was playing calming classic music, the sort Jonas would often put on when he needed to focus and read. Really, it wasn't *ridiculous* to read from the books. If his goal was to convince Ava that she was wrong, after all, then more information would serve him well. The more he knew, the better he would do next time they argued.

Gritting his teeth, the Fox Hunter shuffled over to the bookshelf and plucked a tattered Jewish Bible from the pile.

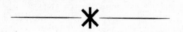

THE DOOR OPENED AGAIN SOME TIME LATER. JONAS looked up, expecting it to be either Ava or the Jakob boy.

When he lifted his eyes from the *Tanakh*, however (which seemed identical to the Old Testament save for a few innocuous variations in translation), he found himself facing a woman ten years Ava's senior. A Jewish woman with plaited dark hair and red-rimmed eyes.

The Fox Hunter stiffened. This stranger looked a little too much like the many pictures of his mother he'd been surrounded by as a boy. He averted his gaze, this time keeping his eyes pinned on the *Tanakh*, staring at the section where the genocidal Haman was hanged from his own noose.

The woman drew close. For a moment, Jonas was certain she would attack him, but instead she glanced from the captive Nazi to the little chair and slowly took a seat.

"Av...Black Fox One sent you," Jonas mumbled after a few moments of silence passed between the two of them. He could feel the woman's sorrowful gaze upon him, burning right through his chest. He had faced tearful women before: hysterical women who would cling to his coat and beg him to show their husbands or their children or themselves mercy. Training himself to ignore their pleas, to stop his eyes from turning the strangers' faces into Ava's, had been a difficult task, but he had managed.

Something about this woman was different, though. Her tears were partially dry, her eyes red, and she emanated a strange sort of sorrowful serenity. No frantic desperation, no pleas, no screams. It seemed that she knew nothing could faze her because the worst thing imaginable had already happened.

"No," the woman mumbled. "They told us not to speak with you. They said you were important."

Despite himself, Jonas smiled. *Important, hm, Ava?*

The Jewish woman before him spoke, and his smile died on the spot: "I just needed to look one of you in the eyes."

"An SS man, you mean," Jonas said, at last lifting his gaze from the *Tanakh* and giving the woman a smug smirk. He gestured towards his filthy plainclothes. "Apologies if I'm disappointing."

"Yes, you *are* disappointing," the woman mumbled. "You look human when you're not in uniform."

"Human?!" Jonas scoffed. It seemed that this Jewess didn't know who the subhuman in the room was.

The woman's azure eyes darkened. She trembled so terribly that he worried the chair might turn to splinters.

"Your kind used my baby for target practice," she said. Her tone wasn't accusatory. Confused, agonized, but not accusatory. "And they laughed. And when they laughed, it sounded like a demon laughing. I thought all of you must be devils disguised as humans."

Jonas dug his nails into the hardcover. Target practice? Jewish children died, of course, he had known that all along, but he had been under the impression that the SS carried out their duty with the solemn severity it required. The SS were intellectual knights bound by a code of honor, not Vikings who took pleasure in butchering their enemies' babies.

But he knew a liar when he saw it, and he knew that the woman wasn't lying.

"I...that's not protocol..." Jonas muttered. It almost sounded pathetic, the Fox Hunter trying to make an excuse on behalf of his comrades...and to a subhuman, no less! He shouldn't have needed to explain himself, but he felt compelled to say something in the face of the grieving mother before him.

Grieving mother? His inner SS man reprimanded him for humanizing the enemy so thoroughly. *Not a grieving mother, a Jewess. Those SS men did the right thing, even if their methods weren't appropriate.*

But though Jonas' training assured him that his comrades' actions were entirely justified, the woman spoke, and he felt his chest swell with involuntary disgust.

"They grabbed him out of my arms and threw him into the

air...they shot him, and then they stepped on him to finish him off...*stepped* on him. Is *that* protocol?"

"N-no..." Jonas muttered. He'd seen gristly things in his years of service, but even imagining bringing his boot down on an infant's skull made his gut churn. Subhuman or not, there was no excuse for such unnecessary cruelty. Toughness was one thing, but sadism was supposed to be a Jewish trait. Germans were supposed to treat all creatures humanely, even animals. Even subhumans.

"That's..." he muttered. "I'm..."

Sorry? He was, but he couldn't say that to a Jewess.

You said it to Ava, he reminded himself.

Ava is different, another part of him argued. The bereaved woman was looking at him, eyes wide, expectant, a strange mix of dread and hopelessness clashing in her irises.

"I don't condone that." Jonas tried to keep his tone even, neutral, but the slightest lilt of softness made its way into his voice.

He was surprised when his words seemed to only elevate the woman's sorrow. Somehow, he had made an insufferable situation worse. She broke down, sobbing, and it was a strange sound. He had heard women sob before. From fear, from terror, but he had rarely stayed and listened to the weeping of the bereaved.

This wasn't even that: not the sob of a woman mourning her child, but the wail of someone who had just lost their faith. Instructually, he found himself drawing the *Tanakh* closer to his person. He buried his face in the book, but while he could look away, he couldn't stop himself from hearing those wrenching wails. Every sob she unleashed struck at his soul.

Did Ava cry like that when she realized she was a Jew?

When she lost her family?

117

As though summoned by his thoughts, Black Fox One ran in. "Ruth...Ruth..." she whispered, gathering the woman into her arms. "Come on, I'm sorry, whatever he said..."

Ava turned her masked face to the Fox Hunter, and he gave her a wide-eyed look, a silent plea of innocence. She shook her head and ushered the woman out of the room.

Jonas heard her sobs even after she was gone.

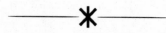

THE NEXT STRANGER THAT INVADED HIS SPACE WAS the sort that he had been expecting: the angry, violent sort. The intruder kicked down the door, awakening Jonas from a nightmare where he'd crushed a baby's skull with his boot.

"You bastard!" the stranger shouted. For a moment, Jonas' sleep-addled brain thought he was looking at his own reflection. True, the Jew invading his cell was ensconced in ragged civilian garments rather than a pristine SS uniform, but his features were German. His light blue eyes blazed with the sort of righteous fury Jonas only ever saw in the irises of SS men readying themselves to round up a pack of wicked Jews.

The Jewish man grabbed the small chair, and now it seemed that one of the Fox Hunter's "guests" finally intended to beat him to death with the flimsy piece of furniture. Jonas, by instinct, glanced about for a means to defend himself, but there was nothing he could use as a weapon. Even the bucket was empty, and the heavy books that might have made for decent shields were too far away.

With nothing else to use for self-defense, Jonas grabbed his pillow and held it over his head, hoping that would be enough to save him from enduring any permanent damage.

"Ava!" the Fox Hunter cried, hoping that his shout would bring his fiancée running. He was surprised by the sound of his own voice: frantic, frightened, the sort of tone he had never *himself* used but had *heard* many times. It was the sort of cry that Jews would let out when they called to their God or one another, begging for a savior.

Unlike them, however, Jonas was rescued, but not by Ava. Another boy about a year younger than the furious intruder ran in. The second Jew had Semitic features: curly dark hair, brown eyes, a big nose. Classic Jew, really. Clearly full-blooded, and yet he didn't join his friend in assaulting the helpless *Fuchsjäger*. Instead, he leapt between the attacker and the captive Nazi, shielding Jonas with his own body.

"Aaron, Aaron, stop!" the dark-haired Jew begged, grabbing the chair legs and trying to wrestle it away from his friend. "Aaron!"

"Don't you fucking dare, Eitan! Don't you fucking dare!" Aaron snarled as he tried to wrench the chair from the smaller teen's grasp.

The two Jews struggled, and while it seemed that Aaron, who was easily a foot taller and twenty pounds heavier than Eitan, should have been victorious, Eitan managed to hold his ground.

"*Stop*, Aaron!" Eitan commanded. "Black Fox One told us not to touch him!"

"I don't give a *shit* what they said!" Aaron cried, and the fury in his voice gave way ever so slightly, betraying the sorrow that was driving his rage. "His comrades raped my sister!"

The animalistic fear burning in Jonas' chest was replaced with a horrific nausea and a wave of instinctual empathy towards his attacker. Aaron's murderous rage was borne not from simple racial fury, but from a place of honor. Jonas had spent six years worrying about Ava, fearing that she was suffering a similar fate, and vowing to tear any man that touched her apart limb by limb.

"I wouldn't do such a thing," Jonas cried in a tone of empathetic indignation, attempting to plead his own innocence and acknowledge that the Jew was acting with German righteousness. Aaron snarled.

"Fuck you!" Aaron declared, but he either decided that killing Jonas wasn't worth harming Eitan or the Fox Hunter's declaration weakened his resolve enough that his friend was able to yank the chair from his hands and put it back on the floor.

"Come on," Eitan said, grabbing his trembling friend by the shoulders and embracing him. "Come on, don't pay him any mind, forget him..."

Aaron shot Jonas a tear-filled glare, but bowed his head and nodded, letting his friend lead him out of the room.

With the danger gone, Jonas' inner SS man crawled forth and chastised him for the empathy and admiration burning in his chest. *What's wrong with you? Jews have no honor. They're not human. There's nothing a Jew doesn't deserve.*

Jonas had often had nightmares of Ava being brutalized by subhumans, but now when a nightmare encroached upon his sleep, the monsters of his imaginings were no longer Jews or Black Foxes but cackling SS men.

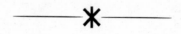

THE NEXT STRANGER WAS A RABBI, BROUGHT BY curiosity. Jonas expected the most vitriol from this one, but the

Rabbi sat in the little chair and noticed with a small smile that *der Fuchsjäger* was reading from the Talmud.

"I see you've only got two-thousand and six-hundred pages left!" chuckled the Rabbi, and Jonas grunted. The Rabbi was practically the manifestation of all things the Fox Hunter had been taught to hate: a Jew with curly sidelocks and a long beard. He was a dirty, disgusting, strange creature, and yet Jonas, unbathed and chained up and stripped of his rank, suddenly found himself sitting a few feet from the Jewish holy man and feeling...small.

The Fox Hunter lifted up one of the many books of the Babylonian Talmud that Ava had provided.

"Is the whole thing like this?" he asked.

"Like what?" the Rabbi said, head tilting slightly sideways, dark eyes twinkling almost impishly.

"It's...*arguing*. Isn't this supposed to be a book of law?" Jonas muttered.

"It's an examination of the Torah by the great Rabbis of the era. It provides a glimpse into the actual practices..."

"Yes, but they're just...arguing about minutiae," Jonas interrupted.

"As Jews are wont to do! Really, the silliest thing about Nazism is its belief that we Jews could possibly operate a global conspiracy. Even if we wanted to, the whole thing would fall apart in five minutes because we'd never be able to agree about how Seychelles should be run."

Despite his training, Jonas snorted and glanced back down at the Talmud. He wouldn't call the great tome inspiring, but it was also relatively innocuous so far. He had peered between the lines, searching for the segments he'd been told about: the segments that instructed Jews to abuse gentiles, the segments that instructed Jews to embrace their inner wickedness.

Nothing. He almost wished he didn't know Hebrew or else he could have dismissed it all as deception by way of inaccurate translation, but he could read the Hebrew and the German translations, and both were merely filled with Rabbis arguing about every single punctuation mark in the Torah. It was boring, certainly, but it wasn't particularly vile.

Jonas glanced up at the Rabbi and bit his lip. Asking the Jewish man anything would be wrong. Even if he hadn't found the passage that explicitly instructed Jews to lie to Germans yet, surely it was *there*. Not on the page, but in the Jewish soul.

But curiosity had driven the Rabbi to come and sit with the SS man, and now curiosity gnawed at the Fox Hunter until he couldn't help but inquire.

"There's a section," Jonas said, holding up the book. "There *should* be a section, I haven't found it yet, it's supposed to be called '*Libre David*'..."

"Alfred Rosenberg told you that?" the Rabbi guessed, a bitter lilt in his voice even though his smile didn't falter when he dropped the name of the Nazi chief ideologue, the man whose writings had filled Jonas' SS curriculum. The Fox Hunter nodded.

"And I looked, but I can't find it..."

"And that's the chapter that supposedly teaches us to be evil bastards and cheat the gentiles." Still, the Rabbi's smile didn't falter even as the bitterness in his tone became biting. Jonas suddenly felt like he was back in school and had just given the most bumbling, stupid answer to the teacher in front of the entire class. The Rabbi's icy gaze felt like an audience of eyes. The Fox Hunter nodded again, and the Rabbi heaved a mournful sigh.

"That 'chapter' doesn't exist, son," the Rabbi declared,

slowly rising to his feet. "Look for it if you don't believe me. You've been lied to."

With that, the Rabbi left the room. Jonas watched him go in silence.

As soon as the door was shut, the Fox Hunter scurried to his bookshelf, grabbing every volume of the Talmud he had been provided. For the next four hours, he tore through every book, searching desperately for the chapter of *Libre David*, looking for evidence that a page or several had been ripped from the books in a desperate attempt to hide the truth.

But the Rabbi was right. He looked and looked, but the book of Jewish law which Nazi propaganda supposedly quoted, the books his teachers had told him about, did not exist.

For a moment, Jonas felt like his insides had been stuffed with cotton, like he was going to be ill. Then, just as quickly, a flare of anger consumed his chest. A familiar feeling, but with an unfamiliar target: furious anger, righteous anger, but not directed at the Jews.

They lied to me...they lied right to my face. My teachers, my comrades, they all lied to me!

He dug his nails into the edges of the book and stared at the intricate Hebrew lettering. His corneas burned, and fear joined anger in his chest.

If they lied about that, what else did they lie about?

"Dummi...psst! Herr Dummi Nazi."

The nightmare of stomping on a child's skull until it was little more than mush beneath his jackboot hadn't left him alone, and so when Jonas awoke to a child's voice, he did so with a yelp and a start, sitting up and almost, *almost* letting a sob escape his throat.

It was little Jakob again. The boy was standing near his bookshelf, wide eyes glowing with confusion. He gawked at the terrified Nazi as though Jonas Amsel was a tiger that had just transformed into a house cat.

"You...had a nightmare?" the child muttered, picking at the fresh bandage on his cheek. Jonas shoved his hand under his blanket, touching the box with the swastika ring. He huffed when he found that the gesture did not comfort him. Being near the symbol of National Socialism did not give him a burst of strength, it merely reminded him of his doubts, of the lies he knew were lies and the truths he was uncertain about now.

"Why are you here?" Jonas muttered, and his tone was less harsh than it had been the last time he had seen the child. Jakob rocked back and forth on his heels, humming softly as he picked at his band-aid.

"Black Fox One says we're leaving tomorrow morning and you're gonna be here all by yourself," the child mumbled. "Is that why you're having a nightmare? 'Cause you don't wanna be alone?"

The Fox Hunter gritted his teeth and realized that the mystery of what a Nazi feared was too tempting. The boy wouldn't let up. Better that lie than the gruesome truth. Jonas nodded.

"Do you have a family?" the boy asked. "A mama?"

"My mama died when I was little," Jonas muttered, tightening his grip on the little box even though it practically burned his palm. "I have a papa."

"Oh..." Jakob's tone was morose.

"Black Fox One said you were an orphan," the Fox Hunter said. The boy shook his head.

"No, I have a papa," Jakob mumbled. "Well, I *had* one. He's not dead, but he hates me and Mama."

Jonas lifted a brow. "Why?"

"'Cause we're Jews and he wasn't, so he gave us to the SS and got a new family." The boy seemed strangely cavalier about the whole thing, and the Nazi worldview that the Fox Hunter was beginning to doubt crumbled a bit more.

"He abandoned his own wife and child?" Jonas said, fury forcing its way to his voice. Again, the boy affixed him with a perplexed expression.

"No, he turned us in, he didn't *abandon* us," Jakob said.

"That's unacceptable," Jonas hissed.

"But...are you *actually* a real Nazi, or are you just *really* confused?"

The boy's query struck him worse than any blow he'd suffered during his service. Jonas' head throbbed worse than it had when he'd first awoken in this room after Ava had knocked him out.

Jakob's father had done the right thing. The National Socialist Party demanded such sacrifices. Engel had been right to kill his traitorous wife, Naden had wrongly tried to save his.

But nothing in the universe could have convinced Jonas to throw Ava away. If they had married and had a child, he *never* would have abandoned them. He would have shed his SS uniform and followed them into the ghetto, into the worst concentration camp.

A brutal bout of realization struck Jonas. If he and Ava had become parents early, like he had always wanted, their child would have been a mongrel, a half-breed exactly like Jakob. He probably would have looked just like Jakob. A mere few nights ago, the Fox Hunter had dismissed the idea of his potential child being anything like the little subhuman, but he had been wrong again.

The boy shuffled close, too close: no other visitor besides Ava had dared get so close to the Nazi. A small part of Jonas was tempted to grab the boy and try (probably in vain) to use him to escape. He would make a decent hostage.

But the nightmares of crushing Jewish children made the idea of doing harm to little Jakob odious. The mere notion made Jonas' gut roil.

The child waited a moment, lingering within the Nazi's reach with his lips slightly parted, as though he was ready to let out a scream if the Fox Hunter suddenly grabbed him. When Jonas instead merely met his gaze and inhaled sharply, Jakob offered him a small smile and reached into his pocket.

"Here," the boy said. "Since you didn't hurt any mamas."

He handed Jonas a little foil-wrapped something-or-other. Gingerly, Jonas took it, wincing when his calloused hand brushed against the boy's as he did so.

"I..."

"It's chocolate," Jakob said. "Black Fox One got it for us, but you didn't get any. I was gonna save it, but you can have it."

Jonas gazed down at the slightly melted candy and felt his palm burn and his throat go dry. The Fox Hunter had assumed he hadn't killed any mothers except his own, but he had certainly *hurt* many mamas over the years. Even thinking of eating the little wrongfully offered reward made guilt and nausea assault his guts.

"I...I'm allergic to chocolate," Jonas lied, dropping the candy back into the boy's palm. "But...thank you."

"Oh! Sorry you're allergic. Chocolate's really good."

"Enjoy it, then."

126

"Mmm hm!" The boy shoved the sweet back into his pocket.

"It will melt if you leave it in your pocket," Jonas noted. "You should eat it now. If you keep saving it, you might lose it."

"Oh! It melts?"

"You've, ah...never had chocolate before, have you?"

"Just a few times, and we ate it right away. Papa used to say chocolate was too expensive."

"Hm. I didn't have much candy when I was your age either. Do you want to know a secret?"

Jakob had taken the chocolate out of his pocket and was unwrapping it. He paused his task and glanced up, eyes shimmering with eager curiosity as he bobbed his head.

"Me and Black Fox One were friends when we were children," Jonas confessed. Jakob nearly dropped his chocolate bar in shock.

"Really?!" the child exclaimed, and Jonas nodded.

"Yes. We were neighbors. We used to run around the streets looking for coins people had dropped. Sometimes, we'd even pickpocket a few Marks off some rich folk. Then, when we'd get enough money, we'd buy a lollipop and share it."

"Yuck! That's gross! You'd lick her spit!" the boy cried, wrinkling his nose. An amused smile pulled at Jonas' lip, and he was so, *so* tempted to say something that would fly over the child's head, but he controlled himself.

"Well, that didn't matter to me much," Jonas muttered. "We were very poor."

"Sooo...if you two were friends, is that why you're not evil like the rest of the SS? That's why you're just confused? You didn't turn her in like Papa turned Mama in, right?"

"No, I wouldn't do that to her," Jonas said, shaking his head. The boy's smile widened.

"That's good! You know, if you wanna fix your brain so you're not confused anymore, you should zap it and that'll make it better, and then Black Fox One can let you out."

"That's...ha!" chuckled Jonas, though his amusement turned to discomfort when he remembered the empty insane asylums dotting the *Altreich*, their ill patients no longer treated with electroshock therapy but instead banished to gas chambers. The Rabbi's dire warning echoed in his mind again. *You were lied to.*

"You should probably go to bed," Jonas muttered. The boy slipped the little piece of chocolate into his mouth and smiled, nodding.

"Ok'ah!" the boy said, his mouth full. He gave the German a small wave and darted from the room with a little bounce in his step.

When Jonas laid his head down again, he found himself unable to sleep until he had taken the ring box out from beneath his pillow and set it under the bed.

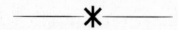

AVA LEFT WITH THE JEWS, AND JONAS WAS ONCE again alone.

The solitude was not welcome. The Fox Hunter found himself missing the shrieks of children and the Yiddish songs and conversations that spilled from the main chamber. He kept glancing at the door, waiting for another visitor, and felt a pang in his chest when he remembered that nobody would be intruding.

He didn't spend the time studiously avoiding his bookshelf and pondering how to convince Ava to leave the Black Foxes. He forced the little voice of his SS training, which seemed quieter now, to silence itself completely as he continued trudging through the Talmud and perusing the other books she had left. He didn't chuck anything at the radio in a desperate attempt to shut Papa Fox up, but felt grateful for the noise, be it the forbidden American jazz, classics, or even Papa Fox's diatribes against the Third Reich. It was nice. It made him feel less alone.

When Ava returned, this time by herself, she tore off her mask and greeted him with a smile.

"Oh, shit, you found the comics!" she chuckled when she saw what he was reading. He smirked. Tucked in one book on Jewish ethics, he'd found a small magazine made up of illustrations. He'd heard of comic books before: the SS magazine *Das Schwarze Korps* had mocked the Jews who created the ridiculous figure of Superman, dismissing it as Judaic tripe that would rot the brain of any intelligent person who picked it up.

The comic Jonas had uncovered was written and illustrated by someone named Bernie Hoch. *The Breathtaking Adventures of the Black Foxes, Issue 1*. It was about Ava, though of course Hoch presumed that the illustrious Black Fox leader was a dashing young man who could take on an entire battalion of SS men unarmed. Somehow, Comic-Black-Fox-One managed to punch half the hierarchy of the Third Reich by the time the book was finished, including a fanged Adolf Hitler.

"You like it?" Ava chuckled. "You're smiling."

It wasn't high art, but if nothing else, it was amusing. It did put a smile on his face, watching a completely inaccurate rendition of Black Fox One defeat cartoonishly devilish villains.

The Fox Hunter's heart sank a bit as he glanced at one

panel, which featured "Black Fox One" knocking a snarling SS man to the ground. He stared at the demonic blond caricature and raked a hand through his own sand-colored hair.

"Where did you get this from?" Jonas asked.

"Contact."

"Can't say more?"

"Nope! Artist is apparently a fan of ours. Been writing for years, even before America was in the war. It's...flattering, I guess. Plus, the kids like them when they can read them."

"Can *you* read them? They're all in English, and I remember how you used to make me do your English homework for you."

"Low blow, Dummi! I can make it through a comic book! There are barely any words in it anyway! Half of the words are punching noises, and that's a universal language."

"So...is this what being Black Fox One is actually like?" Jonas teased, shutting the comic, and tossing it onto the foot of the bed. Ava chuckled.

"I wish! A chance to deck Hitler in the face would be nice, and if I could take out that many men just by myself...well, things would be easier."

Ava's shoulders slumped slightly, and she glanced almost wistfully out the door.

"Have you had missions fail before?" Jonas queried.

"Thought you read all the reports."

"It was difficult to parse which attacks were you since you didn't leave survivors...none besides me, that is."

"I've had...problems," Ava confessed, gloomily looking into the eyes of the gas mask in her hand. "Rescuing Jews is the easy part, but getting a whole troop of kids and girls to safety..."

Images came unbidden to Jonas' mind: the Rabbi who had

told him the truth, the honorable Jew seeking to avenge his sister, little Jakob and his propensity to disobey Black Fox One.

"The Jews you just moved, did they all make it out all right?" The question came from his lips before the ever-weakening National Socialist within him could even hope to suppress it. Ava gazed at the Fox Hunter for a moment, her eyes glistening like they had when she was an ignorant teenager dreaming about winning gold for Germany.

"Everyone got out just fine," she said, a smile stretching across her face as she glanced from the crumpled comic book to her ruffled fiancée.

And although the grievously battered loyal SS man inside him tried its hardest to stop him, Jonas Amsel declared: "Good."

NINE

For a few days, they remained together, Ava preparing for her next rescue mission, Jonas still perusing the books she had given him and chipping away at his SS training with every page he read and every debate he had with his fiancée. She left one day and returned with another troop of Jews, and he found himself feeling strangely grateful that the Bunker was noisy again.

New strangers came into his room, drawn by anger or curiosity or amusement. The procession of Jews continued on, each of them different, each of them horrifically human. And with every visit and strained conversation, the Rabbi's morose declaration grew louder, more vicious, more overwhelming.

You've been lied to. You've been lied to.

JONAS AWOKE AFTER A LONG, ACHING PERIOD OF silence. At this point, he wasn't sure what he found more painful: the absence of rescuees or their presence.

When he awoke to the sound of Yiddish songs and laughter, he sighed. The battered remnants of his Nazi training fought valiantly against the relief in his chest. He felt a strange sense of satisfaction at listening to the happy laughter of the Jews and undesirables Ava had saved. Jews like Jakob and the Rabbi. Jews like Ava herself.

Jonas glanced down at his ankle and was completely shocked to discover that his shackle had been removed.

What...? Jonas thought, wringing his leg and then pinching himself to be sure this wasn't a dream.

He didn't wake up on the same bunk with the shackle locked around his ankle. Which meant it was a test. Maybe a trick. Maybe as soon as he left the room, Ava would bash his skull in.

Well, at least this time he would be expecting it.

The Fox Hunter hopped off the mattress, hesitating before he stooped down, grabbing the dusty ring box hidden beneath the bed, and sliding it into his pocket. He didn't see anything he could use as a weapon and so he grabbed the little chair, hoping that it would make for an effective bludgeoning instrument if the need arose.

Carefully, he nudged the door open. When nothing happened, he used the chair to push it open the rest of the way and braced himself. Nothing.

He slipped into the barely illuminated hall and started towards the exit, spinning about every time he heard a sound too close. A rat skittered past his legs, and the singing continued its cheerful tempo, but Ava did not emerge and stop him from fleeing.

Maybe she's waiting right outside? Jonas thought as he reached the entrance hall and caught a glimpse of the hatch, shivering as the strange silver eye graffiti stared at him. That was likely, but if he bolted, he could probably make it out.

And then what? Jonas thought, shaking his head. *That'll do you no good. You're here to save Ava, not run from her. If this is a test, you're better off passing it.*

Sighing, he turned on his heel, ready to march back to his cell.

"Hey! Hey, friend!"

Jonas tightened his grip on the little chair and winced as an unfamiliar voice called to him. A man emerged from the shadows, gruff and filthy with a slight Dutch accent. The Dutch resistance fighter's green eyes flitted from the ragged Fox Hunter to the door. Jonas readied himself for a fight, but the Black Fox merely gave him a gentle smile and beckoned for him to come close.

"Hey, c'mon, let's take that chair back to the others. Don't do anything stupid now. I get it, but a chair won't beat a Nazi."

Jonas' heart hammered as he realized that the Black Fox didn't think he was an escapee. *Ava didn't tell them about me this time. He thinks I'm one of them...*

"I'm not a Jew," the Fox Hunter blurted, almost sounding like a child as his voice became high-pitched. He looked down at his rumpled civilian clothes and realized why the Black Fox might have assumed he was a fugitive undesirable: he was just as disheveled and dirty as the rest of them now.

"Neither am I, friend," the Black Fox said, drawing close and clapping Jonas on the shoulder like he was a comrade. The swastika ring in Jonas' coat pocket suddenly felt excruciatingly heavy.

"Still, even if you don't know Yiddish, some of the songs

can be catchy!" the Black Fox said, gingerly leading the Fox Hunter away from the exit and towards the sound of celebrations.

"So, what's your story, friend?" the Black Fox asked. Jonas bit his lip.

"I...ah...would rather not say," the Fox Hunter said, his gut writhing as the Dutch Black Fox smiled at him. *You would have killed him without a second thought a few weeks ago.*

"Eh, that's fine, I get it," the Black Fox said. "Look, you don't have to worry: the enemy of my enemy and all that. The others won't begrudge you unless you were a traitor."

Traitor. He *was* a traitor. He should have run, run and reported Ava, but he would rather betray his nation than betray her. Jonas shivered and stumbled as the Black Fox led him into the largest room in the Bunker.

It was absolutely packed with people. This transport seemed to mostly consist of women with a smattering of children and older folks. A sea of dark hair with the occasional blonde scurrying by, a din of song and shouting, laughing and crying, of German and languages he couldn't decipher.

Jonas looked this way and saw a woman comforting a little girl that had skinned her knee. That way: two women whispering excitedly about their husbands who were fighting their enemies. Another way: a few older gentlemen chit-chatting with one another. A few people were singing, some cheerfully in celebration of their liberation, others with a sob caught on every syllable.

"Come here, philosopher
With your cat's brain
Come sit at the Rabbi's table
And learn some sense

Bim ba bam, bimba bam
Bim ba bam bim ba bam!"

"Hey, friend," the Dutch Black Fox said, jabbing Jonas in the shoulder and making the Nazi jump.

"Y-Yes?"

"You look spry enough to sit on the floor. Mind handing the chair over to Old Man Menachem? I don't imagine sitting on the floor is good for his knees."

The Black Fox pointed towards an old man sitting on the cold ground, surrounded by a few young children. Menachem was reading them something, though it seemed most of the little ones were distracted by the hubbub around them. That or they simply weren't able to hear him over the Yiddish folk song.

"A–all right...uhm..." Jonas glanced at the Dutch Black Fox. "Have you seen Black Fox One?"

"Aha!" chuckled the Dutch man, clapping Jonas' shoulder again. "Was *that* what you were looking for? You're wasting your time, friend: she won't be interested. Trust me, I've tried."

"What's *that* supposed to mean?!" yelped Jonas a bit too loudly, drawing the attention of several Jews. His cheeks turned scarlet, and he shook his head.

"Er...never mind. I just...needed to speak to her, that's all."

"She's around here somewhere. Took off her uniform. She might be hard to find. Knows how to blend in, One does. That's how she gets half her work done. Walks up to a troop of SS men: 'Help, help, I'm a feeble young woman!' Then, *bam!*" The Black Fox smacked his palms together and chuckled.

"I'll give Menachem my chair and look around," Jonas muttered.

"Sure thing. If you need anything, just yell, 'Fifty-Six!' and I'll come running."

The Dutch man, Black Fox 56, gave Jonas a slight shove towards Old Man Menachem before scurrying off to have a drink with a few of his fellow resistance fighters. Jonas followed Black Fox 56 with his gaze, but he didn't see Ava standing amongst the Black Foxes. Sighing, the Fox Hunter stepped up to Old Man Menachem.

"Sir," he said, and his inner SS man, whose voice was no longer a powerful cry but now little more than a hoarse whisper, harangued him as best as it could for treating a worthless Jew with anything resembling respect.

Old Man Menachem looked up. Jonas had never met his grandfather, but Dieter had described him as a gentleman with an impressive beard and twinkling eyes who could put one at ease with a smile. Jonas swallowed. Menachem fit that description perfectly.

And your father would send him to one of the camps he designed.

Jonas felt like a beast was clawing at his stomach as he offered the old man his chair. "For you, sir...the floor can't be good for you."

"Aha!" laughed Menachem, tucking the book under his arm. One of the children helped him stand and shuffle towards Jonas. The Fox Hunter set the chair down, and Menachem got comfortable.

"Bless you, son!" the old man said. "Much better! I was just about to say that I couldn't keep reading. Now where was I? Ah! Right! King Asmodeus the Great Demon..."

The old man thumbed through the tattered tome, trying to find the proper chapter. Jonas glanced at the cover: it was some sort of fairytale book. The cover bore an image of a horrific monster raising its claws above a defiant young Jewish man brandishing a black sword.

"You're welcome," Jonas muttered, and then he scurried away, desperately not wanting to hear whatever story Menachem was reading.

The Fox Hunter tossed himself into the throng of Jews, searching for his fiancée.

"Ava!" he cried, but she didn't emerge from the horde. He tried to pick her face out of the crowd, but it was impossible: too many pretty faces, too many dark-haired beauties, so many sets of dark eyes.

"Ava!"

He felt a hand on his shoulder and relief flooded his chest before he turned. "Ava..." Jonas muttered, and for a second he was certain the Jewess that had grabbed him *was* Ava. She looked so similar. She was different, and yet too much the same.

"Sorry, sir, did you lose someone?" the Jewess said with a gentle smile. "It's so crowded in here! I think most of the kids are..."

"I-I don't need help!" Jonas yelped in the sort of desperate manner that he immediately realized made his declaration utterly unbelievable. He broke away from the girl and continued through the grand chamber, desperately trying to find his Ava. If he could just find her, pick her out from the throng of subhumans, then he could keep believing that he was *right* and the echoes of *you've been lied to* could *stop*.

But it was useless. He couldn't find Ava. It wasn't plucking a needle from a haystack: no, his task was akin to finding one particular stalk of hay among thousands.

Not special. Not *different*. His training died with a whimper and the warning became reality. *You've been lied to.*

139

He felt uncoupled, like a locomotive that became unteth-
ered from its hefty cargo cars and continued forth down the
tracks, unburdened and incomplete. It was at once liberating
and terrifying, leaving an empty feeling in the pit of his chest
that was swiftly filled with a toxic swell of anger.

I was lied to, he thought, and in the name of that lie he had
killed. Murdered. Nausea took hold of him, and he almost
collapsed. He was angry. Angry at his father who had lied to
him, at the nation which had lied to him, at the lying system he
had served.

Anger turned from the state to himself, and his eyes
burned with furious tears. He had killed on behalf of a lie, and
while his self-interested instincts begged him to regard this as
an excuse—*you're a victim too, you were lied to*—memories of
actions past made him squeeze his eyes shut and shake his head.

Yes, he had been lied to, but he wasn't stupid. He could
have known better if he had just looked, listened. Instead, he
had embraced the lovely lie and now he had innocent blood on
his hands. The swastika ring felt like it was scalding in his
pocket, and he was almost tempted to throw it into a dark
corner of the Bunker. But when he reached up, he felt a
calloused hand grip his wrist.

"Hey, Dummi!"

Jonas couldn't see through the tears that had accumulated
in his corneas, but he knew her voice. Ava must have been
watching him the whole time. He might have been self-
conscious any other time and wiped away his tears, but he had
no desire to look her in the eye right then. She slipped her hand
into his, and though guilt made him hesitate, he gripped it.

"C'mon, let's talk."

Blindly, Jonas let her pull him away from the main chamber. Before he knew it, he was sitting on his bed, taking in

sharp breaths and drying his tears on his pillow like he was eight years old again.

"I'm sorry," he gasped, and for a moment that was all he could say. She sat beside him, grasping his shoulder. When she spoke, her tone was strange: relieved and morose all at once.

"I know it hurts," she assured him. "Come on, you're okay, breathe..."

Jonas was anything but *okay*, but he nonetheless obeyed, forcing his eyes to stop pouring tears. His vision finally cleared, and he looked to his side. Ava had indeed shorn her Black Fox One uniform in favor of a black dress. If his soul hadn't felt like it had been torn to shreds, he might have been tempted to kiss her right then, but instead he bit his lip hard.

"God, fuck, I didn't...I can't believe I..."

"Jonas, Jonas, come on, it's okay..."

"It's not!" He didn't intend to snap at her, but his voice became tinged with anger. "I've been hunting these people for *years*, Ava! God knows how many people are dead because of me!"

"And I knew you would realize that if you just got a chance. I believed in you, Jonas, and I'm glad I did."

"I..." Jonas hiccupped. "How forgiving is Judaism?"

She laughed, but it was a bitter laugh. "Remember how our pastor used to prattle on about original sin? The idea that humans are born stained, sinful. I always thought it was bullshit. Judaism doesn't believe that."

"So what does Judaism believe?" Jonas queried, eager, desperate, to think of anything besides what he'd done and what he was.

"Humans come into the world pure and whole, free from sin," Ava explained. "But we all have two inclinations, one towards evil, the *yetzer hara*, and one towards good, the *yetzer hatov.* Rabbi Gedaliah said that even the worst soul in the universe has a *yetzer hatov.* He said there was no such thing as the Devil. Then again, he never met Heydrich. I don't think there's even a pinprick of good in *him.* It would take a miracle to get him to listen to his *yetzer hatov.*"

"A miracle or someone very special..." Despite himself and the terrible ripping sensation in his gut, Jonas managed a fondly teasing tone and smiled at his fiancée. Ava chuckled and patted his arm.

"Don't sell yourself short, Jonas," she said. "Much as I'd like to take all the credit, I knew it would take more than just me to make you see the truth. I think almost anyone can change, but just because of love? No. Not when you think you're acting on behalf of your *yetzer hatov.* See, the thing is, even the *yetzer hatov* and *yetzer hara,* they're not just an angel and devil on your shoulder. The *yetzer hara* is more like...base instincts. Animal instincts. It can be bad if you *only* listen to it, but without the *yetzer hara* you'd lie down and starve to death."

"So the evil urge can be good?"

"Yes, and the *yetzer hatov* can be used for evil. It's not necessarily *good,* it's more like...the part of you that ate from the Tree of Knowledge. The higher intelligence, the urge to be like God. That can be good, but a *yetzer hatov* can also be... misled. Corrupted. A corrupt *yetzer hatov* is far worse than an out-of-control *yetzer hara.* The old kings of Europe were driven by their *yetzer hara,* but these days every awful human thinks he's an agent of God. The *Wehrmacht* has it on their belts: *Gott Mit Uns.*"

"You think people in the SS are actually listening to their *yetzer hatov*? How about Hitler?"

"I think he really believes the bullshit he spews...so, in his mind, he's always following his *yetzer hatov*. I doubt he'd ever admit he's wrong, though, even if God Himself told him so. He thinks *he's* God. Everyone tells him he's a God, after all. Really, though, I think everyone gives Hitler too much credit. By himself? He'd just be a madman raving on the side of the road. But the people who listen to his ravings, believe his ravings, kill for his ravings, people like Heydrich..."

"People like me," Jonas said, a shiver wracking his body. "It's our fault. It's *my* fault."

"Jonas, you don't have a bad bone in your body," Ava assured him, squeezing his arm a bit too tight. "You've got a strong *yetzer hatov*, it was just...misdirected."

"Does it matter?" Jonas said, nearly hissing. "Hitler may very well think he's listening to his *yetzer hatov*. That's no excuse."

"But you've *really* listened," Ava argued. "You could have just shut your ears and refused to see reality, but you've listened. I can tell you want to make things right."

"I wish I could," the former Fox Hunter mumbled, reaching into his pocket and squeezing the little ring box, gritting his teeth. "But nothing can make things right."

"Maybe not...there is a way to make it *better*, though."

"Better?" Jonas took his hand out of his pocket and clasped his hands together as though to plead for a way out of this sinful muck. Ava grasped his wrists and pried his hands apart, pulling him towards her.

"Help us," she begged, pressing his hands to her chest as though she wanted him to feel her frantically hopeful heartbeat. "Help *me*. Use that *yetzer hatov* for true good. You're a talented man, and you have insight into the SS. You could help us..."

"You want me to be a spy for you," Jonas said, a lilt of

disappointment making its way into his tone. He would do so happily, but the thought of returning to Heydrich and pretending to believe a word he said...

"No!" Ava exclaimed, tightening her grip on Jonas' wrist so much that he could barely feel the blood flowing to his fingertips. "I don't want to let you out of my sight, and I don't want you to ever have to put on an SS uniform again. I'd rather you figure out a way to lure Heydrich here so we can nab him and make him spill his guts. I'd like you to stay with me. Work with me."

"Ava, I'm the Fox Hunter, nobody would ever accept..."

"I'm Black Fox One. If I tell Papa Fox, he'll give you a chance. Trust me: you wouldn't represent the first time someone from the SS offered us help."

"I don't know how much help I can realistically be," Jonas confessed. "I want to help, but there's no way Heydrich will follow me anywhere. Not if I don't return with you as my prisoner."

"And that's not going to happen." Ava released her fiancé's wrists, and he put his hands on her shoulders.

"Never," he vowed.

"It's all right," Ava assured him, offering him a dazzling smile as she put her hands on his thigh. "We'll figure something out. It's good to have you back."

"Ava..." Jonas started to let his arms fall to his sides. She grabbed his wrists again, yanking him into a fierce embrace.

"I'm sorry..." he hiccuped as sobs conquered his body once more. "I'm sorry, I wanted to do the right thing..."

"I know, Jonas, I know..."

TEN

Panenské Břežany

"Ah, Major Amsel. Please follow me. The *Reichsprotektor* and Major Engel are in the garden."

As Dieter Amsel climbed out of his car, he smiled at the young servant that stood between the two SS men guarding Reinhard Heydrich's manor. He stepped back, slightly into the road, and gazed at the entrance to the villa. The Heydrich family had once lived in Prague castle, but the cold, dreary structure had been unsuitable for the Hangman's children. Heydrich's wife had insisted they move far from the bloody streets of Prague, and the Lower Chateau in the village of Panenské Břežany had provided a perfect home for the Blond Beast.

The manor had once belonged to a Jewish sugar mill owner and was more than suitable for the man who ruled Bohemia and Moravia: sprawling and grand, yet isolated from the riffraff. Plenty of space for the children to play, but a mere thirty-minute drive from his office in Prague. It was at once cozy and grandiose, and more than that it was safe. Reinhard Heydrich wouldn't have to worry about assassins crawling about his yard or Black Foxes kidnapping his children. The well-guarded estate would protect his daughter and his sons.

Dieter's gaze shifted about. There were two young men standing in the greenery a few yards from the gate. They were picking handfuls of overgrown grass and shoving it into rucksacks. Not unusual: they were likely gathering food for rabbits. Dieter had seen the same men loitering about the Heydrich estate before, and he might have been concerned if the Hangman himself hadn't previously declared that the men were harmless, well-trained Czechs that respected their German master. ("Besides, they do good work plucking the weeds," Heydrich had said with a smirk.)

One of the Czechs looked up from his labor and offered Dieter a polite Nazi salute, which the Major returned brusquely before he turned away from the peasants and faced the front gate. Two SS men stood on either side before a set of somewhat strange statues: on the left was a bear with wide, almost pained eyes, and on the right was a boar tending to its young.

"Sir, watch out!"

Dieter yelped: he had been too distracted gawking at the statues and hadn't noticed a truck coming around the sharp bend. If it weren't for the young Czech servant, he likely would have been flattened, but he slammed his body against his closed car door and narrowly avoided being run over.

"You all right, sir?" one of the grass-pickers cried. Dieter had suffered worse near-death experiences, and so he recovered quickly and nodded at the Czech, thanking him for his concern. The Czechs returned to their grass-picking while Dieter strode up to Heydrich's smiling young servant.

"Someone's going to get killed one of these days," the servant sighed. "Are you all right, Major?"

"Just fine," Dieter chuckled, lying through his teeth. The Major was anything but fine, though his mood had nothing to do with this near accident. His son had been missing for weeks. The Fox Farm was set to open in days and Jonas was gone, gone in search of Black Fox One. Gone in search of Avalina Keller.

As he followed the Czech girl through the iron gate and up the pathway, Dieter reached into his back pocket and touched the silver watch he had brought with him. He knew when he had been summoned to Heydrich's home, ostensibly to discuss the opening of the Fox Farm with the future Kommandant Engel, that the Hangman was displeased. The Major hoped that the gift would please the Butcher of Prague enough that he would be willing to give Jonas more time.

Dieter smiled and waved at the heavily pregnant Lina Heydrich, wife of the Blond Beast, who was bustling about, overseeing a few servants who were remodeling the grounds. It was a true struggle to even offer his chief's wife a modicum of politeness when worry and guilt were burning in his soul.

Jonas was still chasing after his fiancée in a foolish attempt to save her. Dieter had always been willing to accept that his boy had a dangerous profession, but he had never feared for him more than he did now.

What if he's dead? She wouldn't kill him, would she? She's a Jewess, of course she would.

Dieter had always loved the Kellers. When he had discovered the truth about Ava's bloodline, he'd been utterly shocked.

147

Shocked and furious, for he had become convinced that the Kellers had been lying to his face for more than a lifetime. It might have hurt his soul to threaten them if he hadn't been so angry and, more than that, so afraid. Dieter loved his son, he loved his nation, and he had always thought he would never have to choose between the two of them. But Jonas was too much like his mother. Stubborn and romantic.

You did the right thing, Dieter assured himself for the millionth time. *If you hadn't sent her off, Jonas would have stayed with her. He'd be on his way to a camp right now. He'd be dead by now. You saved his life.*

Perhaps. And maybe everything would have been fine if Ava hadn't returned, and as Black Fox One no less. And now Dieter's son was determined to rescue his supposedly innocent, supposedly Aryan fiancée.

Dieter bit down on his tongue. A part of him had wanted to confess before his boy set off, but he had been too cowardly. *Jonas would hate you if he knew what you did...*he had thought, and so he'd kept his mouth shut and simply held on to the hope that Jonas would return from his hunt empty-handed, that Ava would prove impossible to track down.

But now...now Dieter felt lost. If Jonas was alive, then he had either been captured or he had failed and was simply biding his time before he dragged his feet back to a thoroughly disappointed Butcher of Prague.

And if Jonas returned a failure, he would no longer be in Heydrich's good graces. That by itself would be dangerous, especially if the Hangman then decided to investigate the Amsels. Dieter had done his best to expunge all evidence of the Kellers' existence. He had covered his tracks thoroughly, but he didn't doubt that Heydrich could find something if he decided that looking would be worth the effort.

Thus, appeasing the Blond Beast had to be priority number one. And so as soon as he drew near to the Hangman, Dieter plastered a smile onto his face and pulled the wrapped gift from his back pocket.

"Ah! There's our architect," Heydrich said when he saw Dieter. The Butcher of Prague was sitting on a small lawn chair with a table covered in files resting at his side. He was wearing his uniform—a rarity for him in his home where he preferred to eschew the uncomfortable outfit, but since this was technically a matter of business as much as it was a playdate for the Engel and Heydrich children, he must have decided to be halfway formal. No medals, just his uniform jacket and jackboots.

Engel sat on another chair near Heydrich, a sketchbook in his hand and a thoughtful expression on his face as he drew a structure of some sort. He lifted his green-blue eyes and smiled in greeting.

"Hello, Major!" Engel said, raising up his hand. "Heil Hitler!"

"Heil Hitler," Dieter replied. A slight movement made his eyes shift, and he realized there was a teenage boy sitting at Leon Engel's side: Norman Engel, the now-fourteen-year-old who had handed his own mother over to the Fox Hunter. The teen looked far too much like Jonas: sandy blond hair and dark blue eyes. Norman stood up and clicked his heels together, offering the Major an eager Hitler salute.

"Heil Hitler!" the boy barked zealously, and his father grinned in a painfully prideful way that was familiar to Dieter. He had smiled that way whenever Jonas achieved a victory for the Cause. Always, every time his precious boy climbed higher in the ranks, Dieter's pride would be tinged with guilt because he knew Jonas wouldn't have chosen the safe, good life of an SS hero if he'd known the truth.

And Norman...that steely, empty expression was too familiar, and so frightening on a cherubic young face. Dieter hastily returned the greeting and turned his attention away from Engel's son, glancing at the other children scampering about.

Engel's daughters, eight and nine respectively, were playing with Heydrich's sons. Dieter glanced at Heydrich's middle child, Heider. Eight years old with tidy blond hair and blue eyes like his father, Heider Heydrich was a shy and sensitive lad, oddly quiet and oddly anxious. Dieter wasn't sure he'd ever seen the boy without a slightly befuddled expression on his face.

Dieter's eyes flitted to the Hangman's firstborn, Klaus. It was rare to see one Heydrich boy without the other, though Klaus Heydrich was very different from his shy brother, much more like his father. Not in wickedness, for the ruby-cheeked boy with slightly messy blond hair didn't have a bad bone in his body. Dieter still remembered how terribly Klaus had cried when he'd seen a rat caught in a trap. No, Klaus had empathy, unlike his cold-hearted father, but he was also devilish in a way that mirrored Reinhard. Always wont to break rules and get his poor younger brother into trouble.

Unlike shy Heider, Klaus was an outgoing ball of energy, and in addition to everything else, he seemed to have inherited his father's womanizing habits. The boy always strove to woo any little girl he came across, much to his mother's exasperation and his father's obvious pride.

At the moment, it seemed that Klaus was doing his darndest to impress Liesel and Gretchen Engel. The boy was standing halfway in the stables, grabbing his pony Xaver by the reins and trying to drag him out to show him off. The girls watched, giggling as they fiddled with flower crowns. Heider had his back against a tree and clutched two wooden swords in both hands, holding them slightly upwards as though he intended to use them in self-defense when the horse snapped.

"Klaaaaus, he's gonna kick you!" Heider shrieked, and Klaus turned to the girls, flashing a bright smile.

"He won't!" Klaus promised them. "He's a good boy, he's a great steed! C'mon, Xaver!"

But though Klaus tugged and tugged, the horse would not budge. It dug its hooves into the ground and let out an aggravated snort. Klaus made a noise that was almost the same.

"Klaus, my boy," Heydrich said, his high-pitched voice taking on an amusedly paternal firmness. "Leave Xaver be."

"Papa, he's being stubborn!" Klaus huffed, letting go of the reins and casting a scowl at his pony as Xaver turned and trotted back into the stable. "He's *my* horse! He should listen to me!"

"Yes," Reinhard agreed with a nod. "But nevertheless, if you keep trying to force it, then either you'll hurt him, or he'll hurt you. Better to leave him be, Klauschen."

Klaus winced at the suggestion that he would hurt Xaver and glanced back at the horse, offering him a conciliatory, apologetic smile. "Okay, Papa!" the boy declared, and with that, the children turned their attention to the Heydrichs' German shepherd, a one-eyed police dog named Odin. They chased him about, the boys pretending he was a dragon, the girls trying to put a flower crown on him.

All the Heydrich children were accounted for save one, the youngest, and since she hadn't been in Lina's arms, she must have been nearby. Reinhard Heydrich would never allow his beloved daughter to be left alone with filthy Czechs.

Dieter looked at the Hangman again and found her: Silke

Heydrich, just barely three years old, was sitting at her father's feet, leaning against his jackboot and humming happily as she played with a Little Red Riding Hood doll.

Silke was a blonde, blue-eyed, adorable little girl that was the only entity Dieter knew of which could soften the Hangman's iron heart. He remembered when she'd been born: it had been almost hilarious watching the cold-eyed Blond Beast glow with paternal pride as he showed her off to absolutely everyone.

The contrast between the little cherub cloaked in white and the demonic Beast in ash-grey, between the tiny child and the giant Butcher, was startling. Heydrich clutched a memo about the Fox Farm in one hand while the other brushed the top of his child's head, and when he elicited a giggle from the girl, Dieter saw the edges of the Hangman's lips edge upwards into a genuine, gentle smile.

Dieter was grateful for the girl's presence. Heydrich's one weakness was his children, and Silke more than the boys would put him in a merciful mood.

"Shall we get down to business?" Heydrich asked. Dieter decided to get off on the right foot straight away and handed the Hangman his gift.

"From me and Jonas!" Dieter declared. "I was going to give it to you during the ceremony for the opening of the Fox Farm, but I thought it might be useful now since you have so many important meetings! Your time is valuable!"

"Ah, thank you, Dieter. Hopefully, Jonas will return soon to present me a different gift," Heydrich said, carefully tearing away the paper and opening the box. He gave a small nod of approval when he looked down at the watch.

"Ah, and it has my rune," Heydrich noted, pulling the pocket watch out of the box and examining the engraving as he held it by the chain. "Very considerate."

"Papa!" Silke craned her neck all the way back to look up at her father, smiling wide and batting at the pocket watch like a kitten might a string. "It's pretty! It's...uh..."

Silke seemed to lose her train of thought for a moment, shifting from side to side and babbling something under her breath that was completely incoherent. Nonetheless, Heydrich leaned down a bit, listening to her lispy little voice and nodding in feigned comprehension. His cold eyes had thawed completely, and when she finally finished her blabbering, he rewarded her with a fond chuckle and a pat on her golden locks.

"You think so, sweetheart?" he crooned. Heydrich's voice, odd enough when he spoke in curt snaps, seemed even stranger when it softened for Silke. It was like hearing a tiger purr.

"Well, Dieter, it has Silke's seal of approval. Thank you," Heydrich said, tucking the watch into his pocket. The Major chuckled, smiling down at the little girl, who had gone back to fiddling with Little Red's frayed cloak. *Thank you, Silke!* Dieter thought.

"Let's get to it!" Engel said, setting his sketchbook on a small table and patting his son's shoulder. "Norman, my boy, why don't you go play with your sisters? Keep them protected from that vicious hound!"

"Oh, Engel, Odin's harmless!" Heydrich insisted. "Poor Daxi, rest his soul, that's the dog you would have had to worry about."

"Odin gives kisses!" Silke announced cheerfully, holding up her doll. Heydrich patted her cheek.

"Yes, sweetheart, very good!" he said, but when the Hangman looked up, his gaze fell upon Norman and hardened. The boy stiffened and leapt from his chair as though he'd suddenly realized that he was sitting on a poisonous spider.

"I'll go," Norman said. He saluted Dieter and gave a particularly enthusiastic salute to the Blond Beast, who returned it casually. Silke saw her father lift up his arm and imitated him innocently, earning a fond smile and gentle praise from the Hangman.

"You should be proud of your boy, Engel," Heydrich said once the teen was out of earshot. Engel watched Norman skitter over to the younger children.

Klaus, who seemed to be of the belief that any playmate was a good playmate, immediately tried to welcome the teen into their fold. He offered Norman a wooden sword and cheerfully invited him to be on the boys' team ("I'll be on the girls' team, so it won't be unfair!" the nine-year-old offered, winking at the girls and eliciting a chuckle and a "that's my boy" from his father.)

Norman, however, regarded the boy's invitation with a squirm of discomfort and a quiet murmur before he went to stand by a tree and simply observe as the smaller children ran about. Dieter saw Engel's smile falter and his eyes...Dieter knew that look. The look of a man who didn't know what sort of father he was.

"I am proud of him..." Engel muttered, and he sounded almost uncertain.

"Reinhard." Lina Heydrich swept in, saving Engel before the Hangman could notice his faltering. "It's six-o-clock. Naptime for Silke."

Lina reached down and tried to pick up her daughter, but Silke yelped and dropped her doll, looping her arms around Reinhard's leg and desperately clinging to him.

"No! No! No!" the girl shrieked, sobbing as though naptime was merely a euphemism for death. When she screamed, Dieter saw the Hangman wince. Heydrich's eyes, always seemingly narrowed in suspicion, widened as though merely hearing Silke's typical childish distress was physically painful.

"Oh, Lina, let her stay," the Hangman said, tossing his papers aside and reaching down. He picked up the girl and lifted her onto his lap. Silke threw her arms around his neck and squeezed tight, as though she was afraid that her mother would wrench her from her father's arms.

A familiar posture, that one. A child clinging to their father, holding tight and braced for separation. Dieter had seen so many daughters ripped from their father's arms. For a moment, he almost hoped Lina would insist and yank her daughter out of the Hangman's grasp. It wouldn't be the same, but it would be a shadow of that suffering. A tiny fraction. Better than nothing for the man who had heartlessly refused to return Viktor Naden's daughters, who could take Dieter's own child away from him with only a word.

But Lina clutched her dress and sighed, glancing uneasily at the documents. "Reinhard, your work..."

"We'll speak politely, *schatzi*," Heydrich assured his wife, stroking his daughter's untidy golden locks. "She won't understand a word of it."

"I understand lots!" Silke argued, burying her face in her father's chest. Heydrich chuckled and kissed the top of her head.

"Of course, *kleine*, you're just too smart," he said. Lina must have realized that separating the father and daughter would be a fruitless venture at best and conceded defeat, returning to her gardening and offering to take Silke if she became too troublesome.

"Let's begin, then," Heydrich said. One hand embraced his daughter, who nestled against him, while the other pointed to some of the papers on the little desk. "The wall was unfeasible?"

"The soil wouldn't support it, sir," Engel declared. "Too moist. Since the rest of the camp was already constructed and the location is really ideal, we didn't want to move it all just for one feature."

"Disappointing, but reasonable. Dieter, you've compensated with heavy use of electric fencing?"

"Three layers. Nobody will be able to escape," Dieter assured him.

"Excellent. And the armaments factory will be up and running?" Heydrich said, patting Silke's head.

"Yes, sir...do, ah, do you think it's wise to allow Black Foxes to build weapons?" Dieter asked. "We could utilize slave labor for a separate sector, and we wouldn't have to worry..."

"The purpose of the Fox Farm is to break their spirits," Heydrich noted. "I can think of no better way to do so than to make them construct our guns and bullets. They'll effectively be forced to..."

His eyes flitted to his daughter, who seemed to be drifting off despite her insistence on not wanting naptime. Reinhard chose to censor himself for her sake: "They'll build the weapons and the bullets that will take down their own comrades."

"The guards at the Fox Farm are well-trained, and the armory is impenetrable. Little chance of sabotage, absolutely no chance for rebellion," Engel said, beaming with pride as he glanced down at the picture of his future camp.

"Rebellion *is* a concern, but we've taken that into

account," Heydrich proclaimed. "The Black Foxes will receive extremely low rations. Starving men and women make for poor soldiers."

"Resistance occurs in other camps with rampant starvation," Dieter pointed out.

"True," Engel said. "But there's also the children. We'll be placing the little Black Foxes and the children of Black Foxes we've captured in every barrack. No separation, no..."

He glanced at Silke. Reinhard's eyes narrowed.

"No *processing*," the future Kommandant said, earning a nod from Heydrich. "The plan is to allow the children to receive better rations than the adults."

"Some adults will be desperate and foul enough to steal from the children," Heydrich explained. "This will sow discord. Additionally, the prisoners will hesitate to start a rebellion because they'll be afraid of harming the children."

"And the children will eventually be turned into informants. We'll tie their rations to their compliance. Since they'll be everywhere, we'll always know what's happening in the barracks," Engel declared, almost snickering.

"Very clever," Dieter mumbled.

"Carrot and stick," Heydrich said, smirking proudly and squeezing Silke a little tighter. The girl was fast asleep now, clinging affectionately to the mass murderer.

"Those who cooperate will be rewarded," Engel proclaimed. "Those who do not will be..." Again, he glanced at Silke. Heydrich looked down to make sure that his daughter was asleep and nodded, giving Engel permission to speak without using euphemisms.

"Brutally suppressed," Engel said. "We'll want to avoid killing where we can since the goal is suppression of the whole and not extermination of the captured: we have some of the best interrogators on staff. A little torture will teach the Black Foxes not to resist."

"Every once in a while, I plan to allow one person, preferably a young teenager, to 'escape,'" Heydrich added. "They'll return to their Black Foxes and spread the word of what will happen to them. I think it will go quite far in reducing their reach and appeal."

"Brilliant, sir," Dieter said, and it was. A few months ago, he had helped build the Fox Farm with absolute enthusiasm, but now there was a decent chance that Jonas could end up behind the barbed wire...

"Shall we toast, gentlemen?" Engel's offer tore him from his thoughts. Dieter shook his head and smiled politely.

"Not really in the mood, Engel."

"Shame. Heydrich? Oh, right," Engel chuckled, pouring a glass of cheap booze for himself when Heydrich shook his head and dipped his chin to gesture towards the child in his arms.

"Frankly, Engel, if I drink, I don't drink that swill," Heydrich said. "Since you refused my offer of wine..."

"Meant no disrespect, Chief!" exclaimed Engel. "Wine and me have never agreed. Don't like...grapes. I'll have to bring my own drink to the opening ceremony, so I won't be the only sober man at the party!"

"I'll be sober," Heydrich announced.

"Sir, you should celebrate! This is your achievement!" Dieter chortled.

"I'll be giving a speech and posing for the camera," Heydrich noted, shaking his head.

"Ah, true. Don't want to give Goebbels any ammunition," Engel muttered. "Speaking of which, will he be there?"

"No, but he'll be sending a crew. I only hope our star attraction arrives on time..."

"Special Agent Amsel is still in deep cover, correct?" the future Kommandant said, glancing at Dieter with a smirk. His tone was laced with mock concern, a verbal prod.

That was how it was in the SS—men of equal rank would tousle before their superiors, pointing out flaws in the politest way possible, trying to topple their comrade, their competition. Out of the corner of his eye, Dieter saw the edge of Heydrich's lip curl even as he pretended to busy himself with his sleeping daughter.

Fine, Engel, thought Dieter, flashing a vicious smile of his own. *Two can play at that game.*

"Jonas will be back promptly, I'm sure," Dieter said. "In the meantime, the Fox Farm is full to bursting. There are plenty of V.I.P.s to show off. I *would* suggest we execute Katja Naden, but of course that won't be happening."

A predatory gleam came to Heydrich's eyes before they flitted to Engel. The Kommandant-to-be forced his smile to remain in place even as his eyes communicated his discomfort. Everyone had heard of Viktor Naden's family, everyone had compared Naden to Engel, and no doubt being reminded of the *Einsatzgruppen* Captain made the ex-husband of Black Fox 25 uncomfortable. Engel's green-blue eyes briefly darted to his morose son.

"Oh?" Major Engel said, and it was clear that he was fighting to maintain a casual tone.

"Black Fox Ten was executed two days ago, along with her daughter Nadine. The youngest, the five-year-old, was just transferred to the Fox Farm. Heidi Naden," Dieter said. "What do you think, Reinhard? Think she'll make for a good informant?"

"Certainly," Heydrich said, patting Silke's shoulder and letting his lake-blue eyes shift from the squirming Major Engel to the two Engel girls, who were pretending to be princesses while the Heydrich boys played knight.

"I thought the purpose of the Fox Farm was to break their spirit, sir," Engel murmured. "Is there a reason we put them down before the camp was even opened?"

"Orders," Heydrich declared simply.

"Viktor Naden was fool enough to actually go all the way to the Berghof," Dieter elaborated. "Went right up to the Führer and fell to his knees. Degraded himself completely. Begged him to show Katja and Nadine mercy. Needless to say, the Führer wasn't impressed. Practically heard him all the way from here: 'Traitors like them deserve no mercy!' Ordered them to be shot, only spared the youngest to keep Naden in line, then sent him to the front lines. I'm sure he'll be mincemeat soon."

"I warned him," Heydrich said, wrapping his other arm around Silke and speaking in an almost sing-song voice. Engel let out a non-committal hum and downed another shot, glancing at his daughters.

"He gets what he deserved," Engel finally declared, his voice halting. Dieter smirked victoriously. Major Engel was ruffled.

"Indeed," Dieter concurred. "You should be grateful. It reignited the memory of what happened with your traitor wife. What was her name? Anniska! Right! Well, everyone is talking about Naden and how he's *nothing* like you. You or your boy."

Every SS man's eyes shifted to Norman, who sat in the shade watching Klaus and Heider clash with their wooden swords. There was an aching emptiness in the teen's eyes as he spectated.

"I...have to take a leak, gentlemen, pardon me," muttered Engel, surrendering by casting a scowl at Dieter. He downed the last of his drink and followed a Czech servant towards the manor.

"He seemed uncomfortable," Heydrich observed, and Dieter nodded. Alone with the Hangman at last. With Heydrich's sons happily playing close by and Silke slumbering in the Butcher's arms, Dieter couldn't think of a better opportunity to fish for that elusive sliver of mercy.

"In truth, I pity him," Dieter said. "He raised his son well, but I can't imagine it was easy, killing the woman he loved. I pity Naden even more: he was a fool for disobeying you, Reinhard, but it was worse for him than Engel. A wife is one thing, but his children...I cannot imagine being forced to choose between my nation and my own children. Typically, we work for both. Our nation's interests and our children's interests are usually interconnected; to serve one is to serve the other. We forget how easy it is for our children to fall from grace. Your boy, for example..."

He pointed towards Klaus, who was blushingly trying to help Liesel repair her broken crown of flowers. "Little charmer he is," Dieter said. "You must be very proud."

"I am," Heydrich confirmed, and Dieter's heart somersaulted with hope when he heard the Hangman's tone: soft, almost thoughtful. The Butcher of Prague gazed at his son with cloudy eyes.

"You're an excellent father to him, Reinhard. I'm certain he'll take after you when he grows up. He'll want to make you proud. But...things *do* happen. If your boy were to bump into a Jewess with pretty eyes and fall head over heels, well, you know Klaus. What would you do if he came to you and declared that he loved a Jewess?"

For a moment, Reinhard appeared to actually contemplate the question, his eyes losing their coldness completely before he shook his head.

"A ridiculous idea," Heydrich said. "That will never happen. I won't allow it."

"Of course," Dieter sighed. "I know you won't. We have to protect our children from outside forces, yes, but sometimes we also have to protect them from themselves, from letting their souls become corrupted."

"Precisely," Heydrich agreed.

"Nevertheless, it isn't always that easy, is it?" sighed Dieter. "They do things behind our backs. Naden's daughter, for example, joined the Black Foxes. From good racial stock to an undesirable like *that*."

Dieter snapped his fingers, and he could have sworn he saw Heydrich wince.

"And if that happens before you can do anything to prevent it, what then?" Dieter queried. "A man's first obligation is to his children. But we must also be loyal to the Cause. It's a terrible thought, that even the purest among us could become an Enemy of the State. Even your little Silke..."

He gestured to the tiny girl nestled against the Hangman's chest. Heydrich put a hand on the back of her head, tightening his embrace and glancing down at her with a strange expression, something between affection and anxiousness.

"God forbid, if your girl was an undesirable, what would you do?" Dieter asked. "What would you choose?"

The Blond Beast's eyes flashed. Dieter inhaled sharply. He had pushed too far.

"I don't deal in hypotheticals, I deal in *reality*," Heydrich hissed. "These maybes and what-ifs are a distraction. We have a job to do for our nation *and* our children. That is *all*."

"Of course, Reinhard, forgive me. I didn't mean to offend," mumbled Dieter. "I merely wanted to illustrate why one might be inclined towards sympathizing with Naden and Engel. Both of their actions, I think, are understandable."

"Understandable, yes, but only one of them was *right*," Heydrich declared. He kissed his daughter one more time and called for Lina to come get her. Once Silke was out of his arms, a cold aura descended upon the Hangman as his heart turned to iron once more.

Engel returned after only a few moments, and the SS officers discussed the Fox Farm and the opening day ceremony. After the three men had hammered out a few more details, they wrapped things up. For a moment, they sat and watched the children play, but when Liesel Engel cut her hand on a thorn-bush and Leon ran to dress her minor wounds, Dieter decided to escape.

"I feel out of place at this playdate. I should go," Dieter declared. "Thank you for inviting me to your home, Reinhard, always an honor."

"Let me walk you to your car. Come along, I know a shortcut," Heydrich said. Dieter knew immediately that it wasn't an offer and smiled, following his superior as he led him away from the children, away from the gardens, and into the manor.

"Ah, the place looks lovely, Reinhard," muttered Dieter as they trudged through the marble-lined halls. He pretended to be very interested in the ornate carvings and did his best to suppress his nervousness when Heydrich suddenly stopped and turned to him with a smile.

"You haven't been here in some time," Heydrich noted, and Dieter chuckled.

"Aha! Apologies, everything has been very overwhelming.

Once the Fox Farm is up and running, I'll have more free time and we can go horseback riding."

"Yes. When your son returns. Assuming he does."

"Aha...Reinhard..."

"Assuming he hasn't run off with that Jew fiancée of his."

Dieter's heart stopped.

"W...wha..." the Major choked. Heydrich, towering a foot above the older man, stepped forward. The Hangman was smiling. Not the gentle fatherly smile he had given Silke; it was a merciless smirk. The expression of a cat that had been lying in wait for hours and had finally pounced on his prey.

"You think I'm very stupid, don't you?" Heydrich said, and the mirth in his tone made his taunt almost sound like a giggle. "Did you really think I didn't notice you fiddling with my files? Did you think I didn't notice that you removed every trace of the Keller family? Oh, yes, Dieter. I knew about your son's liaison with a Jewess. Haven't you wondered why I was so willing to trust him?"

"You had dirt on him..." Dieter barely managed to gasp, his mind racing until it burned with realization.

"If he'd stepped a toe out of line, I would have had a string to pull," Heydrich confirmed with a slight flourish of his long fingers, like he was tugging the wires of a marionette.

"Of course...*der Oberverdachtschopfer,*" Dieter muttered, anger temporarily taking the place of terror when he realized that over a decade of camaraderie was built on lies. "You *never* trusted Jonas, or me! You only let us get this far because you knew you could control us if you needed to!"

"Correct," Heydrich said proudly. "Jonas has never given me reason to use that information."

"Until now."

"No, Dieter," the Butcher of Prague said, shaking his head. "Not against him. Not *yet*."

"Reinhard..."

"That's *Reichsprotektor* Heydrich to you." Heydrich's proud tone gave way to coldness. "Only my friends may call me by my first name."

"You don't have any friends," said Dieter before he could help himself, but fortunately, the Hangman regarded the insult with a chuckle, his lake-blue eyes flitting towards the door that let the cheerful shrieks of his children seep into the stolen manor.

"I have what I need," Heydrich declared, a slight hint of warmth in his voice before his smile became an icy scowl as he gave Dieter his undivided attention. "I *don't* need a traitor."

"I'm *not* a traitor!" Dieter cried, gesturing proudly to the polished swastika pin on his breast. "I have no sympathy for the Jews, I was only trying to *protect my son*. As you would in my shoes."

Dieter pointed towards the open door to emphasize his point, trying to appear confident and defiant even as he felt like he was about to collapse from terror. Heydrich's frosty eyes flitted from the open door to the Major, and Dieter felt his frantic pulse steady slightly when the Hangman offered a conciliatory nod.

"Indeed," Heydrich said, and Dieter felt it safe to keep pushing.

"I wanted to get rid of them, not help them," he explained. "I wanted to make sure my son would have no reason to empathize with undesirables."

"And in the process, you attempted to deceive me." Heydrich's tone became biting again as he turned away from the door and crossed his arms imperiously behind his back.

"Your son will decide his own fate now. He'll return to me as either a traitor or a patriot, and then I'll know what to do with him. I knew your son was hiding something when he returned from his first blunder. The only reason Black Fox One would spare him, the only reason he would return so shaken, would be if Black Fox One turned out to be a familiar face. However, I also know that his fiancée's father couldn't be Black Fox One, nor her younger brothers."

Dieter did his best to conceal a shiver that snaked up his spine as the depth of Heydrich's knowledge made horror grip his heart. "And you know that because...?"

"Because I had them shot." Heydrich smiled again, and it was the smile of a snake that had swallowed a rat whole. Dieter felt his heartbeat stall.

"You..."

"The men would only be a nuisance," the Hangman explained with the casual coolness of a man describing a pesky infestation of ants. "The women could be used against you and your son if the need ever arose. Unfortunately, we only captured the older woman. She's being held in the Fox Farm as we speak, but it would have been more useful if we could have caught the Jewess fiancée. Avalina Keller. The only Keller that Jonas could have possibly encountered under that mask."

"You...you knew..." Dieter gasped, and Heydrich's smirk morphed into a scowl.

"*Suspected*. I didn't wish to believe it at first. A woman is Black Fox One? My men have been getting thrashed by a little Jewess? I'm almost tempted to keep the cameras away from the Fox Farm for opening day."

"Have...have you been trailing Jonas?" Dieter asked, and now his fear on his son's behalf tripled. The Black Foxes were one thing, but the Hangman of Prague...

"No need," Heydrich said, stalking forward, forcing Dieter to back up until the Major's spine was pressed against the cold marble wall of the confiscated manor.

"I don't need the Fox Hunter to capture Avalina Keller," Heydrich declared, leaning over the shivering Major. "I can flush her out just as well myself. As for you...I think it's time for some honesty."

ELEVEN

"**K**its and kittens, while I hate to start off the day with bad news, Black Fox Radio tells you the truth, the entire truth, and only the truth no matter how much it hurts. And this news is going to hurt: we've received confirmation that Black Fox Ten and Black Fox Twenty-Seven have been executed on the orders of Butcher Heydrich..."

"Oh, no...Jonas..."

Ava leapt to her feet and fled from the main chamber, where her comrades and several of the Jews she had rescued were gathered around the radio, listening to Papa Fox's latest announcement with grim sighs and muttered prayers. A few scowled at her as she slipped away from the pack. She had finally told her comrades and the rescuees about Jonas' real identity. They had all taken it better than she had thought they would: a few had desperately wanted to kill the Fox Hunter, to avenge their captured and murdered comrades, but all of them had respected Ava enough to stay their hand at her command. Now they were mulling over the information Jonas had provided and debating whether or not he could be trusted to be an asset. If not...

Ava sighed heavily and entered Jonas' room. At her comrades' insistence, she had returned Jonas to his prison, though he was no longer chained to the wall. Without a chair, the Fox Hunter sat on the ground beside the radio, lapis-colored eyes overflowing with guilt as Papa Fox continued to talk about Katja and Nadine Naden.

"Now, ladies and gentlemen, I don't typically divulge details about Black Foxes for obvious reasons, even post-mortem. However, I feel like this is a learning experience. First: Black Fox Twenty-Seven was a twelve-year-old girl. Hitler will pose with small children and proclaim that he fights for the innocent among us, and yet he personally orders the deaths of little girls. What can be said of a man who puts little girls to death? What can be said of a system that puts little girls to death? What can be said of the men—the cowards—who arrested and ultimately murdered little Nadine Naden?"

"Jonas..." Ava put her hands on her fiancée's trembling shoulders as a sob wracked his body.

"It's my fault," he muttered. "I hunted them down, they're dead because of me."

"You didn't know, you didn't..."

"It doesn't matter. Papa Fox is right." Jonas had never thought he would let those words leave his lips.

"Point number two, and this is directed at the Germans listening in, good and bad alike: your actions rebound. I'd like to remind you children of a story, an old story, a Jewish story—oh no! The story of Exodus, and specifically the story of the tenth plague.

"Pharaoh, he was a man like Hitler. A keeper of slaves, a baby murderer, a Jew killer. He was sitting pretty on his throne,

ignoring all the divine warnings God was sending down. Fire rains from the sky? Well, he's got a marble roof. Plague descends upon the crops? He's got plenty of food. He thought that God couldn't touch him, he thought that he was immune from consequences, the consequences of his evil actions. He thought they would never come back to bite him in the ass. But then the Angel of Death came for his child. And did that child deserve what he got? No. But Pharaoh sure as hell did.

"You men in the SS, you men serving this Reich, you have a lot of excuses. You may think you're doing this for your children, or maybe you don't give a shit and just want a paycheck. Maybe you don't even agree with all of it, but you just want to stay safe. But you're not safe. Nobody is safe, nobody is clean. Viktor Naden is one of the most vicious, fanatical sons-of-bitches I've ever had the misfortune of reporting on, and whatever he's going through right now, he deserves it times ten. But you, you Germans and Nazis who are listening to this, know that you're next. The beast that is Nazism is never sated.

"The Nazi Molech will come for your loved ones and your children. You can burn incense on a swastika alter, you can pretend to be a God, but you can't escape it. From the slave in the stable to Pharaoh on his throne. From the lowest SS man to the Führer himself. It will consume you and yours. Yes, Heydrich, since I know you're listening—even you will one day find yourself facing down your own darkness. And what then? It will be too late. You can cry and plead for mercy, but the Nazi Molech knows no mercy. So fight it now. Resist now. You may think that submitting to Nazism is the only way to keep you and everything you love safe, but the opposite is true. Compliance is death."

"He can really spin things," mumbled Jonas. "Two of his own get executed, but he can still turn it into a call to action.

Ha! I bet he and Goebbels could have gotten along swimmingly in another life."

"Oh, no. Papa Fox is a fighter, not a liar. It's not propaganda if it's reality."

"He *is* right," Jonas muttered. "It came back around for me too. I was lucky...relatively lucky. I still have you for now..."

"You still have me," Ava assured Jonas, sitting beside him and throwing an arm over his shoulder. "And it came back to bite me too."

"You didn't deserve it. I do," Jonas muttered softly, leaning his cheek against her hooded head and grasping her hand, kissing her knuckles. "I certainly don't deserve to have you back."

"Maybe, but I'm pretty great, so *I* deserve to have you back," Ava countered, and Jonas chuckled softly.

"True, I suppose, since you have terrible tastes," he said. "I was there when Naden begged Heydrich for mercy. I felt... somewhere inside me, I *felt* that it was wrong back then."

"Your *yetzer hatov* must have been screaming."

"But I just made excuses. 'The youngest one was put into protective custody.' Bah! God knows where that poor child is now. It bothered me at the time, but I dismissed it. Bought into Heydrich's hypocrite talk."

"You were lied to, Jonas," Ava said, reaching up and putting a hand on his cheek. "And beating yourself up won't change the past. You've done all you can for now to make up for it: you drew out those maps of the Fox Farm. Thank God for your photographic memory..."

"For all the good it will do. The Black Foxes don't have the means to attack any concentration camp, much less a camp made specifically for them."

"It's still helpful. And once I go talk to Papa Fox, I *know* I can convince him to let you help even more."

"You really think he'll trust the Fox Hunter?"

"No, but he'll trust Black Fox One's fiancée."

"Ha...oh...I still have this damn thing," muttered Jonas, reaching into his pocket and pulling out the little box with the swastika ring. "Dunno what to do with it now...do you wanna bring it with you? In case you run into trouble and need to bribe someone?"

"Jonas Amsel, I'm offended! You think I need to *bribe* Nazis? No, no, no. I *kill* Nazis."

"Except me..." Jonas sighed, shoving the ring back into his pocket.

"You're an ex-Nazi as of...well, as of the moment you realized you were lied to," Ava said, raking a hand through Jonas' hair. "Don't let the others tell you different."

Papa Fox finished his monologue, and the music came back on: *Swan Lake Op 20, Act 1.* Ava leaned in, listening closely to the seemingly random pops and bouts of static before nodding.

"That's my cue," she said, clinging to Jonas' hand even as she stood up. "I have to go. I'll be back soon."

"I'll be here," Jonas promised, smirking slightly. "Awaiting news of my fate. Whatever it is, I'll accept it."

"Don't worry: Papa Fox has accepted some weird help in the past. You won't be the most unbelievable story I give him."

"Just...please be careful. Stay safe. And keep those Jews safe too."

"I will. Promise. Just hold down the fort, and don't let the others beat you down too much."

"I deserve what they give me..." the former Fox Hunter sighed, squeezing Ava's hand.

"Yeah, but if they mess up your pretty face, then *I* suffer."

Ava leaned down and planted a brief kiss on Jonas' lips. Despite his heavy heart, Jonas smiled and returned it: their first kiss since she had disappeared so many years ago. He had missed it too much. It hurt that it had to be brief: a quick kiss more appropriate for a wife going to the shop rather than a soldier leaving for battle.

"Stay safe," Jonas said again as she ran out, leaving him alone with the music masking Black Fox code.

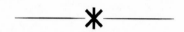

"SO YOU THINK HE'S LYING?"

"Of course he's lying, he's the fucking Fox Hunter! I don't give a shit if he's her fiancée, we should be skinning him alive right now!"

"Black Fox One said..."

"Black Fox Fifteen, Twenty-Five, Ten, all arrested by him! Ten and Twenty-Seven are *dead* because of him!"

"We can't afford to be emotional. It's not like we're above accepting help from monsters. Stalin's our ally..."

"Half the people in the Fox Farm were arrested by Amsel! Even if he *does* really want to help, he's just trying to clean up his own fuck-up!"

"So? Help's help, doesn't matter why it's given."

Either the crack in the wall of Jonas' cell had gotten bigger, or the Black Foxes were simply getting louder. The former Fox Hunter laid on his bed, tossing his ring box into the air and catching it again, gritting his teeth as he listened to Ava's comrades discuss the information he had given them for the thousandth time.

"Maybe it's not his fault," one Black Fox suggested. "Nazi

architecture is always so fantastical. They couldn't possibly build a wall like this on this land, it's practically a swamp."

"Then they've either realized that by now and moved shop..."

"He said the camp was constructed, not the wall. More likely, they'll realize their fuck-up and just loop electric fencing around the place."

"Heydrich won't like that."

"Heydrich doesn't like *anything*."

Jonas smirked and shrugged. Well, Heydrich liked a few things. Being right, being powerful, being a Young God of Death.

"Well, it doesn't matter either way," sighed another Black Fox. "We've never stormed any type of camp before, and even without a wall, this place is gonna be impregnable. Crawling with SS men and with hostages to boot, especially children. Unless we want to provoke a massacre..."

"They're dead in there, they're dead if we rescue them...we might as well *try*..."

"And then we all die too! And then what? More Jews die. One big fuck-up domino. It's just what Heydrich wants. Bet he sent this little shit to provoke us into attacking just so he can butcher us all."

"Hm...there's twenty of us here..."

"Twenty-one."

"Eight-Sixty doesn't count, he's the babysitter."

"Guilty! Though I could throw a few grenades, I guess."

"Psh! You couldn't even pull the pin!"

"Enough, everyone, stop acting like children. Look, we have limited resources. One could help us out in a pinch, but even she can't take on three divisions of SS men on their turf, regardless of what those silly comics claim."

"So...we can't do anything?"

"I didn't say that."

"So what *are* you saying, One-Twenty?"

"I'm saying One might be right when she suggests trusting the Fox Hunter."

"*You're* saying that?! *You*?!"

"One is willing to stand by him, and she's never steered us wrong."

"*Women.* Love One, she's great, but she's letting her emotions cloud her head."

Jonas gritted his teeth, but fortunately, the sound of a slap echoed through the Bunker. Another Black Fox had punished the speaker on Ava's behalf.

"Ow, what the fuck?!"

"As I said, don't be a child. We don't have much of a choice if we want to save our friends. The only way I can see us getting anyone out is if we have a man on the inside. There's no wall, right? If someone could cut the power to the fence at the right time..."

"What about the guards, though?"

"Guard—why are we even discussing this?! Like we should even *consider* working with the Fox Hunter after all he's done!"

"The Talmud says that when the Lord was asked what should become of the sinner, He declared, 'Let the sinner repent.'"

"Nobody gives a shit what that old fairytale book says, One-Twenty, and even if *you* do: Amsel can repent all he wants, that doesn't mean we have to help him."

"The Talmud also tells us to open the door to repentance if we want it to open for us."

"*We* don't have anything to repent for. *We're* doing the right thing."

"In your entire life, you've never questioned your actions? You've never regretted a thing?"

"Sure I have, but I've never been a fucking murderous Nazi! I never thought *you* would be suggesting we turn the other cheek!"

"I'm not. He should be punished for what he's done. So should Heydrich and Hitler and all the rest. But that doesn't mean shutting the door on him completely and refusing to let him help if he genuinely wants to. Even if he can't redeem himself, he can *try*. We should let him *try*."

Black Fox 120's tone was at once sharp and soft, thoughtful and firm. Jonas didn't hear the rest of the conversation, however, as right then the door to his little cell flew open. The former Fox Hunter sat up just as he was tossing his ring box into the air and successfully head-butted the flying container, eliciting a giggle from his guest.

"S-sorry!" the guest said. It was one of the Black Foxes, the smallest of those gathered in the Bunker: a short man with slightly curly onyx hair who wore a scarf that was the precise shade of his turquoise irises. There was a brightness to him that Jonas read as naïveté. He probably didn't get into many battles. In fact, when he spoke, Jonas realized his voice matched that of Black Fox 860, the one that the others had called a "babysitter."

He must be one of the Black Foxes that ferry children, or maybe he just takes care of the ones Ava rescues, thought Jonas, rubbing his head and shoving the useless ring box into his pocket. Eight-Sixty drew close, offering Jonas a half-finished bottle of beer.

"If you're desperate," the Black Fox said. "Got a little chocolate too, if you want."

"I appreciate it, but keep it for yourself, please," Jonas begged.

"I'm not much of a drinker. Except when I have to deal with the others, haha!" Eight-Sixty chuckled, carefully placing the bottle on the ground. "Don't mean to mess up your quarters, just wanted to make sure everything's all right. I assume you heard a lot of everyone's yelling. I'm pretty sure Hitler could hear us screeching from the Berghof."

"It's fine," Jonas sighed. "They *should* be suspicious of me. They'd be stupid not to be. They'd be even stupider if they didn't wanna string me up."

"And it's all the gentile Black Foxes that *really* wanna string you up, even more than us Jews. Aren't you people supposed to turn the other cheek or something?" jested Eight-Sixty.

"You're a Jew?"

"Not really. Guess I am now, though," the Black Fox sighed, glancing at the Judaic tomes on Jonas' bookshelf. "Might as well embrace it. Start doing some of the holidays. Purim always did sound fun, especially the dress-up stuff."

"When Hitler dies, *that* can be your favorite Jewish holiday. You can dress as whoever kills him," Jonas quipped, earning a chuckle from Eight-Sixty.

"I'm sure! He has to die eventually, right? Even if it's not a dramatic death, it'll be something to celebrate. If he dies of something boring, that might be difficult to turn into an outfit, though. If he dies of measles, then what? Don't think it would be a good look, a bunch of Jews dressing as disease."

Jonas nodded, a stone of guilt forming in the pit of his stomach. "I..." the former Fox Hunter muttered, "I don't know what you've gone through..."

"It's been a lot," Eight-Sixty interrupted, fiddling with the end of his scarf. "And I've met a lot of SS men. Some were complete monsters, just wanted to lord their power over me.

But others...others were just lost. Lost and lied to. I have a...a friend that I love a lot who's in the SS."

Eight-Sixty's eyes twinkled, and he clutched at his scarf, wrapping it around his wrist. "And he was like you, I bet. He wanted to do the right thing, he wanted to belong. He's in deep now, but I *know* he's a good person. I'm going to find him as soon as I can, save him."

"You think that's possible?" Jonas muttered.

"I have to," Eight-Sixty replied, wrapping the scarf tighter, so tight that his fingers must have felt numb. "He saved me, saved my friend. He *is* good, just..."

"Confused?" Jonas supplied with a smile.

"Confused," Eight-Sixty concurred with a nod. "Now, you're a bigger fish than my friend, but what you have with Ava, it's familiar. Just so you know: I believe you. I'm in your corner, and it's not just me. A lot of us have gotten help from men like you. You're no Hitler, you're no Heydrich. You're salvageable."

"I..." Jonas muttered, reluctance and gratitude clashing in his heart as he smiled at the Black Fox. "Thank you. I hope you're right."

"Eight-Sixty!" The door flew open again and another Black Fox ran in, brow pinched, untidy dark brown hair doused in sweat. Jonas flinched at seeing the Black Fox's blue eyes, which were a vivid shade of blue. The voice was familiar too: a distinctive Russian accent with the firmness of a preacher. This was the Black Fox that the others had called One-Twenty.

"Sa—err, One-Twenty, everything all right?" Eight-Sixty asked, and it seemed that he was more bothered by One-Twenty's frantic expression than the thought that he had been caught giving words of comfort to the enemy. One-Twenty's eyes flitted to Jonas, and the former Fox Hunter shivered under the Russian's intense gaze. He felt like his soul had been ripped from his body and put under a microscope.

Relief rushed into Jonas' veins when One-Twenty's gaze softened ever so slightly, as though he was satisfied with whatever he had seen in the ex-Nazi. The former Fox Hunter, ever the expert at sensing disquiet, noticed a slight crinkling of the Russian man's brow. One-Twenty rolled his shoulders as though adjusting a heavy weight on his back and cleared his throat, letting his gaze return to Eight-Sixty.

"One's back. Something's wrong. C'mon."

"She's back?" Jonas said, throwing his legs over the bedside and readying himself to follow. "What happened?"

One-Twenty didn't answer but simply started running out of the room. Eight-Sixty followed, giving Jonas a small, comforting smile before shutting the door behind him.

Worry made Jonas want to rush right out, but he lingered in the room just long enough to make sure the two Black Foxes were out of the hall before he leapt to his feet and scurried down towards the main chamber. He crouched behind a wall and listened, his heart aching as he heard Ava's voice: quiet, braced, like she was just barely holding in a sob for the sake of her comrades.

"One, *no*! You can't do this, it's suicide!" Fifty-Six said.

"It's my decision," Ava replied. "I'm not going to ask any of you to sacrifice yourselves."

"You're our comrade! We're not just going to let you march off to your death!" cried another Black Fox.

Death? Jonas's heart started pounding. Papa Fox's words echoed in his ears. *Your actions rebound.*

"And I'm not going to let that son-of-a-bitch execute my mother!" Ava shrieked, and Jonas, unable to stop himself, leapt from his hiding place.

"What's happening with your mother?" he asked, and twenty-two sets of eyes fell upon the former Fox Hunter. Ava was wearing her mask, but he could feel that she was relieved to see him even without seeing her expression. The rest of her comrades were less than amused. (Except for Eight-Sixty, who gave Jonas a warm smile.) Most drew their weapons and one, snarling, marched forward.

"Fucker! This is your fault!" he snapped, and Jonas didn't budge even as the Black Fox grabbed him by the collar. "You told Heydrich her real name, didn't you?!"

"One-Five-Nine, stand down!" Ava commanded. Black Fox 159 did not obey at first, getting in a good squeeze and spitting on Jonas' cheek. When Ava drew near, clearly ready to fight on her fiancée's behalf, One-Five-Nine dropped Jonas. The Fox Hunter landed on the hard ground with a grunt.

"I told you not to hurt him!" Ava snapped at her comrade, grabbing Jonas by the arm and wrenching him to his feet. Jonas wiped the spittle off his cheek and ignored the pain as a bruise formed on his neck.

"Bärchen, what happened to your mother? Where's Gisela?" he asked, grabbing his fiancée's shoulders. Ava gazed at him, her gas mask hiding her eyes while her trembling revealed the terror she was experiencing.

"She...Heydrich has her...there was an announcement on the radio, flyers..." Ava muttered. "He *knows*, he knows, and he has her and he's going to kill her if I don't turn myself in by the end of the week!"

"He knew because someone told him!" One-Five-Nine snapped. "It must have been him!"

Black Fox 159 pointed to the Fox Hunter, who ignored the accusation, squeezing Ava's shoulders and scowling at his own feet.

"Papa," he growled. "It must have been Papa."

"He spilled his guts," Ava hissed.

"Heydrich must have wrung it out of him," Jonas said.

"Or he decided his job in the SS was worth more than you," Ava snarled, but Jonas shook his head.

"No, Bärchen. I know what he did, I know what he is, but he *is* my father, and he loves me. I know he wouldn't have told Heydrich unless he was forced to."

"You shouldn't trust a Nazi family member," another Black Fox said, giving the Fox Hunter an accusatory scowl and crossing his arms over his chest. "Anniska Engel learned that."

"Regardless, your comrades are right, Bärchen," Jonas said, suppressing the guilt that overwhelmed his heart at hearing his victim's name. "You can't turn yourself in."

"Jonas, my mother..."

"Did they say where he was keeping her?"

Ava shook her head.

"If he didn't announce it, then it's almost certainly the Fox Farm. He'd be keeping her close, but Theresienstadt's too porous."

"You would know," grumbled One-Five-Nine, and Jonas, finally becoming exasperated, turned to the Black Fox. There was no anger in the former Nazi's eyes, merely a grim sort of desperation.

"Yes, I would," the former Fox Hunter said. "And I heard what you all were discussing. None of you have the resources to save anyone from the Fox Farm."

"So I don't have a choice," Ava whispered.

"No, you do. We can free her. We can free *all* of them," Jonas declared. "You all were right when you said there's no way of freeing anyone from the outside, but on the *inside* there's an army."

"An army of Nazis!" one Black Fox cried.

"True, but if we can strike from both within and outside, we have a chance. How many other Black Foxes do you think you could corral for a dangerous mission within the week?"

"Besides us?" Fifty-Six muttered. "Maybe...twenty?"

"We're not an army, Jonas, we're an underground railroad. We've never had the ability to attack a camp," Ava said.

"You've never had a man on the inside either. A man whose father *designed* the camp," Jonas countered. "This is risky, but the alternative is to let Heydrich win and to lose your best soldier."

The former Fox Hunter gestured towards Ava, who reached out and grasped his hand, squeezing. He looked at her, smiling, before turning back towards her comrades, still holding her hand.

"I don't deserve your trust," Jonas said. "But Ava deserves your loyalty. And the people I put in that camp, they deserve a chance to escape."

There was silence in the Bunker for a moment save for the static of the radio and the drip-drop of water leaking through the cracks in the structure.

"Do...you really think you'll be able to liberate the Fox Farm?" one Black Fox finally asked hopefully. Jonas sighed.

"I think so, but doing this will take trust, and not just from all of you," Jonas said. "I've been gone too long, and if my father told Heydrich Black Fox One's real identity, then Heydrich has every reason *not* to trust me if I just show up at his door now. We need to play this smart. I have a plan, but I'll need Black Fox One and two volunteers."

"You know I trust you," Ava said, squeezing his hand. "I'll go with whatever idea you have."

"Anyone else?" Jonas asked, suppressing a happy smile at

Ava's trust. Again, there was silence until One-Twenty stepped forward.

"Is there a chance I'll get to spit on Heydrich?" the Russian asked, and Jonas snorted.

"A chance," the Fox Hunter replied. "Though you might get shot if you try."

"Worth it," One-Twenty declared. "I'm in."

"I'm in too!" Eight-Sixty cried, and while that proclamation caused several of his Black Fox comrades to object, begging him to reconsider and even offering to go in the seemingly weak man's stead, Eight-Sixty held firm.

"Like I said before, I believe you. I'm willing to trust you," Eight-Sixty said, and Jonas nodded at him.

"Good, because if this is going to work, you're going to have to go beyond trusting me..."

TWELVE

SS Major Dieter Amsel felt like he should have been dead. Since his conversation (interrogation, really) with Heydrich, his heart had been pounding so hard that he almost couldn't feel it anymore. It felt like he'd had a heart attack weeks ago and was now merely a walking corpse waiting to finally fall.

Numbly, he had returned to his apartment in Prague. Heydrich had given him a generous break, paid leave until Jonas returned. *If* he returned.

Dieter almost wished Heydrich would just shoot him and get it over with. A bullet would be better than sitting in his home, staring at Magda's smile, and waiting to receive news that his son was a traitor. Better to die now, die before his son. Occasionally, Dieter would look down at his Luger and consider putting the barrel in his mouth and blowing his own skull to bits. It would be better than whatever Heydrich would give him.

But cowardice and hope kept him from committing

suicide. And when Heydrich called him into his office, Major Amsel obediently arrived, braced for the worst.

"Ah, Dieter," Heydrich said when the Major strode into the familiar office and lingered by the floral couches. Dieter clicked his heels together and shoved his hand into the air.

"Heil Hitler!" he barked, and he knew that showing loyalty wouldn't help, but he did so, nonetheless. Regardless of what would happen to him and his boy, he still believed in the right-eousness of the Nazi Cause. Heydrich could brand him a traitor as much as he liked, but Dieter Amsel would die a National Socialist.

"Heil Hitler!"

Heydrich didn't return the Nazi greeting, but someone else did. An achingly familiar and strangely excited voice. Dieter had been too focused on Heydrich's ruthlessly icy eyes to even realize that he wasn't alone in the office. Sitting in one of the chairs opposite the Hangman's desk, battered and bruised but bedecked in his SS uniform, was a grinning Jonas Amsel. Very much alive, seemingly cheerful, and clearly not under arrest.

Yet.

A part of Dieter wanted to yank his doomed son into a tight embrace. The other part of him wanted to grab Jonas and flee. Fright and uncertainty kept him planted in place until Heydrich commanded him to sit beside his son. Dieter moved as though the Hangman of Prague held his free will in his spider-like hands.

He sunk down in the chair beside his son, glancing at Jonas and grinding his teeth when he saw the extent of the injuries marring the Fox Hunter's handsome features. A black eye, bruised neck, and it looked like someone had bashed his head against the ground. *SS?* Dieter thought. *No, he wouldn't be smiling like that. He wouldn't be in Heydrich's office, he'd be at the Fox Farm already.*

Suppressing the paternal urge to reach out and touch his son's bruised face, Dieter looked back at Heydrich. The Hangman was leaning back, icy eyes impenetrable, posture at once confident and stiff, as though he knew that Jonas was going to pull something but was confident in his own ability to parry any attack that came his way.

"Jonas returned empty-handed," Heydrich announced. "He called me and claimed that he had set things up to capture Black Fox One, however."

"Yes, sir!" Jonas chirped.

"*Conveniently* right after I announced that I had possession of Avalina Keller's mother," Heydrich drawled, lifting a brow and leaning forward, folding his hands on the desk. "I hope you have a *very good* explanation for that, Jonas Amsel."

Dieter was surprised to feel his heartbeat again, pounding and frantic. Jonas had no clue how thoroughly he had been betrayed. Faced with the Butcher of Prague demanding honesty, Dieter had spilled his guts.

The Major was shocked when Jonas regarded Heydrich's barely hidden threat with a chuckle.

"My father told you everything, I'd wager. Really, it was a mistake to try and hide anything from you, sir."

"It was," Heydrich said, tone proud and curious at once.

"Well, sir, your announcement really couldn't have come at a better time. Gave me the perfect opportunity."

"Start at the beginning, Amsel. Tell me *everything*," Heydrich commanded, his eyes flitting towards Dieter, a smirk teasing the edge of his lip, communicating clearly that if Jonas' story differed in any way from what Dieter had previously confessed, they would both be begging for death before midnight.

"Gladly, sir: as my father probably told you, I was engaged to Avalina Keller. Unbeknownst to me and her, she had Jewish blood. My father hid this from me and attempted to cover up records of her existence, then sent her to America. However, she was turned back and instead ended up in the French village of Annuville. I was never aware of any of this."

Heydrich nodded once, glancing at Dieter, his vicious smirk dissipating as truth tumbled from Jonas' lips.

"Being frank, sir, I operated for years under the assumption that Avalina Keller had been kidnapped by Jews. When I encountered her at the gas station, I thought she had been brainwashed or blackmailed into joining the Black Foxes. I apologize for not informing you of this, sir, but I let my emotions get the better of me. Considering how much harm Black Fox One has done to the Cause and considering the Naden incident, well, I thought it best to have proof that she was acting against her will before I asked you for clemency on her behalf."

"So you *always* intended to assist her?" Heydrich said.

"I intended to free her from Jews, sir. I didn't know she *was* a Jew. My father didn't tell me. I only found out when I managed to track her down and she captured me. She told me about her racial stock, and she told me that she had purposefully joined the Black Foxes."

"And then...?" Heydrich prodded, waving for him to go on. Jonas glanced down at his black-gloved hands, pausing thoughtfully for a moment before continuing his story.

"Truthfully, sir...Avalina wanted to change my mind. She still had feelings for me and hoped to turn me against the Reich, to turn me into a double agent for the Black Foxes. She hoped that my love for her would drive me to betray my nation."

"And she didn't succeed?" Heydrich guessed, almost sneering. Jonas bowed his head in shame.

"It was...it was extremely confusing," the Fox Hunter muttered. "This is my fiancée, a woman that I had always wanted to save and...and I *still* wanted to save her. I tried to convince myself that she was an *Edeljudin*, that she was *different*. Then I started to crack and think that maybe, *maybe* she was right. But..."

Jonas sat up straight, his countenance becoming steely. "I remembered my training, and I remembered what my father had told me before I set off: I remembered that I am German. I remembered Naden, and our discussion about the Engel family, and what you had previously said about hypocrisy. You were right, sir: I'm the Fox Hunter. It would be *wrong* to give mercy to a woman that I love when she is a Jewess, an enemy."

"Love..." Heydrich repeated, and Dieter's pounding heart slowed its frantic beat when the Hangman's eyes thawed ever so slightly. "You're saying you *still* love this Jewess, then?"

Jonas inhaled sharply and bowed his head again, hesitating for one moment before nodding. "Yes, sir, I do. I don't think anything could ever make me stop loving her," the Fox Hunter confessed before looking up at his superior again, expression fixed into a determined scowl. "But the Cause demands great sacrifices of all of us, and this is mine."

The Butcher of Prague's narrow eyes widened almost imperceptibly. Dieter was practically on the edge of his seat, and when Heydrich leaned back and gave a conciliatory nod, he felt like he'd been given new life.

"Go on," the Hangman said, his voice not quite gentle, but verging on it. It almost sounded like he was proud.

"Yes, sir! I decided to play the long con, to earn her trust. Then, hopefully, she would lead me right to Papa Fox, giving me the opportunity to take him down."

"But you didn't succeed?"

"No, sir, unfortunately I didn't. Avalina believed in my supposed change of heart completely and wanted to let me go, but she never took me to Papa Fox, and the rest of her comrades never trusted me. They wanted to execute me. When her back was turned, they would beat me. They only stopped themselves from killing me out of respect for her. Nevertheless, I tried to be patient and waited for an opportunity."

"And that opportunity came when I put out the announcement," Heydrich said.

"Yes, sir, you really did save me with that. As you can imagine, Avalina was rather concerned, but she knew better than to turn herself in. She knew that doing so would merely result in death for both her *and* her mother."

A smug smirk flitted across Heydrich's face. The Hangman nodded.

"Additionally," Jonas continued, "Avalina's identity was compromised, meaning her value as a Black Fox had dropped... as well as my value as a prisoner. The other Black Foxes realized I wouldn't be able to operate as a spy now even if I could be trusted. Calls to execute me grew louder, and Avalina panicked. She didn't want to lose me *and* her mother."

"So she simply let you go?"

"Not precisely. I convinced her that I could help free her mother. Obviously, you're holding Gisela Keller at the Fox Farm."

"Correct."

"But Avalina and the Black Foxes don't know about the Fox Farm yet. Therefore, I convinced her that you would be keeping her mother close at hand, in Theresienstadt. I also convinced her that I could sneak her and two comrades in, then get out with her mother in tow. Tomorrow at five PM, Avalina and her comrades will be waiting at the First Circle, waiting for me."

"But every patron there will be a plainclothes SS officer waiting to arrest her," Heydrich declared, a victorious smile blooming on his face.

"She's alone, abandoned, frightened. It will be too easy. I...I was going to request that I be allowed to stay away from this mission, Chief, for the sake of...my emotions."

"Permission denied," Heydrich said, his tone strangely sympathetic. "You must see this through, Agent."

Again, Jonas drew in a deep breath, squirming for a moment and biting his lip before nodding.

"All right, sir...I suppose I can't avoid it," he conceded. "But please, when she's executed on opening day, don't make me witness it."

"You'll need to be there, Amsel, and more than that: *you* need to drop the noose," Heydrich commanded. "Engel pulled the trigger himself when it came down to it. That's why he's a hero now."

"I..." Jonas whispered, clutching at his chest as though the thought of killing Ava was truly breaking his heart in two. "I don't think I'm strong enough for that, sir."

"You are," Heydrich declared. "If all of this pans out, you'll completely eclipse Engel. For now, however, you're dismissed. Go home with your father. I will set things up at the First Circle and send for you when the time comes."

"Yes, sir!" Jonas leapt to his feet, shoved his hand into the air, and let out a zealous, "Heil Hitler!"

His proclamation of loyalty echoed in Dieter's ears.

Heydrich glanced at the Major as he quietly grabbed his son's shoulder and ushered him out of the office. By 5 PM tomorrow, the Butcher of Prague would decide whether or not the Amsels were heroes or traitors.

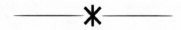

"HAS THE HOUSE BEEN BUGGED?" JONAS ASKED AS soon as they shut the door to their shared apartment, and Dieter sighed, shaking his head.

"No, I checked everywhere."

"Check everywhere again," Jonas said, a reasonable enough demand. Heydrich was Heydrich, after all, and while it would have been hard for him to bug the Amsels' abode in the short time they had been away, it wasn't impossible.

The Amsels tore their already untidy house apart, ripping the cushions from the couch and pulling out drawers, searching for microphones or recorders. Eventually, comforted by the fact that they knew how the SS operated, the Amsels determined that it was safe to talk. Heydrich, ever arrogant, must have decided that it would be a waste of SD resources to spy on people whose every secret he already knew.

"So you told him," Jonas declared, fixing his mother's shrine and turning to his father with blazing eyes. Magda watched her husband from over her son's shoulder, her smile burning Dieter's soul.

"I did, but it didn't matter. He already knew almost everything," Dieter said, putting the cushions back onto his favorite cozy chair and sitting down. He pressed his palm to his medal-clad chest in an attempt to slow the frantic pace of his heartbeat. Jonas was tall, but Dieter had never felt small compared to his son. No matter how much he grew, Jonas had always felt like his little boy.

Not so now. Now, Dieter felt trapped, small, and terrified in the presence of the furious Fox Hunter.

"My boy..." Dieter started to say, but Jonas held up a hand to stop him.

"Don't you *dare* call me that after what you did," he snapped. "You may be my father, but I'm not *yours*. You had *no right* to do what you did to the Kellers or to me."

"Son, listen: you're a smart man, an honorable man. You have no idea how much I respect you, but I also *know* you. I *know* you would have stayed with her..."

"And that would have been *my* decision!" hissed Jonas, gesturing towards his own chest, towards the SS uniform he clearly no longer wore with pride. "Instead, you hurt the woman I loved, hurt her family, and lied to my face for *six years*! There hasn't been a *second* of the day for *six years* that you haven't been lying to me! You knew *everything* and yet you hid it, lied, and kept pushing me further and further into the SS! Do you have *any* idea what you've done to me?! Do you even give a shit?"

Now Jonas' fury was morphing into something else, something that terrified Dieter almost as much as being in the presence of the Butcher of Prague. There was a haunted look to the Fox Hunter, a look of desperate betrayal, like Dieter had torn out a part of his soul and spat on it.

"Jonas, of course I give a shit!" the Major proclaimed, sitting up slightly and curling his hands into trembling fists. "That's *why* I had to do it! Believe me, I hated lying to you, I hated seeing you miserable and heartbroken, but I am your father and I have to protect you always, it doesn't matter how old you are! I had to protect you from her and from yourself!"

You know what would have happened if I hadn't! Hell, you damn near had a child with her!"

"Oooh, is *that* it, then?!" snapped Jonas, throwing up his hands and rolling his eyes. "You didn't want me to ruin your precious, clean bloodline! God forbid the old guard Party members mock you for having a Jewish grandchild!"

"This was *never* about my reputation, Jonas, it was about *you*!" Dieter argued, rising to his feet and taking a cautious step towards his fuming son. "About doing what's best for you! If I hadn't sent her and the rest of the Kellers away, you would have married her, had a child with her, and then what? You would have ended up in a ghetto or a camp!"

"One of *your* camps!" Jonas growled, jabbing an accusatory finger at his father. "The camps you build, the camps you design!"

"Jonas..."

"And you would have just turned the other way and shrugged, eh? If it had come down to that, you would have tossed me and my family into one of *your* camps!"

"No, Jonas!" Dieter cried, his eyes flitting towards a blueprint that they had tossed onto the floor while searching for bugs, a blueprint for one of his many concentration camps. "I *never* would have allowed you to be sent to a camp, if it came down to it..."

"If it came down to it, *then what*? What, Father?" Jonas snarled. "You're saying it's just fine to send hundreds of innocent children to die in your camps, you can sleep just fine knowing that, but if *your child* ended up in a camp, then what? You would resist? Are you a hypocrite or a traitor, Father?"

"You're going too far, Jonas!" hissed Dieter, turning away from his son and forcing his eyes to fall upon the portrait of Hitler that hung opposite to Magda's shrine. The blazing eyes of the Führer filled him with resolve. "I know you're upset, but you have no right to accuse me of such awful things!"

"Accuse?" sputtered the former Fox Hunter. "What have I said that isn't a simple *fact,* Father?"

"You say innocent children die in my camps and ghettos. That is *not* true," Dieter declared with the firm determination of a Christian proclaiming that Jesus was Lord. "Enemies of the State die in my camps and ghettos out of necessity, for the greater good of our children and our children's children..."

"Enemies of the State like my fiancée! If I'd had a child with Ava, *they'd* be an Enemy of the State! *I'm* an enemy of the state! I'm a Jew-lover! You said it yourself: the only reason I'm not rotting away in one of your ghettos is because you lied and hurt the Kellers! You didn't want to save me, you just didn't want to have to choose between me and Hitler!"

"Jonas!" Dieter looked over his shoulder, but did not turn his body, only sparing a brief, withering glance at his son as Jonas himself turned on his heel, facing Magda's portrait.

"What if Mother was alive, Father?" Jonas hissed. "Do you think she would have followed me and my wife and child into a camp? You always talk about her like she was the greatest, kindest woman to ever live."

"She was." Dieter faced Hitler again, desperate to draw strength from the man he knew to be Germany's savior, but the painted Führer seemed to shrink as Jonas continued speaking.

"You once said that she fell in love with you because you were an architect..." the former Fox Hunter whispered, gesturing towards the little models he had played with as a boy that now lay scattered across a shelf. "Because she admired your power to take an ugly pile of bricks and metal and make something beautiful and practical: a house, a bank, something *good*."

"Son, don't..."

"What would she think if she saw your creations now? She married an architect, not a Nazi. A man who made schools, not a man who designs concentration camps."

"Enough!" Dieter turned and started marching towards his son.

"You lied to your own child," Jonas continued. "You tore me away from the woman I love, and now you build cages and slaughterhouses for human beings. If Mother saw the man you've become, she'd be ashamed..."

"Don't you *dare* tell me what she would think! You didn't know her! You only met her the day you kill—!"

Dieter shouted without thinking, rage boiling over into a scream that immediately made regret flood his heart. Jonas whirled around, eyes wide, wincing as though his father had struck him. The Major slapped a hand over his face.

"I didn't mean...I wasn't...I didn't mean that, I'm so sorry," Dieter stuttered.

"Is that it?" Jonas hissed, round eyes narrowing. "I killed your wife, stole your happiness, so you wanted to make sure I stayed alone and miserable just like you?! Is this *revenge*, Father?!"

"No, no, no!" Dieter insisted, stepping towards his son and reaching for him. Jonas all but leapt away from his father's hand, and nothing had ever hurt Dieter as much as his son rejecting his touch like it was toxic. Once again, the Major found himself wishing that he had just put a bullet in his skull before Jonas had even returned, but he forced his cowardice to abandon him and stood under his wife's gaze, clasping his hands before his son.

"My boy, I love you, I promise!" Dieter insisted. "I wanted you to be safe and happy, but if I could only have one, I'd rather you be safe. You're my boy, her boy..."

"You think she'd *want* me to be miserable?" Jonas growled. "You think she'd *want* me to give up on the woman I love?"

"She would want you to be alive!"

"A lifetime of misery is worse than death!"

"I didn't...I didn't realize you felt so strongly, I thought you would move on..."

"Mother has been dead and buried for over twenty years and you haven't moved on! You mourned her every day throughout my childhood! You think I love Ava any less than you loved Mother?! She's my Magda! If you had to choose between Magda and the Reich, are you saying you would choose the Reich?! If someone tried to make that choice for you and threw her away to protect you, would *you* forgive them?!"

The Amsels were lucky the walls were thick and Jonas, even when enraged, managed to keep himself from truly shouting. Instead, he snarled like a furious dog, marching towards his father with every question until the older SS man was all but backed against the cozy chair. Dieter, once more feeling like his heart was beating too fast to function, trembled as his gaze flitted from the photo of his smiling wife to his furious son.

"No. No, I wouldn't..." Dieter finally confessed, falling into the chair behind him and burying his face in his hands, sobs shaking his body. "I'm sorry...I'm so sorry, my boy...I wanted to do the right thing..."

Jonas' furious scowl morphed into an expression of empathy. Sighing, he knelt before his father, waiting a moment for the older man to dry his tears before he put a hand on Dieter's knee.

"I know, Papa, I know," Jonas whispered. "But you didn't. And neither have I. But right now, we have a chance to do the right thing, to *really* do the right thing. I need you to help me."

"J-Jonas, what are you planning?" the Major hiccupped, feeling Hitler's gaze burning the back of his skull. His son's eyes blazed with rebellious fire.

"We're going to liberate the Fox Farm," Jonas declared. "Burn it to the ground. We have the supplies, but we need your help."

"Black Fox One is getting herself captured on purpose..." Dieter muttered slowly, and Jonas nodded.

"And you're not going to execute her." A note of disapproval, almost paternal chastisement, came to Dieter's voice. Jonas' brow pinched, and he shook his head.

"Jonas, this is suicide..."

"Fine." The former Fox Hunter's chest swelled with defiant determination. "I'd rather go out trying to help Ava than spend another minute serving a lie, serving the state that killed the Kellers and turned me into a murderer."

"My boy, you're not a murderer, you're confused," Dieter said, cupping his son's face in his hands. "Please, it's not too late. Maybe we can save Ava, maybe even her mother, but don't drag yourself into this foolish crusade!"

"I'm already in, Papa," Jonas said, reaching up and grasping his father's hands. "And I need you to join me."

"W-What?! Jonas, no, you can't ask me to become a traitor! I will not—!"

"Then my plan will fail, and I'll die. I'll die with Ava, and you won't stop me," Jonas declared, squeezing his father's hands so tight that it hurt. "I love you, Papa, even after everything you've done. I want to trust you, I *have* to trust you. I want to believe that you really do love me more than you love

Hitler. I want to believe that you're not like Leon Engel, that you're not like Heydrich. Please...for me and for my mother. You have a choice to make now, you can't avoid it anymore. Your country or your son. Choose."

Dieter's old words to Heydrich reverberated painfully through his brain. *I cannot imagine being forced to choose between my nation and my own children...*

He looked at the picture of Magda on the wall, her gentle smile, her gorgeous lapis-colored eyes. Her laugh, long lost, echoed in his mind and soothed his hammering heart.

He craned his neck to glimpse the portrait of Hitler. The Führer gazed at him with intense blue eyes, steely and hypnotic.

He looked at his son, who smiled at him with the unconditional trust he had offered when he was just a little boy with a bruised knee, reaching for Dieter, knowing that his father would protect him no matter what.

It felt like a part of Dieter's soul abandoned him when he made his choice, but at the same time, a strange surge of strength filled his soul.

"What's the plan, son?"

"THAT'S THEM?"

"The woman, the man with dark hair and blue eyes, and the smaller man. Three Black Foxes. We'll take them all alive, Chief?"

Heydrich nodded. The Hangman and Jonas stood in the backroom of the First Circle, utilizing a small peephole to keep track of their marks. Jonas pressed his eyes against the hole and studied the three Black Foxes as they sat down. Ava, One-

Twenty, and Eight-Sixty, all dressed in dark plainclothes, sat at a table, trying their best to appear casual even as Jonas could see them squirm from where he hid with the Hangman.

"Let's get on with this," Heydrich declared. "And Amsel..."

The Hangman strode forward, grabbed Jonas' shoulder, and pulled him away from the door. Jonas was by no means short, but right then the three inches Heydrich had over him felt more like three feet.

"No tricks," the Butcher of Prague said, and the unspoken *or else* hung between them. Jonas sighed sorrowfully and nodded.

"No tricks, sir, but can we do this quickly and humanely?"

"Always," Heydrich assured him before rapping on the door thrice with his knuckles, signaling to the SS men waiting that it was time to strike.

Jonas' many years in the SD served him well right then: he had learned how to recognize when people were lying and he knew, therefore, how to lie in such a way that even Heydrich couldn't easily see past the façade. As the commotion went on outside, as he heard Ava quite convincingly cry out in shock, he turned from the door, honing every subtle tick, every clench of his jaw and raising of his shoulders, for maximum believability. Heydrich, a lie-detector of a man himself, was seemingly fooled. He looked at the seemingly distressed Jonas with a smirk.

"Let's go," Heydrich commanded once the SS men outside announced that the Black Foxes were subdued. The Hangman emerged from the backroom like an emperor approaching rowdy subjects. Jonas shuffled behind him, practically hiding behind the Butcher of Prague. He made sure not to let up, wincing when Ava, who was kneeling on the hard floor with her hands cuffed behind her back, let out an affronted shriek.

"Jonas, what the Hell?!" she cried, and pride bloomed in Jonas' belly so intensely that it was difficult to turn his face away in feigned shame. His beloved Bärchen was as good an actor as he: she had learned well from faking injury to pickpocket unsuspecting marks during her childhood and playing the distressed damsel to seemingly chivalrous SS targets as Black Fox One.

"So, this is the infamous Black Fox One," Heydrich said, standing over the young woman. He reached out one spiderlike hand and grabbed Ava's chin, and it was *so* difficult for Jonas to keep himself from putting a bullet in the Butcher's back right then.

"Avalina Keller. Just a pathetic little girl," the Hangman said. "Your romantic little fantasy hasn't gone as planned, has it?"

She wrung her head and tried to bite his long fingers, but Heydrich's reflexes were well honed and he drew back his hand with a chuckle.

"Interesting," the Blond Beast said, malicious mirth dripping from his high-pitched voice. "You fight even when you're caught. My men told me your father didn't fight at all. Even helped them pull your brothers from their hiding places. I suppose not all Jews are as *cowardly* as he."

Immediately, Jonas realized what Heydrich was doing. Dropping that sort of bomb right then, it was an attempt to shock Jonas into letting his mask slip. The Hangman's eyes flitted towards the Fox Hunter for a moment, but Jonas didn't break, and Ava's furious reaction drew Heydrich's attention back to her.

"You killed them! Son-of-a-bitch, I'll rip your damn eyes out!" she snarled, fortunately remembering the scheme even as genuine anger burned in her eyes. "Jonas! Help me! Jonas, you said you loved me!"

"I'm sorry, Ava..." the Fox Hunter muttered, turning away. He knew that Heydrich, the son of an opera writer who had grown up in a music conservatoire, had a particularly sharp ear for voices and their subtleties, and so he made sure that his stutter was perfectly natural as he said, "I-I wish things were different."

Heydrich watched the Fox Hunter carefully for a moment before his lake-blue eyes brightened. Jonas almost smirked. *Bullseye. He buys it.*

"And these two," Heydrich muttered, turning towards Black Fox One-Twenty and Black Fox Eight-Sixty.

Eight-Sixty gazed up at the Hangman, turquoise eyes so wide they all but consumed half his face, trembling so much that the chains on his cuffs clinked against one another. Either Eight-Sixty was an exceptional actor, or simply being in the presence of the Blond Beast was enough to make him quake like a newborn kitten regardless of this being part of the plan.

Heydrich smirked at the smaller man's obvious terror, but when he looked down at Black Fox 120, hesitant curiosity briefly flitted across the Hangman's face. He stared into One-Twenty's unblinking, blazing blue eyes and squinted as though something about this particular Black Fox was familiar to him.

One-Twenty spat at the Hangman's boot, but Heydrich easily dodged the foul projectile. "Khruvina will be avenged, butcher!" One-Twenty snarled, and whatever spell the Hangman had been under broke as he scoffed and turned away from the two male Black Foxes.

"Unremarkable. Take them all to the Fox Farm. Put them all in Barrack One."

The SS men quickly moved to fulfill Heydrich's command,

struggling as One-Twenty and Ava fought back, kicking and, in Ava's case, screaming.

"Jonas! Jonas, how could you?! Jonas! Jonas!"

She shouted his name as she was dragged off, and Jonas made sure to wince every time she did. He felt a hand on his shoulder and looked up to see Heydrich wearing a smile that was somehow arrogant and gratified at once.

"Special Agent Amsel, you've redeemed yourself and your father today," he declared. "Your honor and loyalty are beyond dispute now."

"Thank you, sir."

"Goebbels' team will be at the camp for the execution. It will be hard, but you will be a hero throughout the Reich. And after that? I'm sure you'll find a proper German wife."

"Yes, sir...I just...I'll need some time."

"Understandable. You did the right thing, but it was not the easy thing. Just know that you have every reason to be proud of yourself. I'm very proud of you."

"Thank you, sir. From you, that means the world," Jonas said, looking up and fighting against the disgust churning in his gut as he gave the Hangman a smile. Heydrich patted the former Fox Hunter's shoulder once more before he dismissed him.

"Take some time off. I'll see you at the ceremony."

"Yes, sir. I won't miss it."

THIRTEEN

"Oh, for God's sake, how hard can it possibly be to set up a microphone?! Get moving, the ceremony begins soon! Oh, Reinhard! You're right on time!"

Dieter hopped off the wooden structure that would double as a podium and a set of gallows, strolling towards the cheerful *Reichsprotektor*. Heydrich had gone all out for the opening of the camp: his black SS uniform, which was reserved for ceremonial occasions, was pressed and decorated with all of his medals. His *ehrenring* glistened on his finger as though he had spent hours shining it, and his ceremonial SS dagger was sheathed at his side. The Hangman greeted Dieter with a nod, holding up the silver pocket watch the Major had given him. Dieter chuckled.

"Enjoying your gift, Reinhard?" Dieter said, fighting to keep a casual tone, to make it seem like he was eager to forget their confrontation at Panenské Břežany. Heydrich, seemingly willing to let it all be forgotten in light of Jonas' actions, nodded, slipping the watch into his pocket.

"Very practical," Heydrich said. "Is Black Fox One secure?"

"Tied up like a hog in Barrack One. From what I'm told, she hasn't said a word since she got here. Looks like she's dead inside."

"Good. We wouldn't want her sobbing and hysterical when the noose drops. You know that Himmler can't stand seeing women cry," Heydrich said, jabbing his thumb to gesture towards Joseph Goebbels' little camera crew, all of whom were setting up their equipment and chatting with Leon Engel. Engel was grinning broadly, but even from a distance, both Heydrich and Dieter could see him squirming.

"What's with him?" Dieter asked, and Heydrich shrugged.

"Overwhelmed. So much to do once you turn over the keys. Maybe he's just worried about your son stealing his spotlight."

"As he should," chuckled Dieter. "He won't have to worry about me handing over the keys, however: this damn microphone is the last thing we have to set up. I've been running around all day ironing out the camp's kinks."

"Such as?"

"Barbed wire fence's electricity kept cutting out, so I fixed that. There was a discrepancy at the factory and the armory, but I got that sorted. A few of the watchtowers were sinking a bit since they were built with the old wall schematics, but I checked the structures and it's nothing to worry about. Everything is ready."

"Excellent. Guests should be arriving soon, then we can get this show over with. I'd like to be home by the afternoon."

"Afternoon, sir?"

"Much as I enjoy success, Dieter, I'd prefer to spend some time with my family. Silke heard that today was a big celebration for Papa and got it in her head that it was my birthday. She's going to 'make me a cake.'"

"Ah. Meaning her mother is going to make it and she'll slather it with icing."

"Precisely. Mustn't disappoint my girl," Reinhard said, and a small, genuine smile came to his typically harsh features. Dieter, who knew full well how dangerous the man before him was, who had hoped in a moment of fear-induced vengefulness that the Hangman would have his child taken away from him, nevertheless felt the smallest prick of regret stab at his soul.

"Chief, Major Amsel!"

"Ah, Major Engel. Or perhaps I should say *Kommandant* Engel," Dieter cried, offering Engel a casual salute and then grasping his hand, giving a firm, friendly shake. Heydrich did not offer his underling a handshake, instead merely granting Engel a brusque nod.

"Ready for the ceremony, Chief?" Engel asked. "Lina helped you iron out your speech?"

"Twenty-nine 'uhms' she counted when I recited it last night," sighed the Hangman. "She's ruthless, but effective."

"You're meant for each other!" Engel laughed, letting his gaze turn to Dieter. "And you, Major? Ready for a show?"

"Once these idiots can figure out how to plug in a damn chord and Goebbels' boys get their equipment ready."

"Haven't been on a newsreel in a while!" Engel chuckled, whipping off his death's-head cap and brushing back his golden locks. "How do I look?"

"Perfectly adequate, Kommandant," Dieter said. "Don't worry: I'm sure everyone will be so busy staring at my boy that they won't even notice you."

Heydrich let out a grunt that must have been a repressed chuckle. Kommandant Engel gave a strained laugh.

"Ah, where is your son anyway, Amsel?" Engel asked, and again his shoulders slumped and rose like he was adjusting a hefty backpack. "I was hoping to have a chat with him before we got down to business."

"Feel free to talk to him during my speech," Heydrich offered. "I won't be offended."

"Ah, thank you, sir!" chuckled Engel. "Public speaking... there's a reason why Goebbels gets paid so much. You couldn't pay me twice what he makes to take his job!"

"Hm." Heydrich glanced at Dieter. "Where *is* Jonas? I told him he has to drop the noose. That was an *order*."

"He's getting a drink, sir," Dieter said. "He'll be out soon."

"Very well," Heydrich muttered. "I suppose that's understandable, but he mustn't overdo it."

"Oh, I'm sure he won't, sir."

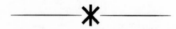

"For the thousandth time: I don't care if you're a hero to the Reich, you can't raid the fine wines."

Jonas heaved a deep sigh and scowled at the single guard standing in his way. His pulse was pounding in his ears: he could already hear the screech of engines as the SS guests arrived. He could hear the rowdy guffaws of the guards who were being given a break to watch the execution of Black Fox One. Pretty soon, the servants would arrive to retrieve the wine. Jonas had to get into the cellar before then. Which meant convincing this severe guard to budge.

"Come on, I'll be in, have a few sips, get out. I won't touch anything too expensive!" cried Jonas. "I'll even pay it back later! I'm about to execute my ex-fiancée, I need a damn drink!"

"Look, comrade, I sympathize," sighed the guard. "But orders are orders, and I do *not* want to deal with a pissed-off Heydrich."

"Heydrich won't notice!" Jonas argued.

"Hm..." mumbled the guard, his eyes nervously shifting to and fro before he leaned closer and confidentially muttered, "Look, if you can make it worth my while..."

The ring! The former Fox Hunter pulled it from his back pocket, hesitating only for a moment before offering it to the guard.

"Here," said Jonas. "This is gold. Give it to your girl."

"That was...?"

"I don't need it anymore," Jonas proclaimed, his tone stern even as he suppressed a smile. The guard grabbed the ring, and the former Fox Hunter felt lighter, liberated, like the guard had taken a little piece of his sinful past away.

"Fine, I'll take this, and you'll put in a good word about me to Kommandant Engel. Deal?"

"Deal."

"Five minutes. Don't overdo it."

"Keep standing guard and knock if someone comes," Jonas commanded, opening the door as the guard stepped aside. The Nazi guard, oblivious to his new role in the Black Fox scheme, smirked and nodded, admiring the ring while Jonas slammed the door to the cellar behind him.

Thankfully, Dieter had planned out the construction of the camp and had plotted out every detail of the opening day celebrations, right down to the wine list. It was easy for Jonas to find the bottles that would be served. He drew a small container from his back pocket.

I hope this works, he thought. *Hold on tight, Ava.*

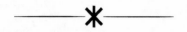

"Hey, Sam..."

"Eight-Sixty..."

"S-Sorry, One-Twenty! You see the Fox Hunter yet?"

"No," One-Twenty said, pausing to glance at his comrade. The two Black Foxes lingered in a corner by the door of the terribly cramped Barrack One. Black Fox 120 had been kept in worse conditions when he had previously been captured by Nazis. The Barrack was crowded, yes, but it was at least good company. Almost entirely Black Foxes, some familiar faces. The Barrack even had a window, though it only offered the captured resistance fighters a view of the gallows. Not a feature installed to give them sunlight, a detail added for maximizing hopelessness. No doubt Heydrich planned on making sure that the prisoners could never hide from those nooses. One-Twenty would expect nothing less of the Hangman.

The Russian Black Fox pressed his face against the murky glass and scowled: Heydrich was examining the nooses, and even from a distance, One-Twenty could practically see the Hangman's arrogant smirk. Hatred burned in his heart.

"Hey..." Eight-Sixty broke him from his furious fantasies, putting a hand on his shoulder. One-Twenty turned with a scowl that softened when he saw Eight-Sixty's expression: determined, but chastising.

"He'll get what he deserves," Eight-Sixty whispered, "But we want him alive."

"Don't worry," One-Twenty said. "Death is too good for him. I won't let him off that easily. Is everyone else ready?"

Eight-Sixty nodded. "As long as the Fox Hunter did his part."

"How's One?"

"When the war's over, she should go into acting. She's really selling the hopeless spurned woman schtick," Eight-Sixty said, refusing to gesture towards their top woman lest he draw uninvited attention to her. One-Twenty spared a brief glance at Black Fox One. Bruised, tied to one of the bunks like a wild animal, burying her face against her mother's shoulder, she certainly looked helpless. Even knowing she was playing it all up, the sight was so pitiful that it made One-Twenty begin to lose heart.

A loud sob drew his attention away from their leader and down to his feet. He hadn't even realized that he and Eight-Sixty were standing near two children huddled against the wall. Little girls, neither one a day older than six. One was unfamiliar to One-Twenty: a girl dressed in a slightly muddy white shirt and shorts whom he almost mistook for a boy with long hair. She brushed her shoulder-length black locks from her eyes and wrapped her arms around the other girl.

"It's okay, Heidi," the black-haired girl said gently, but the smaller child, Heidi, continued sobbing. While the black-haired tomboy was at the very least trying to maintain her personal cleanliness, little Heidi had fallen to shreds. She wore a torn-up pink nightgown caked in grime, her porcelain skin was bruised, and one of her two braided blonde pigtails was undone.

One-Twenty felt his heart leap into his throat when he recognized the sobbing wreck of a five-year-old. Heidi Naden, daughter of the disgraced Beast of Belorussia. Once her Nazi father's precious little princess, now nothing more than another undesirable to be broken.

One-Twenty's soul burned, and he practically shoved his face against the window, ignoring the girls and trying very hard to focus on Heydrich, to get lost in violent fantasies of what he planned on doing to the head of the *Einsatzgruppen* once he got his hands on him. Eight-Sixty, never one to let a crying child go without comfort, knelt before the girls.

"Hey there," he said in the gentle voice he always used to calm children that the Black Foxes rescued. "I'm Amos, but everyone calls me Eight-Sixty."

"Shhh!" hissed the raven-haired girl. "Don't say your name, dummy!"

Eight-Sixty chuckled. "Aha! Sorry, but I figured you were trustworthy. You seem to be doing a good job taking care of your sister."

"Oh, she's not my sister," the dark-haired girl said. "She's my friend, though. She was crying before 'cause her mama got killed, so I gave her a hug 'cause mine's dead too."

"Oh, dear...my mama got killed, too," Eight-Sixty muttered sympathetically. "You were very kind to take care of her, very responsible. I wish I'd had a friend like you when I lost my mama. What's your name?"

"Aliza," the dark-haired girl answered, gesturing to the blonde beside her, whose wild sobbing had petered into sniffling as she gazed curiously at the Black Fox before her. "She's Heidi."

"Heidi Naden, right?" Eight-Sixty said, turning his gaze to the younger girl, whose tear-filled eyes widened. She nodded, wiping her stained cheeks with one grimy palm.

"I knew your mama, Heidi. Well, I met her," said Eight-Sixty. "She actually helped save my life, you know. She was very brave and strong, and your sister Nadine was amazing too."

A shiver wracked One-Twenty's body. Heidi tilted her head to the side.

212

"Everyone said they were bad," Heidi mumbled. "That's why they got killed."

"Everyone, or just the Nazis?" Eight-Sixty queried. "Nazis lie a lot, sweetie, and they definitely lied about your mama. She was very, very good. And she would want you to stay strong. Listen..."

He beckoned for the girls to come close enough for him to whisper a secret. Both did, leaning in.

"Something big is going to happen soon, and I want you two to stay with me, okay?" Eight-Sixty whispered, offering his hands to both girls. "Stay with me and stay with each other. We'll all be all right, okay? I promise."

Aliza grasped Eight-Sixty's hand immediately, nodding, a fiery glow in her chestnut-colored eyes. Heidi hesitated for a moment, glancing from her dirty palm to the Jewish man's gentle smile before hesitantly grasping his hand.

A few moments later, two SS men came into the Barrack. They grabbed Black Fox One, who didn't fight back. Ava's mother put on quite a show, sobbing and wringing her hands. Heidi whimpered. Aliza tightened her grip on Eight-Sixty's hand, shaking with hatred as the SS men dragged Black Fox One outside.

"It'll be alright," Eight-Sixty promised the girls, squeezing their little hands. "Everything's going to be alright."

WINE WAS FLOWING. NAZIS WERE LAUGHING. Heydrich was adjusting the microphone. Dieter was waiting by the gallows.

213

Ava stood with a noose around her neck, her head bowed, muttering a Hebrew prayer.

Jonas tarried at the bottom of the stage's staircase, just out of the cameras' line of sight, stealing glances hither and thither, counting down the seconds in his head. Heydrich hated public speaking almost as much as he hated Jews, and therefore, his speech would certainly be short.

The Fox Hunter glanced at the guards. Most hadn't started drinking yet, but the few who had were already taking their seats, masking their wooziness.

"Gentlemen, comrades..." Heydrich began once the cameras started rolling, and the usual nonsense flowed forth: calls to action against International Jewry, praise of Hitler, the same old lies. Goebbels' crew recorded it all. Heydrich was seemingly too lost in his own egotism to even notice that several of his men were stumbling into their seats. Perhaps he mistook their symptoms for mere drunkenness.

"Special Agent Amsel..." Jonas winced when he felt a hand on his shoulder. He looked to his side and realized it was Leon Engel. They were down to the wire now, and so he didn't bother putting on a fake smile, but that was fine: the newly minted Kommandant wore an expression of severe empathy, like a teacher who was counseling a pupil that was struggling in a subject that he himself had once found difficult.

"Listen," Engel whispered. "Don't look at her. Don't listen. She's just another Enemy of the State. The woman you love is already dead, understood?"

"Yes," mumbled Jonas, disgust and pity writhing in his gut when he saw the look in Leon Engel's eyes: pain masked by zealotry. Engel squeezed the former Fox Hunter's shoulder.

"This won't be easy, but it's *right*, all right? It's the right thing to do," Engel said, and it sounded as though he was talking to himself as much as Jonas. "It'll hurt like nothing else, but you'll look back and be glad that you did it."

"I know."

"Special Agent Jonas Amsel, please come forward," Heydrich commanded, stepping away from the podium and smiling down at Jonas.

"Go," Engel hissed, giving Jonas a slight pat on the shoulder and pushing him towards the stairs. "Do what you have to."

"I will," Jonas vowed, almost smiling as he ascended.

Hardly had Jonas stepped onto the platform when Heydrich's eyes flitted to the audience of guards and Nazi officials. All were sitting, but half were completely passed out. One or two fell right out of their seats and into the dirt. The Hangman raised an eyebrow: drunkenness was one thing, but there was no way that so many well-trained SS guards were *this* plastered. Even the propaganda crew were looking on with concern, mumbling to each other, no doubt debating on whether or not they should stop filming.

Heydrich looked at Jonas. The former Fox Hunter smiled.

BOOM!

And then, in practically one second, utter chaos erupted. Multiple explosions rocked the camp: the warehouse went up in flames, the door to the armory was blasted open, the watchtowers were incinerated. Barely had the explosions abated when the barracks burst open, and the captive Black Foxes swarmed the now-open armory.

Not all of the guards were out cold from the drugged wine, and therefore the prisoners scrambling to grab weapons might have been mowed down. But once smoke rose into the sky, several trucks suddenly emerged from the thicket, smashing through the front gate and the barbed-wire fence, which had been rendered powerless hours ago. The guards of the Fox Farm, the few who were awake, suddenly found themselves battling Black Foxes from all angles.

Buildings were set ablaze. Goebbels' film crew ducked and covered. The undrugged SS men tried to drag their unconscious allies to safety, exchanging fire with both the Black Foxes that had invaded the camp and the newly armed former prisoners.

Heydrich only got to gawk at the chaos for a moment before a curt command claimed his attention. "Hands up."

The Hangman turned to face a smirking Jonas Amsel, who had a gun pointed right at his former superior's chest.

The look that Heydrich gave Jonas almost made the former Fox Hunter wince: murderous didn't begin to describe it. If looks could kill, Jonas wouldn't be dead, he would be halfway through getting his skin surgically removed and rubbed with lemon juice. The Hangman's hatred for Jews was miniscule compared to his hatred for traitors, hypocrites, and men who humiliated him. Jonas Amsel was officially Reinhard Heydrich's worst enemy.

That was a frightening thought, but also good. Like being despised by the Devil.

Heydrich must have felt like making it to his next birthday, however. He did as Jonas said, lifting up his hands.

"Why?" the Hangman asked, barely a hiss, and Jonas's eyes answered for him, flitting towards the gallows. Heydrich followed his opponent's gaze. Dieter was cutting Black Fox One's bonds. Briefly, Jonas' father and Ava exchanged a solemn look, one that communicated their mutual disdain and a silent agreement to sort out their feelings later.

"Any ideology that says Ava deserves to die is an ideology built on lies," Jonas declared. "I won't serve a lie."

The icy countenance of the Hangman broke. His face contorted in fury, and he truly looked like a beast.

"Idiot!" Heydrich snarled. "You think one little Jewess proves anything?! You think *your* Jew is special?!"

"No, Heydrich. She's special to me, but she's not *different*. You were half right before: there can be no exceptions. Ava is worth saving, and so is every other Jew."

Ava's eyes shone in the fire of the camp, glistening with utter joy at her fiancé's declaration. It was a beautiful sight.

It was also a distracting sight.

As Jonas drew near to the Hangman, taking the Butcher's gun and tossing it over his shoulder, he became distracted by his ragged love's adoration. His lapse gave the Hangman a chance to grab at the weapon Jonas hadn't taken: his SS honor dagger.

"Jonas!" Ava shrieked. Jonas leapt back and the Hangman's dagger slashed at his arm. The Nazi motto that was emblazoned on the blade in gothic font, *My Honor is Loyalty,* became stained with the Fox Hunter's blood. The gun fell from Jonas' hand.

"Son!" Dieter yelped, but thankfully Jonas' fiancée was close at hand. Ava lunged forward. With one kick, she struck Heydrich's arm and sent his dagger flying. Another strike knocked the Hangman off his feet and sent him falling onto his face.

Heydrich snarled and tried to stand up, his eyes flitting about, trying to find his weapon. Smoke from the burning camp obscured his vision, but he saw it yards away: it had fallen by the foot of a small girl with raven-black hair.

The girl stooped down, grabbed the dagger, and met Heydrich's gaze. Her dark eyes were wide with the fright of a child spotting a monster in the darkness of their closet. She gripped the hilt hesitantly, like she would have loved nothing more than to rush forth and help her heroes fight the Beast but was kept planted by instinctual fear. Heydrich growled at the child, who winced as though he was an uncaged lion.

"Aliza!" one of the Black Foxes cried, and another rushed forward, the one with strangely hypnotic blue irises. One-Twenty and the Hangman of Prague locked eyes for the briefest of seconds before the resistance fighter grabbed Aliza by the arm, wrenching her away from the battle, towards one of the cars. She went with him, clutching Heydrich's dagger as she weaved past the battling Black Foxes.

"She got a trophy," Ava sneered as she and Jonas pinned the Hangman's hands behind his back.

"I'll take one too," Jonas chuckled, his eyes falling upon the shimmering *ehrenring* decorating Heydrich's right hand. Once upon a time, he had sought the ring for its prestige, for the honor it represented, for the good fortune it seemed to provide the heedless Hangman. Now he desired it because he knew that taking it from the Hangman would be well-deserved salt in the wound, one final humiliation.

"Looks like I get one of these after all," Jonas said, quickly slipping it off the Hangman's finger and tucking it into his pocket. Heydrich growled at the indignity, and the sound was music to Jonas and Ava's ears.

BANG!

A gunshot, one among many, rang out close by. Leon Engel, who had been ducking near the staircase and for once was actually sober, fired off a round. The bullet struck Jonas in the chest. With a gag and a yelp, Jonas fell off the platform.

"*Jonas!*" cried Ava, and as Leon started opening fire on her, she leapt off the platform. Dieter followed her, taking out his gun and shooting at Heydrich as he did so. He wasted his ammunition, however: as soon as Black Fox One was off him, Heydrich rolled to the gun he had knocked out of Jonas' hand and claimed it for himself, taking cover behind the podium and joining the fray which had now turned against the former Fox Hunter and his fiancée.

"Jonas! Jonas, are you all right?!" Ava cried. Jonas could only groan in response. Blood bloomed across his grey uniform, staining the dirt ground. Another bullet, this time fired by Heydrich, nearly struck his head. Ava grabbed her fiancé and dragged him to the wall of the platform, pressing her back against it. Dieter crouched next to her. Their position was completely indefensible, and both Dieter and Ava realized this right away.

"Take him!" Dieter commanded, gesturing to one of the cars. "I'll cover you!"

"Papa..." Jonas managed to groan.

"Take care of my boy, Ava! Go! Don't come back for me!"

Briefly, Dieter and Ava locked eyes, and Black Fox One nodded once. The message was clear: this sacrifice would make them even.

Ava slung Jonas' arm over her shoulder and started dragging him towards one of the vans. Heydrich jumped out from behind the podium and started opening fire, but Dieter climbed back onto the platform, firing at the Hangman and forcing him to duck behind the podium once more. A bullet struck the microphone, making an awful bout of static screech throughout the camp, melding with the shouts of injured SS men and the victorious hoots of Black Foxes as they filled their vans and began their escape.

Dieter fired on Heydrich, embedding bullet after bullet in the podium. Engel shot but missed.

"Forget him!" Heydrich shouted at the Kommandant. "Get Black Fox One!"

Engel nodded and took off after the fleeing Black Fox, but he didn't get far: Black Fox 56 and Black Fox 159 saw their comrade carrying her injured fiancée and hurried to defend her, firing at Engel and forcing him to take cover behind one of the barracks. Ava managed to get Jonas into the truck. Once a few more prisoners piled in, the vehicle took off, trampling the reams of fallen barbed wire and vanishing into the distance.

Realizing that his son had escaped made relief flow through Dieter's adrenaline-pumped body, and again the feeling that he was already dead took hold. This time it wasn't a weighty feeling; he didn't feel like a corpse being dragged about. He felt oddly light, almost liberated.

"You're a disgrace, Dieter!" Heydrich snarled.

"I wish it didn't have to be this way, Reinhard!" Dieter cried, lifting up his gun and realizing with grim resignation that he was almost out of bullets. "I'm still a National Socialist, but I had a choice to make, and I won't regret it! I'll choose my child over my nation, always!"

"Sentimental fool," Heydrich growled, wiping sweat from his brow and trying to calculate how to best fire at Dieter without getting his head blown off.

"I thought I might be able to reach you, Reinhard!" Dieter cried, and he had never imagined that he would shout at Heydrich before. Doing so made him feel even lighter, even freer. The words tumbled out. "But you would never understand! You're not like Naden, and you're not like me! You're no hypocrite! You're the perfect National Socialist! The Man with the Iron Heart! You wouldn't show any mercy in my place! That question I asked at Panenské Březany, I know the answer!

If your precious little girl was an undesirable, you'd slit her throat yourself and you'd feel *nothing*!"

Bang!

Dieter's final word, *nothing*, echoed about the burning Fox Farm. He might have gargled or sputtered, but Heydrich, seemingly without regard for his own safety, left his cover and marched close.

Bang! He shot Dieter again.

Bang! Once more.

Bang! Bang! Bang! He missed thrice as his hand trembled. Dieter was nothing more than a bloody mound of skull and blood. Scarlet consumed the Hangman's vision.

"Chief!"

Engel's voice brought him back to reality. Heydrich spun around and realized that the Black Foxes were gone. The few SS men who remained were scattered about, trying in vain to put out fires and lick their wounds.

But while he should have been burning with a desire to pursue like a hunter, to rebuild the camp into a kingdom of terror twice as awful as what it had been, Heydrich felt hollow inside.

"Thank you for saving me back there, Engel," Heydrich sighed, tossing Jonas' gun aside. "Let's clean up. I want to go home."

FOURTEEN

"He's doing all right?"

"Well...his wound's healed. He hasn't said much."

"I don't blame him."

"Serves him right."

"Two-Five-Eight...."

"All the shit he's done, he deserves to lose someone."

Bitterly, Jonas Amsel found himself agreeing. It was just like Papa Fox had said: his actions rebounded. How many fathers had he taken away? How many orphans had he created? He deserved to lose his father. And for that matter, his father, an architect who built factories of murder, deserved to die.

It was right. It was fair. But it still hurt. In Jonas' soul, he felt an aching emptiness, like a part of his heart had been torn from his body. Bad enough he had lost his father, but he couldn't even shed a tear for him without feeling a tsunami of guilt. *He built the Fox Farm. He built so many camps and ghettos. He made you a Nazi. He sent Ava away. Whatever Heydrich gave him, he deserved it.*

All true, but Dieter had still made eight-year-old Jonas a little village from his spare models. He had still taken care of Jonas when he broke his leg. He'd still laughed at Jonas when he'd had his first drink at thirteen. He'd still helped Jonas learn to ride a horse. A lifetime of unrepentant Nazism could not render those memories meaningless to Jonas, no more than his own activities as the Fox Hunter could make Ava dismiss him as a monster.

He almost wished that the Black Foxes would put him back in his room so he could be by himself, but they had decided that Jonas' actions at the Fox Farm made him worthy of being cared for with the rest of them. They had returned to the Bunker, which had never been so crowded. The injured lay on cots in the middle of the main chamber while the rest of the resistance fighters scrambled about, trying to figure out what to do and where to go.

Jonas took comfort in the chaos, which was as jovial as it was stressful. Children of Black Foxes skittered after Eight-Sixty. Heidi Naden was quickly coming out of her gloomy shell as the others welcomed her into the flock, either ignorant of her father's murderous identity or simply deciding not to foist the father's sins upon the daughter. Occasionally, Jonas would see little Aliza admiring Heydrich's dagger, swinging at the air and pretending to slash at the Hangman's throat before One-Twenty came by and quietly ordered her to put it away before Eight-Sixty saw and confiscated it.

Familiar faces jumped out at him: faces he had once sneered at as he arrested them were now alight with joy as they reunited with comrades. While most of the escapees from the Fox Farm had merely regarded Jonas with suspicion bordering on barely concealed disgust, a few had actually thanked him for his actions.

"I'm glad you changed," one of them whispered, and that was like a dagger to the heart. Jonas regretted almost nothing from the Fox Farm operation except that he hadn't saved his father. If Dieter could have escaped with them, he could have changed too. The Major had done a brave thing at the Fox Farm, but had he changed? No. He had almost certainly died a National Socialist. And now it was too late for Dieter Amsel to see that he had been lied to.

Jonas thought of the eye graffiti in the Bunker's entrance hall. The visual came unbidden and made a shudder wrack his body. He glanced to his side, at a small pile of books from the shelf in his former cell. He had been scouring the holy tomes, trying to decipher what Jews believed about the afterlife, about the punishment that awaited men like the Amsels when they passed. There didn't seem to be one single answer, nothing as simple as a lake of fire. In some schools of Judaic thought, there was a furnace that cleansed souls of their sin, and in others there was simply an eternal void. Jonas could only pray that the latter wasn't reality.

"Jonas..."

A familiar voice made strange through turmoil interrupted his ruminations. Jonas smiled at Gisela Keller as she sat before him, her dark eyes shimmering with the same maternal concern she had offered him when he was little and would show off a scraped knee.

In six years, it seemed that Gisela had aged twenty: her dark hair was streaked with silver, lines of worry were etched onto her face, and she was awfully skinny from her many years as Heydrich's prisoner. Nevertheless, there was a brightness to her eyes. Not precisely the vicious vivacity of her daughter, but a light of hope. Jonas and Gisela hadn't gotten a chance to talk very much since they had been reunited, but when they had, Gisela had declared that she was proud of him.

"Hi, Frau Keller," Jonas said, greeting her as he always had. She chuckled.

"You really should just call me Gisela. I suppose you'll be calling me Mama one day anyway."

"If Ava will still have me."

"She will. Have you seen the look she's been giving you? I'm proud of her, but she's *truly* proud of you."

"I don't think I deserve that..." Jonas muttered, his gunshot wound suddenly burning. Gisela put a hand on her future son-in-law's arm.

"You wouldn't feel that way if you didn't," she declared. "My parents really tried to drill that Talmud nonsense into my head. Did my best to forget most of it, but I remember one quote. Something to the effect of 'repentance turns an intentional sin into a mere stumbling.'"

"Do you still hate Judaism?" Jonas queried. "Ava's taken a liking to it."

"And *you've* taken a liking to it?" Gisela mused, her eyes flitting to the little pile of books stacked at Jonas' bedside.

"I don't believe in fairytales about talking snakes and splitting seas, but there are parts of it that I agree with having read it. Rosenberg and the SS just invented fake quotes whole-cloth to make us hate it and hate Jews by extension...but you *actually* grew up with it."

"Yes, well...a version of it. An awful version of it. There are six-hundred and thirteen commandments, and my parents expected us to perform each one thoroughly. That being said, I was sixteen when I ran away from home and met Otto. Teenagers, you know, they're not precisely well-known for seeing shades of grey. For a very long time, even hearing a word of Hebrew was traumatic for me."

"And now?"

"I suppose you could call Theresienstadt forcible therapy in that regard. The only Jews I knew before were my family and congregation. The worst sort. I thought it was a black-and-white choice: freedom and secularism with the Germans, or forced marriages and shame with the Jews. But there are all sorts of Jews in the world. Even some of the more religious ones aren't all terrible. That One-Twenty fellow, he can quote every book of the Torah yet he's a reasonable man. When I was in Theresienstadt by myself, there were Jews of all sorts, some good, some bad, and I would have never survived without the good, even with Heydrich trying to keep me alive."

"I know you don't want to think about it, but...I'm curious why you never told your husband, at least," Jonas said. "He was a National Socialist. Why didn't you tell him? Or Ava? She was marrying an SS man, you must have known *someone* would find out..."

"At worst, I figured Ava and the boys would be counted as half-breeds. I thought it would be a problem, but not a deadly problem," Gisela whispered, clutching her heart. "Unhappy coincidence that Otto happened to be a blood Jew too. *I* didn't even know that. Maybe it was for the best, though: how many people would be dead now if Ava was a happy Nazi housewife and you were still serving Heydrich?"

"Gisela..." Jonas reached out and gripped her shoulder. She batted his comforting hand away and offered a smile.

"I'm proud of you for many reasons," Gisela declared. "Because you proved me wrong. I didn't tell Otto because I loved him, and I was worried that his love would be condi-

227

tional. I worried he would hate me if he found out. When he *did* find out, he was furious. We barely talked until..."

She bit her lip and shook her head. "When everything happened with Dieter, Ava was tempted to go to you, but I told her not to because I was afraid for her. But your love for her was more powerful than your hate for Jews. For that, no matter what else you've done, I'm proud of you."

"I'm proud of you, too."

"Bärchen!" Jonas exclaimed, smiling at Ava as she appeared before him. She had eschewed her gas mask, giving her a chance to offer both Jonas and Gisela a dazzling grin.

"Dummi," she said, her voice bright. Ava stretched out her hand and he grasped it. When she leaned forward and planted a kiss on his lips, he was surprised and slightly flustered—several Black Foxes stared, a few children including Aliza gagged, but nobody scowled. Feeling a surge of boldness, Jonas returned the kiss.

"Need to borrow him for a moment, Mama," Ava said once she broke away from him. She pulled her fiancé to his feet.

They set off towards the Bunker entrance, smiling as they looked at the new graffiti that the children had left on the walls and averting their eyes from the warning and the flaming eye. Once they were out of the Bunker, Ava dragged her fiancé to a small radio set resting under the living tree that guarded the hidden entrance to their old hideaway.

Jonas glanced at Ava, who offered him a radiant smile. A million stars of pride shimmered in her night-black eyes, and he had never felt freer. Whatever the Black Foxes decided to do with him, it was worth it.

"Hello," the former Fox Hunter said into the receiver, and a familiar voice, the one he had been forced to listen to on the radio for weeks, replied with a chuckle.

"If it isn't our worst enemy," said Papa Fox. *"One's told me a lot about you."*

"I imagine she's been too kind, sir..."

"No, she mostly called you a dummy."

"Ah...that's fair. That's Ava," Jonas gave her a look that was half a scowl, half a fond smile. She punched his arm, and he barely held in a small grunt of pain.

"But she also told me about that stunt you two pulled. If you'd bothered to ask my permission, I'd have laughed in her face and then shot you myself."

"S-Sorry, sir..."

"But ain't that the beautiful thing about the Black Foxes? We're not the SS, and I'm not the Führer. If we'd done things my way, the Fox Farm would be operational and all the people that are free would be worse than dead. So...maybe I judged you too harshly."

"No, no, I deserved everything you said about me, sir..."

"Quit callin' me, sir, Amsel, it's nauseating. Gedaliah's about to bust a gut listening to you simper like that."

"Gedaliah's there? Tell him I said hi!" Ava chirped.

"Ava says hi to Gedaliah," sighed Jonas.

"One! What have I told you about eavesdropping?!"

"Sorry, pops," Ava cackled.

"Regardless: Gedaliah's here, and he's the forgiving sort. Between him and Ava, and considering what you've done, I think some trust is in order. Most of my men and ladies won't like it, but you're an asset. You were willing to die to right some of your wrongs, and in doing so, you lost something. Gedaliah says that the price of sin is sacrifice. The only thing I want to know is this: are you willing to sacrifice even more?"

"Yes, s—Papa Fox," Jonas declared, gripping the receiver

tightly and glancing at Ava, giving her a smile. "For Ava and to make things better, I'll do whatever it takes."

"Well, then, Jonas Amsel, I never thought I'd say this, but welcome to the Black Foxes."

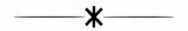

"THIS IS A DISASTER!"

"I'm well aware, Doctor Goebbels, I just want to know how we're going to resolve this..."

"Resolve this?! There's no resolving this, Heydrich! You're lucky that everyone had their hands in the Fox Farm! You're lucky the Führer is blaming the Amsels and not you! Himmler won't stop calling me!"

Reinhard Heydrich typically regarded Panenské Břežany as a sanctuary of sorts: no work that he didn't wish to do would follow him beyond the guarded gates. He could settle down, relax, and didn't have to deal with Joseph Goebbels.

The Fox Farm incident, however, was such a disastrous affair that Heydrich had been sitting in his home office for what felt like an eternity, listening to the hysterical propagandist and continuously casting his gaze out the window, taking comfort in the cheerful squeals of Klaus and Heider as they played out in the garden. He wished he could simply hang up on Goebbels and forget the whole affair, go outside and join their silly games, but he had responsibilities. Black Foxes to catch and, alongside Goebbels, an agenda to reinforce to the masses.

"Black Fox Radio won't be quiet about it," Heydrich grumbled. "What's the messaging on our end?"

"We're lucky that we never actually got an opportunity to

spread word of the Fox Farm, so we're going to play it off as a small detention center and nothing more. I think we should add that the Black Foxes used children as human shields. What do you think?"

"Fair," Heydrich said, the mention of children drawing his eyes to the window. Klaus had Heider in a headlock. The younger boy squirmed and turned blue, but Klaus refused to show mercy until his brother choked out a surrender. Heydrich smiled fondly.

"We'll play it down. Anyone who mentions the incident will be harshly rebuked," Goebbels said. "In the meantime, there's the matter of Amsels."

"Apparently, Jonas Amsel's joined the Black Foxes," Heydrich hissed, turning away from the window and setting his gaze on a portrait of Hitler hanging on the opposite wall. The Führer's frozen, intense blue eyes bore into him in a way that they typically didn't.

"I'm going to put out a reward for his head," Heydrich said, and Goebbels let out a noise like an offended chicken.

"No! No, you will not!" squawked the propaganda minister, his voice so onerous that Heydrich held the receiver slightly away from his ear.

Lina Heydrich opened his office door right then, peeking her head in, her blue eyes widening with worry when she saw her husband's disgruntled expression. Reinhard offered her a smile and pointed to the receiver. *Goebbels*, he mouthed with a roll of his eyes. She smiled and slunk in, shutting the door behind her.

"Listen to me: the Amsels, especially Jonas, they're too well-known. We've had over a dozen newsreels made about Jonas Amsel!" Goebbels shouted so loudly that even Lina winced. "What *exactly* do you think the masses will think if they hear that he turned traitor?! What about our men?! We've held him up as an example, and now our example has joined the Black Foxes! People will wonder *why* he switched sides. People will *ask questions.*"

Heydrich let out a small, affirmative grunt. Lina slunk behind him, cradling her swelling belly with one hand and affectionately massaging his shoulder with the other. Reinhard glanced up at her and didn't smile but gave her a soft look that communicated he was grateful for her presence.

"As far as we're concerned, Jonas and Dieter Amsel both died at the Fox Farm. Anyone claiming to be him is a liar spreading enemy nonsense, a fraud," Goebbels declared. "The reputation of the Amsels as National Socialists *must* be preserved. I don't care if that means you have to attend their funeral and lay a wreath of gold on their graves: the message is going to be that they died for the Cause. Understood?"

Again, Heydrich grunted in agreement. It would hurt his pride, but for the Cause he would do it. A small part of him was ruefully amused. *Well, Dieter, I suppose you get to die a National Socialist after all.*

"Himmler is going to make sure that the SS officers who were there know the protocol," Goebbels continued. "In the meantime, even disregarding the Amsels, we have a morale problem. No matter how much we play this down, it will spread to the other men in the camps and ghettos. It was relatively harmless when the Black Foxes only smuggled Jews out of the Reich, but we've never had an attack on that scale from them before. We all need to reassure the men in the camps and ghettos that they have nothing to fear."

"Already taking care of that," Heydrich declared. "I'll be attending a party for some of the guards and kommandants outside Theresienstadt tonight."

Reinhard felt Lina squeeze him tightly and heard her let out a little sound of discomfort.

"Good," Goebbels said. "Do that, try not to scare them. Get in, improve morale, get out."

"You don't trust me to be charismatic, Doctor?" Heydrich asked, his tone almost verging on impish.

"I have work to do, *Reichsprotektor!*" sighed the Propagandist. "Heil Hitler!"

"Heil Hitler," Heydrich replied, hanging up. Hardly had he done so when Lina spoke up, her voice tinged with worry.

"Do you *really* have to go to that party?" she asked. "It's next to the Ghetto. Someone could..."

"No Jew would be suicidal enough to sneak *into* a gala of SS officers, Lina," Reinhard assured his wife, grabbing her hand and squeezing tightly. "Nothing will happen."

"You said the same thing about the Fox Farm, and you said the same thing when Himmler yelled at you about driving around without an armored car..."

"Lina, *schatzi*, the Fox Farm was a fluke, and my Czechs wouldn't dare hurt me," he assured her, saying "my Czechs" like they were trained hounds and nudging his head in the direction of the servants' quarters.

"You worry me, you know. You're so reckless sometimes," Lina sighed, placing a hand on her belly. "I don't want the children to grow up hearing *about* you instead of *knowing* you. I don't want to have the baby without you..."

"Ah, you just want to put me through the trauma again. My arm *still* hurts from where you grabbed me when Klaus was born," Reinhard joked, patting her stomach and letting his eyes flit towards the window, landing on his eldest son. Lina snickered.

"You don't get the right to complain about that, you volunteered!" she said. "And you didn't seem traumatized at the time. I remember you even helped the doctor cut the cord. *I* was the one who was traumatized."

"Serves you right for insisting on an at-home birth, Lina," Reinhard teased. "Klaus was just teaching you a lesson."

"Heider was easier. Heider is *still* easier. The hospitals in Prague are decent, right?" She sounded nervous. Reinhard stood, kissed her forehead, and patted her shoulders.

"We'll fly in a proper German doctor for the baby," he promised.

"I just hope we don't have to fly in a proper German doctor for *you*," Lina said, her tone teasing, but still carrying with it a lilt of concern.

"I'm *fine*, Lina! All this worrying can't be good for the baby. Go sit with the boys and relax."

"Sitting with the boys and relaxing do *not* go together, love," Lina chuckled. "Be careful tonight, all right?"

"Just for you."

That assurance satisfied Heydrich's worried wife for the moment, and she left him to do his work.

A few hours later, Heydrich stood before a mirror, adjusting his uniform. Mirrors were an old enemy of his. When he had been little and committed some sort of sin, real or imagined, his mother would force him to stand before the mirror, sometimes for up to an hour, staring at his own pathetic, sniveling reflection and repeating over and over again: "I am a sinner, I am a sinner..."

He lingered before the reflective plane out of necessity: he had to look perfect, as perfect as he could. His uniform had to be perfect, his medals correct, not one hair out of place. Anything less would be a flaw, a sin, an opening for attack. The absence of his ring made his hands tingle, made him feel incomplete, like a small part of his soul had been ripped away, but he would have to bear it until Himmler sent him a replacement.

Just as he was about to step away from the mirror, convinced that he looked like the perfect National Socialist that he was, a sound struck his ears.

A scream.

Silke!

Heydrich barely felt himself move as adrenaline pumped through his body. His death's-head cap flew off his head as he ran out of his room, shoving a maid out of the way as he burst into his daughter's room, one hand on his sidearm.

A cursory glance about the nursery revealed that nothing was out of place. Silke was curled up in her crib, her back against the gate, sobbing wildly. Sighing, Reinhard forced his pounding pulse to slow and scooped his daughter into his arms.

"Papa!" Silke yelped, crying into his shoulder. It was an awful sound, her sobs: each one tore at him worse than any bullet, stirring paternal protectiveness in his heart.

"Shhh, shhh," Reinhard muttered, stroking the back of her head. "Don't cry, my girl, it's all right, you're safe, I'm here, shhh…"

When Silke had calmed down enough to release her grip around his neck, she leaned back a bit, wiping her eyes with her little hands and then pointing towards the closet.

"There's a monster," she squeaked pitifully. Reinhard smiled, kissed her cheek, and set her back down in her crib.

"Don't worry, sweetheart. Papa will scare away all the monsters," he vowed, patting her cheek and wiping a stream of tears away with his thumb. She gazed up at him with her wide, adoring blue eyes that always made him putty in her little hands. He could only get such affection from his little girl: pure, untainted, unconditional, *safe*.

Reinhard marched towards her closet with a purpose, like he was investigating a Black Fox hideout, smiling as he felt her concerned gaze upon his back. He strode into the closet and pretended to thoroughly search about before he turned and grinned at his child.

"No monsters in here," he assured her. "They must have run away when I came in. Monsters are afraid of Papa, you know."

Silke smiled widely and nodded, letting out a little sigh of relief. Reinhard strode back to her and coaxed her under the covers.

"Sleep now," he commanded gently, brushing her messy blonde locks from her face. "Nothing is going to hurt you."

"M'kay..." yawned Silke. "I love you."

"I love you too, *kleine*," he declared, kissing her head and slowly tiptoeing out of her room.

For Silke's sake, he was late. He ran back to his room, hastily tried to change into a uniform without wrinkles or tearstains, and in his haste to run to the car, he ended up grabbing the first pocket watch he found in the drawer. Heydrich sat in the back of the car and paused to catch his breath, sparing a small smile and a wave at the two grass-pickers who enthusiastically Heiled him as he passed them by in his open-topped Mercedes. After he greeted the Czechs, however, Heydrich decided to check the time and realized that he had made a mistake.

He held the pocket watch in his hand. The watch engraved with his personal rune. The watch that Dieter had given him. Heydrich had been too overwhelmed with trying to clean up the Amsels' mess and had forgotten to dispose of it.

A part of him was tempted to chuck it out the side of the car, let one of the grass-pickers have it, but Lina would never forgive him for being so wasteful. It *was* silver, after all. Perhaps he could scrap it for parts, though that seemed beneath him. It bore his rune, so regifting wouldn't do.

Heydrich opened the watch and winced when he beheld himself in the reflection offered by the shimmering glass face. His many minutes spent before the mirror had been wasted because of his child's imaginations: his hair was ever so slightly messy, his uniform not perfectly pressed, his medals crooked. Heydrich smirked a little recalling his daughter's wide, worshipful eyes. It would be worth looking a little imperfect for her. Silke took precedence over everything.

Even your duties? A treasonous little voice that sounded a bit too much like Dieter Amsel teased him from the corners of his mind. Heydrich felt his heart of iron fracture as he recalled Dieter's relieved smile in the burning Fox Farm. *I'll choose my child over my nation, always.*

Questions Reinhard hadn't answered echoed about his brain unbidden as he stared down at the little watch. Imaginations of his own took hold as Silke's frantic sobbing echoed in his ears. Silke standing in the fiery ruins of the Fox Farm. His girl being pursued by monsters of a different sort, the sort that he wasn't already fighting. Blue, burning Hitlerian eyes turning wrathfully upon her.

What would you do? Dieter had asked. *What would you choose?*

His child. He would choose her. He would tear Hitler limb from limb if he ever hurt her. He would burn the Reich to the ground to protect his little girl.

Reinhard felt the iron encasing his heart crack at the treasonous thought. *It will never happen*, he told himself. *Whatever that fool Papa Fox says. It's all hypotheticals and what-ifs.*

But still, he knew what his choice would be, and that knowledge invited an accusation. *Hypocrite*, a voice decreed in his head, at first his own, but then different, familiar and frightening but strangely quiet. **Hypocrite.**

Heydrich pushed it down, buried it, silenced it. He stored it in a little forgotten space in his mind where he would store it for the rest of the night. He forced himself to forget, becoming the Man with the Iron Heart again.

EPILOGUE

"**B**lack Fox One! You're back! Is the ball-and-chain dead yet?"

"No, Fifty-Six, he's still here," chuckled Ava as she descended into the safehouse basement, tearing her gas mask from her face and beaming at her comrade. "He's just checking the perimeter."

"He's so particular, it's the SS in him," Black Fox 56 sighed, slapping Ava's shoulder. "Drop-off went well?"

"They'll be in Switzerland by the evening. Jonas got us out of a bind with some guards, funniest shit I've ever seen. Apparently, the SS have all been told that Jonas is dead, so he literally pretended to be a ghost and scared them off. He'll tell you about it when he gets down."

"Much as I wanna hear about that, we've got bigger news: don't suppose you heard what happened to Heydrich?"

"Heydrich?"

"Ah, there he is!" Ava laughed. Jonas Amsel descended into the safehouse, shutting the door behind him. The former Fox Hunter was bedecked in a uniform much like that of his fiancée: black garments, a black hood, and a gas mask. He tore the mask off, offering the Dutch Black Fox a worried expression.

"What happened with Heydrich?" Jonas asked, shoving a hand into his pocket and running his gloved fingers over the runes of the *ehrenring* he'd stolen from the Hangman. "Is he on our tail?"

"Oooh, no!" laughed Fifty-Six, and Jonas felt the worry in his chest evaporate when he saw the grin on his comrade's face: news about Heydrich never elicited a smile, which could only mean that something deservedly awful had happened to the Butcher of Prague.

"We don't have much info right now," said Fifty-Six, leading the couple away from the front door and towards the rest of their comrades. "But he got hit a few days ago on his way to his office."

"By us?" Ava asked, grasping Jonas' hand and squeezing. Fifty-Six shook his head.

"Czech resistance, not affiliated," the Dutch Black Fox explained. "Again, we don't know much, but we *do* know that he's been in the hospital for a little over a week."

"So he's not dead?" Ava sighed in disappointment.

"Papa Fox just said he's receiving more info..."

"Shut up, all of you!"

Jonas, his fiancée, and Fifty-Six entered the main chamber and were immediately yelled at by One-Twenty, who was huddled closest to the radio, scowling at the speakers as they offered only a static rendition of *Anything Goes*. A few of the other Black Foxes, including Eight-Sixty, offered Ava a quiet greeting as she entered, but only Eight-Sixty gave Jonas a smile. Most of the Black Foxes were still reasonably mistrusting, and while at Papa Fox's insistence they had allowed him to become a comrade, it would take more than one or two missions for the former Fox Hunter to truly earn their trust.

Nevertheless, they were willing to give him a seat at the table metaphorically and literally: they scooted over, giving Jonas and Ava a spot by the radio. Gisela kissed her daughter and future son-in-law, and the three of them sat amongst the anxious Black Foxes, awaiting news of the Hangman's fate.

Finally, after the last cheery note of *Anything Goes* ended and the Black Foxes were beginning to squirm with impatience, Papa Fox's voice made them all lean in. His tone spoke volumes: boisterous and relieved.

*"Kits and kittens, do I ever have news for the lot of you. I mentioned before the last song that we were about to receive a report on the condition of our old pal, Billy-Goat Heydrich, the Butcher of Prague. Or should I say the **former** Butcher of Prague? Ladies and gentlemen, kits and kittens, Europe is short one shithead today courtesy of the incredible bravery of a few Czech partisans. Ding dong, the Hangman is dead!"*

Papa Fox's next few sentences were drowned out by the applause of the Black Foxes. Hats were tossed into the air, shots were downed, and Ava yanked Jonas into a celebratory smooch that sent a bolt of fire shooting through his body.

"He's dead!" Ava cried happily, tears gathering at the corners of her eyes. "That fucker's dead!"

Gisela was sobbing and laughing all at once, clutching her heart as the knowledge that her sons and husband had been avenged made joy course through her body. Jonas unleashed a sigh of relief and wrapped an arm around Ava's shoulders. It wasn't the fall of the Reich, but it was a step closer to victory. He and Ava wouldn't have to worry about the Hangman hunting them down any more.

Jonas kissed Ava's forehead and shoved his hand into his

pocket, chuckling when his fingers found the grinning skull of the stolen *ehrenring*.

"I'm keeping this ring," he whispered in Ava's ear. "I stole it from him and only a few weeks later he finally goes down..."

"Hell of a lucky charm, but I won't stop you!" Ava giggled, patting his wrist. "Just don't you fucking dare try to propose with that shit."

"What do you take me for, the Fox Hunter?" Jonas joked, stealing one more kiss before the Black Foxes' jubilations calmed down and One-Twenty, who seemed strangely pissed-off despite the good news, shouted for everyone to shut up so he could hear.

"*Now, ladies and gents,*" Papa Fox continued. "*I'd usually follow up the program with some classics, but for news as good as this, well, I think this calls for a special treat. You all get to hear me sing.*"

"Oh, *this* I have to hear!" Ava laughed in that vicious way she had when she was a little girl ready and raring to tease Bruno Ackerman for having a big nose.

"He's got a good voice!" Jonas argued.

"Yeah, for speaking!" Ava snickered, but evidently Papa Fox must have practiced since she had last heard him sing ("Being fair, when I heard him sing, he was pretty drunk," she would say later in an attempt to defend her previously disparaging tone.) When Papa Fox sang, his voice was melodic as ever.

Gisela hiccupped as she sang along. One-Twenty, lips thin, sat with a disappointed faraway expression, refusing to utter a word even when Eight-Sixty scurried over and sat beside him, quietly conversing. Ava and Jonas held hands and joined the rest of their comrades in singing with Papa Fox, celebrating the death of the Man with the Iron Heart.

"Ladies and gentlemen, let's say farewell
To Heydrich the Hangman who's burning
    in Hell
That chained-up Czech lion broke free and
    rebelled
And sent that damn Butcher
Straight down into Hell..."

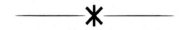

"CONGRATULATIONS, YOU'RE DEAD."

The shift from sleep to death was a slow one for Reinhard Heydrich. First, he was drifting in a drug-induced stupor, his thoughts flitting from his children to his nation, from his father to how much it hurt but how little he wanted to seem weak.

Then, briefly, a pain which was intense enough to break through his tolerance. Like something was being ripped from his brain and his chest all at once.

Then, there was darkness, a suffocating sensation like someone had shoved a pillow in front of his face. If he had been capable of cognitive thought, he might have been concerned that one of the Czech hospital staff had finished him off when no one was looking. He felt like his brain was filled with cotton, like he was nothing more than a thoughtless stuffed animal.

And then he was standing in a white room, ruffled and bloody, strangely enough back in the uniform that he had been wearing when the Czechs had attacked him (he cursed himself for sparing those damn grass-pickers.)

A woman—at least he *thought* that it was a woman judging

by her voice—sat at a small desk in front of him, bedecked in a grey cloak and hood with a warped mirror mask covering her face. Heydrich faced his own distorted reflection, and the pain left him right away, replaced with a keen sense that he was in danger.

Heydrich's instincts took hold, and he quickly surveyed his new environment: white marble floors, a banner featuring an eye with a flame for a pupil hanging above the woman's head.

Escape route, he thought, and he swiftly found the one available door: decorated with two golden triangles, one pointing up and the other down, and guarded by two petite figures bedecked in red hooded cloaks and mirror masks. The child-sized guards seemed to only have wooden swords for weapons. While arrogance told him that he could easily over-power such miniscule soldiers, something about them made Heydrich hesitate to bolt. It felt like they were living tornadoes of fire whose power was only barely restricted.

Toot!

The grey-cloaked woman drew his attention away from the duo of scarlet guardians as she suddenly tossed a handful of confetti in his face and blew on a floating party horn. Heydrich side-stepped the colorful paper and scowled viciously at the woman, but she didn't look up, continuing to read off a little slip of paper pinched between her fingers despite the fact that her mask should have rendered her blind.

"Your emotional state is very important to us, Soul Number 5664-788206109107738, aka Reinhard Tristan Eugen Heydrich..."

The angel in grey lifted up her chin, finally looking upon the deceased Butcher of Prague.

"Oh, damn," she said, and a small part of Reinhard

Heydrich was proud: his reputation evidently preceded him even in the halls of the afterlife.

That satisfaction was short-lived, however, as the woman swept the papers off her desk and slammed her gloved hand on a red button. "Cherubs!" she snapped.

Heydrich felt a burst of warmth and turned just in time to see the two red-cloaked guards draw their wooden swords from their sheaths. That alone might have merely snatched an amused chuckle from the Hangman, but then silver fire erupted from the creatures' fingertips. They drew their hands along the blades of their weapons, and the wooden swords became engulfed in an unearthly silver flame.

Heydrich might have been able to escape if there had only been one: he narrowly dodged a swipe from the first and made for the triangle-clad door, but the Cherub's partner struck him with its flaming sword and...

Pain pain pain worse than anything worse than having a soul ripped from its body hurts hurts can't breathe smell of almonds and sweat and something so awful and pungent can't breathe hurts can't see crushing hurts hurts hurts can't breathe can't breathe please just let me breathe can't...

"Husk status negative."

"You're kidding! *He* has a *yetzer hatov*?!"

And then he was back in the white room, kneeling and shivering like a newborn puppy as the echoes of a pain worse than anything he could have ever imagined wracked his soul. For a moment, the Hangman was too disoriented to do anything more than take deep, desperate breaths.

What was that? Heydrich thought as he finally looked up. The Cherubs' swords were no longer on fire. They sheathed their weapons and returned to their posts. Two more angels had come into the room, both bedecked in blue cloaks, wearing mirror masks just like the others and holding lanterns filled with silver fire.

The woman at the desk sighed, threw up her hands, and gave a dismissive wave. In the blink of an eye, the two angels in blue were gone.

"What...?" Heydrich finally managed to gasp, pain ebbing into anger as he snarled at the angel in grey. "*What* is going on?"

The angel in grey tilted her head sideways. He wished that he could see her expression, get a hint at what she was thinking, but the mirror shielding her face only allowed him to view himself. The reflection that had been slightly distorted became clearer for a fraction of a second.

His reflection smiled. He didn't.

"Friend...you're about to *wish* you felt nothing," the angel said, and though he would never admit it, the Man with the Iron Heart was absolutely terrified.

To be continued in *Adiel and the Führer*.

SAMPLE CHAPTER
ADIEL AND THE FÜHRER

Adiel Goldstein had always wanted a little brother. A little sister would do too. Really, he just wanted a friend.

But his mother Rebecca would sigh sadly every time he requested a brother or a sister, and his father Natan would smirk and say that one Adiel was plenty.

Every birthday, Adiel begged for a sibling, and every year he was rebuffed, given a fancy toy or more paints instead. Which was all well and good, but toys were less fun without anyone to play with, and paints were pointless when there was nobody to paint for.

In a better world, Adiel wouldn't have been so lonely. The village they lived in was small, but there were plenty of children. In a better world, Adiel, ever eager for companionship, would have been swimming in friends.

But Adiel was the only Jewish child in the village. And in the last years of the 1800s, even in a nation as cultured as Germany, being a Jew made him an outcast. At best, he was offered a cold shoulder. At worst, he was driven away with stones and jeers whenever he tried to approach a group of boys his age. Even little children three years his junior had been trained by their parents to spit on the kippa-clad boy when he drew near.

But today...today was the day before Adiel's seventh birthday, and he was hoping beyond hope that today would be the day that he would finally make a friend.

A new family had finally moved into the house next door: the Goldsteins lived in a manor that stretched and stretched so far that it was almost a five-minute walk from the edge of their property to their front door. Beyond the trimmed bushes that surrounded the Goldsteins' estate, however, there was a run-down old ramshackle cottage, a structure that might have once been servants' quarters but had evidently been sold separately. Nobody had lived there before. Nobody wanted to, and the little village so rarely had new people move in.

But today the little house was a home again; home to a pudgy couple that had a golden-haired boy Adiel's age. A child potentially uncorrupted by the ancient hatred permeating the rest of the village.

Adiel's plan was seemingly foolproof, his weapons carefully chosen. First, a drawing, painstakingly painted with all of his best and most colorful paints that showed himself, helpfully labeled "Adiel," and the new blond boy, labeled as "Adiel's Best Friend." Additionally, he had carried out a fair amount of reconnaissance and had deduced that his target loved mud and cars, and so he'd selected his best, shiniest toy car as an offering.

Adiel was ready. His heart was pounding so hard that it felt like it was going to combust, his little hands were so sweaty that he feared he would smudge his beautiful picture, but he was ready. He told his mother that he would be out playing and began his journey.

Eventually, Adiel spotted his target: the apple-cheeked, sunny-haired new boy covered in mud and sporting ripped-up lederhosen. He was kneeling in the dirt and making engine noises as he smashed two hastily constructed wooden cars together.

Adiel knew that he would lose heart if he hesitated, so he made sure his kippa was straight, checked his picture to make sure it was still beautiful, and then marched right up to the boy. The new neighbor looked up with bright, curious blue eyes almost the exact same shade as Adiel's, and the Jewish boy blurted out his practiced introduction in one breath.

"Hi, I'm Adiel and I live next to you, and I like drawing, and tomorrow's my birthday, and I drew you this picture and got you this car, do you wanna be my best friend?"

In the future, when he was old and accomplished enough that childhood memories were less painful, he would laugh, remembering this bungled word-vomit. The way he tried to sell himself like a desperate worker, the way he shoved his painting at the boy like he was offering a resume. The kippa on his head felt like it was scalding his skull, but the neighbor boy only gave it a cursory glance before his eyes fell on the toy car that Adiel offered.

"Okay!" squeaked the neighbor boy, grabbing the car with a smile. "Can I play with the nice car first? I made a track, but if we're gonna have a race, we've gotta make it wider. Oh, and I'm Rupert."

Adiel's little heart soared to new heights. That moment would be bitter in the future because he would know that it ranked among the times he had been happiest. Right up there with the day his wife agreed to marry him, the day she *did* marry him, and the day she would give him a daughter that would be his real best friend.

But right then, six-year-old Adiel, who had never gotten love from anyone except his parents, felt like he wasn't even touching the ground. And it didn't matter that he didn't particularly like playing in the mud, and it didn't matter that his drawing would probably get dirty. He was prepared to kneel down and build an amazing racetrack with his brand-new best friend.

"Rupert!"

But then a woman's voice broke through the birdsong and the happy buzzing in his ears. The joyous moment came crashing down as Rupert's mother emerged from the tiny house, wearing an expression that Adiel knew too well. It was the expression that he saw on the face of nearly every gentile in the village every day.

"Rupert!" the woman said, grabbing her son by the arm and wrenching him to his feet. She pried the toy car from her son's grimy fingers, and though the blond boy argued and whined, she tossed it at the slack-jawed six-year-old Jew's feet.

"We do *not* associate with Christ-killers! Don't you remember what I told you? Jews like him kill good little Christian boys and drink their blood!"

And there, the seed was planted. Perhaps in the past, when Rupert had been warned about the evil of Jewry, he hadn't listened because it was a vague threat, like the threat of cavities if he didn't brush his teeth. But now it was real, solid. Adiel was right there, flesh and blood, and Rupert looked at him with wide-eyed fear.

Adiel barely felt it when the woman spat on him, barely felt the dollop of spit dribble from his forehead down his face. He only vaguely heard her scream, "Go to Hell, Jew!"

But then Rupert giggled, stepped forward, and copied his mother, spitting and echoing her: "Go to Hell, Jew!"

It was then that numb sorrow became white hot fury, like Adiel was a pot that had been boiling too long and needed to explode.

"FINE!" Adiel screamed, and in two swift motions, he ripped the picture in half and kicked dirt right in the ugly, horrible woman's face before turning on his heel and running back to the Goldstein family's grand home.

Adiel was angry. *So* angry. He'd been angry before, but now he felt like something inside of him was straining, near snapping, like his soul was an overburdened horse and its spine was just about to *crack*. He *hated* that lady, and he *hated* Rupert, and he *hated* everyone in this village.

"I hate them!" Adiel screamed as he flew into the house, tears streaming from his face.

"*I hate them!*" he howled as he shoved a table over and sent a vase tumbling to the floor. It shattered. Breaking things helped. It felt like he was letting out the fire, and so he kept at it.

"*I hate them!*"

CRASH!

"*I! Hate! Them!*"

SMASH!

"I HATE THEM!"

Adiel was generally a well-behaved boy, and his parents were indulgent enough that he rarely threw a true tantrum. Not that he wasn't occasionally destructive; he was a six-year-old boy, after all, but his destruction typically served a purpose. When he had been three years old, for instance, he had torn up every pillow in the house so that he could cover himself in feathers and pretend to be the great Ziz Bird Monster of Jewish folklore, an action that had resulted in Natan dubbing his son "little monster."

Natan's epithet had never suited Adiel so well, however: the boy who typically only ever wanted to create set about in a torrent of destruction across his house. Bookshelves were toppled, fine china shattered, vases and decorative statues were hurled to the floor. He screamed and screamed and kept breaking things in a desperate attempt to make the fire in his heart fade.

But then he heard something: sobbing that wasn't his own.

The fire cooled into curiosity, and Adiel stopped himself from tossing a plate into a pile of broken shards. He perked up his ears. A woman was crying upstairs. Adiel realized right then that he must have been horribly loud, and yet his mother hadn't come down to investigate what he was doing.

"Mama...?" he muttered, worry and love quickly taking the place of anger and hate as he scrambled up the staircase. He followed the sound of sobbing all the way into his parents' room, noticing right away that his mother's walk-in closet was slightly open.

He peeked inside without announcing himself. Adiel had been inside the closet on occasion, mostly during bouts of hide-and-seek with his father. During such games, he had often noticed the presence of a large, ancient-looking wooden chest buried behind a few long dresses. Adiel had tried to open it once or twice, but his attempts had been unsuccessful, and he'd given up on the venture.

When Adiel peeked inside now, he realized that his mother was kneeling before the wide-open chest, looking inside and wailing wildly.

"Mama!" he squeaked, worrying that something inside the mysterious chest was somehow hurting his mother. He knew for a fact that parents weren't supposed to cry. Parents were invincible, and therefore, only a truly monstrous force could possibly make his lovely mother sob.

Becca Goldstein moved so quickly that, to Adiel, it seemed like time itself sped up: one moment she was kneeling before the chest, and then she was slamming the chest shut, locking it, standing up, and tucking the key into her apron.

"Adiel!" Becca cried, quickly wiping her tears away and offering him a wavering smile as she brushed her curly dark brown hair back into place. Adiel acted on his very first instinct, scurrying forward and throwing his arms around her.

"Mama, what happened?" he squeaked, patting himself down and huffing in disappointment when he realized that he didn't have a handkerchief in his pocket to offer her. "Please don't cry!"

"Ah, it's all right, sweetie, it's all right..." Becca muttered, her voice cracking slightly. "Mama was just thinking about sad things."

"Don't do that again, okay?" Adiel begged, squirming and clinging tightly to her apron, casting a frightened look at the chest that had somehow, as though via magic, made his ever-smiling mother cry. Becca let out a small, genuine laugh and ushered her son out of the closet.

"Yes, sir, Adiel, sir," she said, shutting the closet door behind her and then kneeling before him, brushing her thumb under his eye. "Looks like you were crying, too. Why were *you* crying?"

If his mother had been hoping to shift the subject away from whatever had made *her* cry, she was completely successful. A dreadful feeling even worse than fiery hatred welled up in Adiel's chest, like he was being weighed down by a thousand bricks. Guilt. His poor mother was already sad and crying, and he'd wrecked her house even though it wasn't her fault that nobody except her and Papa loved him, and now she'd be even more sad because she'd have to pick everything up, and she'd cry again, and it would be his fault, and...

And that was how they ended up downstairs, with Becca chuckling as she observed the wreckage left behind by her son's tantrum. She held the wailing boy in her arms as he blurted apologies.

"You really did a number on the place!" Becca giggled, carefully tiptoeing over broken shards of pottery and setting her son down in a cozy chair. She knelt down in front of him and offered the corner of her apron as a makeshift tissue. "No wonder Papa calls you little monster! Is this what you two do when I'm not at home?"

"Noooooo," hiccupped Adiel, blowing his nose on the apron. "I'm sorry, Mama! I got angry because the neighbor boy Rupert spat on me and called me a Christ-killer 'cause his mama ruined the friend-plan, and I *hate* her, and I *hate* him, and I *hate* them!"

Briefly, Adiel felt the fire flare again, but it was quenched when his mother shook her head with a gentle, chastising little smile decorating her now-dry face.

"See now, Adiel," Becca said in that voice she used whenever she needed to teach him something very important. "They shouldn't have done that. That was really terrible. And you definitely have a right to feel upset and sad about it. But anger and hate, you shouldn't ever feel anger or hate for anyone, no matter what. You see what happens when you do..."

She gestured to the Goldsteins' ruined home and shattered possessions. "See? You hurt yourself and the people you love first. Hatred, Adiel, it's a fire, and it burns you before it burns them."

Adiel reached up and touched his chest, nodding slowly.

She was right, of course; the evidence was all around him. He promised her right then that he would studiously avoid anger and hatred, and if he felt it spark in his soul again, he would extinguish it straight away. He never wanted to be the reason that his mother cried.

Becca happily accepted his apology and helped him get to work cleaning up. Natan Goldstein came home to an almost-clean house, but the investor nonetheless let out a low whistle as he stumbled into the living room and saw broken bits of china littering the floor.

"Hey, little monster, did a storm pass through here?" Natan quipped, tugging on the cuffs of his sweat-soaked shirt. Even though it was a warm spring day, Natan was wearing long-sleeves. Not out of any work-related obligation; Natan was such a talented investor that he probably could have shown up naked to work and they wouldn't have fired him. Adiel didn't know the reason he had never seen his father's bare arms, but he could only assume it was either simple personal preference or, more likely, modesty borne from a birthmark or scar that he wished to conceal.

Not that the almost seven-year-old cared, of course. Adiel would love his father no matter what, and right then, he only cared about Natan's feelings. Adiel ran up to his father, begging him not to cry and promising that he wouldn't get angry ever again. Becca gently explained what had happened.

"You're lucky I just made enough money to replace all this fancy stuff, little monster," chuckled Natan. "Or we'd have to cancel your birthday tomorrow and sell all your gifts."

"Natan!" cried Becca, rolling her eyes.

"We'd have to sell your birthday cake, too. Do we even have any plates left?"

ELYSE HOFFMAN

"I left a couple!" Adiel assured Natan, and his father teasingly tugged on one of Adiel's dark brown locks.

"Me and Mama are gonna eat all your cake," Natan joked. "You're gonna have to starve, little monster."

Natan did not, in fact, force Adiel to starve. The next day, they celebrated Adiel's seventh birthday with a big chocolate cake and a smattering of expensive toys. Natan and Becca also offered the boy good news: they would be moving within the week.

Adiel would remember the day before his seventh birthday, the pain of Rupert's rejection, long after they left behind the little village, long after they moved into a majority Jewish neighborhood where he finally made friends, where his neighbors treated him like a human being instead of a byword. He would always remember that day, and he would always remember his mother's counsel against anger and hatred.

Adiel Goldstein would follow his mother's guidance until the end of his life.

A NOTE TO MY READERS...

Thank you for reading *Black Fox One*! If you enjoyed it, please tell your friends. I'd love to hear your thoughts on *Black Fox One*, and reviews help authors a great deal, so I'd be very grateful if you would post a short review on Amazon and/or Goodreads. If you'd like to read more stories like this and get notifications about free and discounted books and short stories, follow me on Twitter, Facebook, Amazon, and sign up for my newsletter at elysehoffman.com! You can also follow me on Bookbub!

HISTORICAL NOTES:

While the Black Foxes, the Fox Farm, and the Amsels are fictional, Reinhard Heydrich is sadly not. Reinhard Tristan Eugen Heydrich (1904-1942) is often considered one the "darkest figures of the Nazi regime."[1] Heydrich began his murderous career as the chief of the *Sicherheitsdienst,* the intelligence wing of the initially miniscule SS.[2] However, Heydrich's duties soon expanded, and he became the executive director of the Gestapo in 1936.[3]

While Heydrich's crimes are extensive and sometimes bizarre (for example, the Salon Kitty brothel mentioned by Jonas in this novel did indeed exist and was indeed run by the Gestapo Chief)[4], Heydrich is most well remembered for his role in organizing the Holocaust.

During the early stages of the Holocaust, before the construction of the mass death camps such as Auschwitz and Treblinka, the Final Solution was primarily carried out by bullets.[5] The *Einsatzgruppen* mobile killing units roamed the Eastern Front, initially shooting political enemies and Jewish men, but eventually adding Jewish women and children to their killing roster.[6] Of the six million Jews who died during the Holocaust, about 1.3 million were killed by Heydrich's *Einsatzgruppen.*[7]

The *Einsatzgruppen,* however, was not Heydrich's only contribution to the massive scale of the Holocaust. On January 20th of 1942, Reinhard Heydrich chaired the infamous Wannsee Conference.[8] At this conference, the formal Nazi plans for the "Final Solution to the Jewish Question" were outlined. This was the conference where the Holocaust as it would come to be known—the deportation, subjugation, and ultimate murder en masse of Jews in concentration camps— became official Reich policy.[9] Heydrich, however, would barely live long enough to see this genocidal scheme implemented.

In September of 1941, Heydrich had been named the *Reichsprotektor* of occupied Bohemia and Moravia.[10] As the Nazi overseer of the occupied Czech lands, Heydrich set about subduing resistance with a combination of brutality and carrot-and-stick methods, offering jobs and increased rations to Czechs with "good race and good attitude."[11] However, the Czech government-in-exile decided that Heydrich, the Butcher of Prague, needed to be eliminated, and thus a plot was hatched to assassinate him.[12]

The details of the assassination, Operation Anthropoid, have been shown in many books and films. The two assassins who would ultimately ambush and attack Heydrich during his commute from Panenské Břežany to Prague Castle were Jan Kubiš and Jozef Gabčík. Both of these assassins were the "grass pickers" referenced earlier in this novel. As noted by Nancy Dougherty: "For weeks on end, Gabčik and Kubiš had loitered near Heydrich's country chateau, observing his movements. Openly, they picked grass by the roadside, for food was still scarce in Prague, and many Czechs grew rabbits to eat, fattening them up for the kill with free, country greenery. Bystanders often prudently retreated to their houses when the car of the Reich protector went by, but Kubiš and Gabčik 'always greeted Heydrich politely and with respect.'"[13]

Of course, this "respect" was a ruse, and Heydrich would ultimately be mortally wounded by the two brave resistance fighters.

Another historical note: the ship that Ava was on which went to America and was subsequently turned around is based upon the real, infamous history of the St. Louis. The St. Louis was a German ship whose passengers, over 900 in total, were seeking to escape Nazi Germany in 1939.[14]

The St. Louis initially tried to let its passengers seek safe harbor in Havana, Cuba only to be turned away. The ship was similarly turned away from the United States and Canada.[15] Ultimately, the St. Louis was forced to return to Europe, and the Jewish passengers sought refuge in Western Europe. This, of course, was only temporary salvation for many, and while some 288 passengers managed to escape to Great Britain, the rest scattered throughout France, Belgium, and the Netherlands. 254 would subsequently perish in the Holocaust.[16]

The incident that Ava recalls concerning the gentleman who slit his wrists is based upon the real history of the St Louis, where one passenger, Max Loewe, "slit his wrists and jumped overboard. Loewe, the recipient of an Iron Cross as a veteran of World War I, walked with a limp, the result of a severe beating at the hands of Nazi guards in Buchenwald. After landing in the waters of the port of Havana, Loewe was rescued by the Cuban police and taken to Calixto Garcia Hospital, where he remained when the St. Louis pulled out of the harbor on the morning of June 2."[17]

HISTORICAL NOTES:

1. Williams, M. (2018). *Heydrich: Dark Shadow of the SS* (1st ed.). Fonthill Media.
2. Gerwarth, R. (2012). *Hitler's Hangman: The Life of Heydrich* (Illustrated). Yale University Press.
3. *Id.*
4. *Id.*
5. Rhodes, R. (2007). *Masters of Death: The SS-Einsatzgruppen and the Invention of the Holocaust*. Vintage.
6. *Id.*
7. *Id.*
8. Longerich, P., Sharpe, L., & Noakes, J. (2022). *Wannsee: The Road to the Final Solution*. Oxford University Press.
9. *Id.*
10. MacDonald, C. (2007). *The Assassination of Reinhard Heydrich*. Birlinn.
11. Dougherty, N., & Lehmann-Haupt, C. (2022). *The Hangman and His Wife: The Life and Death of Reinhard Heydrich*. Knopf.
12. MacDonald, C. (2007). *The Assassination of Reinhard Heydrich*. Birlinn.
13. Dougherty, N., & Lehmann-Haupt, C. (2022). *The Hangman and His Wife: The Life and Death of Reinhard Heydrich*. Knopf.
14. *Voyage of the St. Louis*. (n.d.). Holocaust Encyclopedia. Retrieved October 29, 2022, from https://encyclopedia.ushmm.org/content/en/article/voyage-of-the-st-louis
15. *Id.*
16. *Id.*
17. Ogilvie, S. A., & Miller, S. (2010). *Refuge Denied: The St. Louis Passengers and the Holocaust* (1st ed.). University of Wisconsin Press.

ALSO BY ELYSE HOFFMAN:

Where David Threw Stones: A Haunting WW2 Tale of Courage, Love, and Redemption

⭐⭐⭐⭐⭐ "If you enjoy reading WWII historical fiction and are looking for something a little different, this is the book for you." – Michael Reit, author of "Beyond the Tracks"

West Germany, 1968

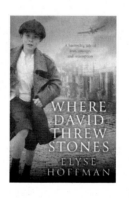

When ten-year-old David Saidel's parents are murdered, he is sent to live with his grandfather in the anti-Semitic village of Brennenbach. Miserable and lonely, David finds solace in his kindly Grandpa Ernst, who has one strict rule: never go out after midnight.

When David breaks curfew to search for his missing dog, he discovers why Ernst is so serious about his curfew: Brennenbach is cursed. When midnight strikes, the town is thrown back to 1943, the height of Hitler's reign.

The Nazi ghosts that infest Brennenbach are just as dangerous as they were in life. They're hunting for David, thinking he is the last member of a family they've been ordered to destroy.

Through the help of a little girl named Maria Rahm, David sets out to end the Curse before it claims more victims.

Award-winning author Elyse Hoffman has crafted an expertly woven tale of World War II's horrors - perfect for readers of Marcus Zusak's "The Book Thief," or Michael Reit's "Beyond the Tracks."

Fracture: A Heart-Wrenching Story of Forbidden Love and Torn Allegiances

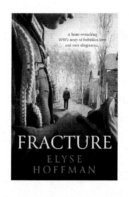

Franz Keidel is a monstrous SS soldier: loyal, hateful, and devoted to Hitler. With a cold heart, he hunts down his Führer's enemies, but one fateful mission will fracture his shield of ice.

While hunting for Jews, Franz stumbles across a familiar face: Amos Auman, his childhood friend. Amos is the only source of joy in Franz's life, but he is also a Jew. Unable to bring himself to kill his friend, Franz vows to protect Amos from his fellow Nazis.

As Franz spends more time with Amos, bringing him food and books, he falls in love with his kind-hearted friend. How could he fall in love with a man, a Jew? How can he continue to hate Jews when a Jew has thawed his icy heart?

And what will Franz do if he has to choose between Amos and his loyalty to Hitler? What choices does he have when he is already beyond redemption?

The Book of Uriel: A Novel of WWII

"An otherworldly tale with indelible characters in a realistic wartime setting. Hoffman's novel sublimely fuses world history and Jewish folklore."---Kirkus Reviews

"A truly unique work of fantastical, historical fiction set in Nazi Germany that will keep readers engaged and invested in the characters and their fates."---Booklife by Publisher's Weekly

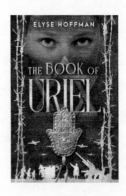

In the fires of World War II, a child must save his people from darkness...

Ten-year-old Uriel has always been an outcast. Born mute in a Jewish village known for its choir, he escapes into old stories of his people, stories of angels and monsters. But when the fires of the Holocaust consume his village, he learns that the stories he writes in his golden notebook are terrifyingly real.

In the aftermath of the attack, Uriel is taken in by Uwe, a kind-hearted linguist forced to work for the commander of the local Nazi Police, the affably brutal Major Brandt. Uwe wants to keep Uriel safe, but Uriel can't stay hidden. The angels of his tales have come to him with a dire message: Michael, guardian angel of the Jewish people, is missing. Without their angel, the Jewish people are doomed, and Michael's angelic brethren cannot search for him in the lands corrupted by Nazi evil.

With the lives of millions at stake, Uriel must find Michael and free him from the clutches of the Angel of Death...even if that means putting Uwe in mortal danger.

The Book of Uriel is a heartbreaking blend of historical fiction and Jewish folklore that will enthrall fans of *The Book Thief* and *The World That We Knew.*

Barrack Five: A Prize Winning Holocaust Story

Winner of the 2021 Readers' Favorite Silver Medal for Short Stories.

The ghosts of the past don't always stay silent...

When Vilém Rehor takes a security job at a former concentration camp, he assumes it will be dreary, but uneventful. But when someone starts carving their name onto the walls of Barrack Five, his supposedly boring job becomes more than he bargained for.

Though he tries to catch the vandal, Vilém can't figure out how they're making their marks—he never sees anyone, but that doesn't mean he's alone...

As he delves deeper into the mystery of the vandal, he realizes that the Holocaust isn't over for everyone. The spirit of a girl long gone reveals herself, desperate to be heard.

Can Vilém help this restless soul?

Made in United States
North Haven, CT
18 August 2024

56252606R00162